PRAISE FOR KATY EVANS

"Katy Evans's books are like a roller coaster; the excitement, anticipation, and absolute thrill of the ride keep me coming back to her awesome romances time and again."

—Kylie Scott, *New York Times* bestselling author

MILLION DOLLAR
MARRIAGE

OTHER TITLES BY KATY EVANS

MILLION DOLLAR SERIES

Million Dollar Devil

MANHATTAN SERIES

Tycoon
Mogul
Muse

WHITE HOUSE SERIES

Mr. President
Commander in Chief
White House—Boxed Set

MANWHORE SERIES

Manwhore
Manwhore +1
Ms. Manwhore
Ladies' Man
Womanizer
Playboy

REAL SERIES

Real
Mine
Remy
Rogue
Ripped
Legend
Racer

MILLION DOLLAR
MARRIAGE

katy evans

Montlake
Romance

Published by Montlake Romance, Seattle

www.apub.com

Amazon, the Amazon logo, and Montlake Romance are trademarks of Amazon.com, Inc., or its affiliates.

ISBN-13: 9781542007252
ISBN-10: 1542007259

Cover design by Letitia Hasser

Cover photography by Wander Aguiar

Printed in the United States of America

To life, an expert at tearing us open
when we need to grow

It was a fake marriage.
At least, that was the plan . . .

THE MOMENT OF TRUTH

December 17
Nell

I'm going to lose my lunch.

It's the live finale the entire country has been waiting for. The arena is packed to the gills with reporters, cameras pointed at us. Flashbulbs go off, and my future seems to flash through my eyes with them.

Everything depends on what will happen in the next hour. We could give our answer in a split second, but not now. I know the announcer will drag things out to the point of sheer madness. Recaps of poignant moments from the season, interviews with contestants, performances by "special celebrity guests" who are also fans of the show.

It's all meant to build up to the moment of truth.

Every one of the people in this arena, every one of the thirteen million people watching at home—they're all waiting on the edge of their seats with the same question.

Will they . . . or won't they?

I wish to god we could just give our answer and be done.

He's so close, but he might as well be a million miles away. Our fingers entwined, he waves at the crowd cheering our names. His hand isn't the least bit clammy. I manage a peek at him, his chiseled features, his relaxed smile, and my throat catches.

No wonder the world is in love with him. No wonder he's been the fan favorite since week one.

This is it. The end. Or . . .

I look over at him and say, "Luke . . . I'm not . . ."

He shakes his head almost imperceptibly. "It's okay," he murmurs, his fingers stroking my palm. "Breathe, Penny. Just breathe."

So I do. But air is not the only thing I need to make me okay right now.

We've been through so much, more than most couples will go through in entire lifetimes.

And now we're about to make the decision that will shape our future.

To think, seven months ago, I didn't even know Luke Cross. Three months ago, I despised him. But somewhere along the line, things changed.

Somewhere along this crazy little adventure we've been having, played out on television for the entire world to see, I did what I told myself I'd never do.

I don't even know how it happened, but as I look back, it seems so inevitable. Like I couldn't have stopped it, even if I'd tried.

But just because it was meant to happen doesn't mean it will last forever . . .

HALF A MILLION DOLLARS IN DEBT

Nell

> *I really don't know why I'm here. I'll probably be the first person voted out. If we vote people out? I don't watch television, so I have no idea how these competitions work.*

—Nell's Confessional, Day 1

Seven months earlier

I'm lying on the floor of the living room of my off-campus apartment. I think I might be having a heart attack.

Courtney comes inside and looks down at me with a pout. Kicks me a little with her pointy-toe flat. "That bad?"

She sees the torn envelope, the trifold statement lying on my abdomen.

She knows exactly what time of year it is and what this means.

And yes, she also knows how bad this is.

But for the past few years, I've been very good at living in denial, ignoring the approaching day of reckoning, the day when the crap hits the fan.

Which is totally today.

"I can't breathe," I moan out. "I'm dying."

She goes to the fridge and grabs a handful of grapes. "Hmm. If you die, is someone else responsible for your student loans?"

I sit up and scowl at her. But only for a second because suddenly I feel weak again. I might be coming down with something. I lie back down and stare up at the old dusty crystal chandelier in our crap apartment. The crap apartment I'd chosen to *save* money. It's not like I've lived like a princess all these years. I've been frugal, dang it!

She crouches and picks up the letter. "Wow. $500K, huh?"

Ugh. Hearing it out loud like that only makes it seem more insurmountable. I push my butt into the ground, hoping the floor will swallow me up. "How did I get here?"

She taps her chin. "I don't know. It might have to do with not getting a job when you graduated from college four years ago."

I sit up and stare at her. My best friend, Courtney, majored in education, obtaining her undergrad degree at Emory at the same time I did, and she has a real job now. She's not making big bucks, but at least she can pay down her student loan debt each month and doesn't have to put her half of the rent on her credit card. Plus, she can afford little luxuries, like . . .

Courtney catches me eyeing her iced vanilla bean Frappuccino and hands it over. I greedily take a sip. "You poor thing."

I scoot my legs into crisscross applesauce. "How do you expect me to get a job? I'm still trying to finish my PhD!"

She laughs. "In comparative literature. I don't even know what kind of job you can get with a degree like that. You said you don't want to be a professor."

"I don't." It's not that I wouldn't. Actually, teaching sounds like fun. But getting up in front of a lecture hall full of college students and speaking? Even the thought gives me hives. I hate being on display like that. "But I've graduated with honors from all my classes. There are plenty of jobs available for someone with my education."

I may be deluding myself. I'd kept myself firmly out of the career counselor's office at college. Never did a thing to brush up my résumé. I'd been perfectly fine, advancing my education at Emory University, first with my undergraduate double major in philosophy and art history, then my master's in anthropology, and then my PhD. That's because when Penelope Carpenter starts something, she finishes it. When I was a kid, I asked my parents what the furthest was that I could go with my education, and I made plans to get there, taking the classes that interested me. I said I was going to go all the way, and I did—on my own terms.

I'm made to go the distance. Unfortunately, I amassed a little bit of debt along the way.

But god. The real world? It gives me a panic attack. School is where I shine, where I feel comfortable. Books are my safety. And life? Well, that's anything but.

Ugh, just thinking about it, I feel the red welts popping up on my face.

Which is why I really wish there were another degree I could go for. A megadoctorate. Maybe I can go for my JD? Postpone the day of reckoning even more?

"You're coming to the ceremony on Thursday, right?" I ask her.

She pulls off her blazer. "Of course, *Doctor.*"

I smile at her. Good. I don't make friends easily, so she's the only thing close to family I have here in Atlanta. All the rest of mine is up in New England, living the hoity-toity high life. And no, they made it pretty clear to me that if I wanted to go to a school that wasn't Harvard, I was on my own when it came to paying for it, which I've been doing—poorly—by picking up tutoring gigs here and there. My dad was self-made and wants his children to be as well. He cosigned for me on my credit card and apartment lease, but he expects me to pay him back in full when I get the money. My mom thinks I'm making a terrible mistake by endlessly advancing my degrees and doesn't hesitate to tell me every chance she gets. My father has told me that my inheritance is actually going to his alma mater, Harvard, when he dies. So I didn't even invite them to my graduation. Not that they would come anyway.

I pick up the folded paper by one corner like it's dirty, then let it fall to the ground. "You think Gerald will be there?"

She snorts. "No."

"But—"

"Nell. The Gerald train has not only left the station, it's in another country, speeding far, far away from you."

Way to be blunt, Nee. But yeah. I knew that. Still, I always hold out hope where his big blue eyes are concerned. I'd never taken an interest in guys before him, but I kept bumping into him at the library. He ended up asking me to study together, and I've been smitten ever since. He's cute as heck, a fencer, a wine connoisseur, an art and classical music lover, and my all-around perfect man.

He's also a resident now at the Atlanta Children's Hospital and engaged to some brilliant med student in a Barbie package. It's been nine months since we broke up. You'd think I'd have gotten the hint and would've stopped texting him every week by now.

But no, that would be what a girl who has her life together would do.

And all Nell Carpenter has, clearly, is a giant black hole of debt.

I stand up, throw my student loan statement in the trash, wrap myself in my cushiest blanket, and fall onto the couch, dead.

Courtney looks at me with pity. "Aw, honey. You know what? *Millionaire Bachelor* is on tonight. Why don't I get changed, we heat up that frozen pizza, and we watch together? We can make fun of how pathetic all the contestants are."

I don't even answer. She knows I never watch that stuff. Never eat frozen anything. My form of entertainment is reading. Listening to classical music. Tooling around on my harp. Cleaning the house. And

I eat clean. Some people would call it OCD. But I'm not. I just set high standards for myself.

It's hard to believe we've lasted as roommates. It's a good thing she isn't a total slob. But Courtney is one of the few people who can stand my quirks. Part of it is that she's pretty easygoing, and part is that she was forced to. We were thrust together as roommates our freshman year at Emory and have roomed together ever since. When I said I don't make friends easily, I lied. Actually, I don't make friends *at all*. Sure, there may be a value in it, but I've always said that education is my priority, which is why I never went to a party or engaged in small talk or hung around in the common room. But it was almost like I *had* to make friends with Nee, because our proximity, sharing a tiny ten-by-ten room, dictated it. I even resisted it the first few months, but Courtney is bubbly and sweet and impossible not to like. Eventually we ended up going to the dining hall and studying together and becoming best friends.

"Well. Fine. I'm going to eat pizza and watch. You can just sit there and mope."

So I do. I sit in my cocoon and whimper miserably as she gets a Diet Coke and frozen pizza and sits on the sofa next to me, watching the crap show. I try to ignore it, but eventually the hot, built millionaire catches my attention. Especially when he gets a couple's massage with one girl one night, then ends up hot-tubbing with another girl the next.

I squint at the screen as he starts making out with the girl in the hot tub. "What a charmer. How can you watch this trash?"

Her eyes are so glued to the screen that I don't think anything short of a nuclear holocaust will tear her away. "He's hot."

"Also, a douche."

That doesn't stop her. She's practically drooling. She has a sweet, wonderful boyfriend who treats her like gold, and she's pining away for this douche?

A commercial comes on, and she goes to pop some popcorn in the microwave. I reach over and take a taste of her pizza. Ew. Cardboard tastes better. When I throw my head back on the pillow, I see something on the TV that makes me stop with little tendrils of fake cheese slipping down my chin.

"Calling all Atlanta residents ages twenty-five to forty-nine! Want to make a cool million dollars? Come on down to the auditions for our newest hit reality TV show . . . *Million Dollar Marriage*! Do you have a unique personality and the spirit of adventure to win it all? Join us at the Atlanta Convention Center, noon to five on May fifteenth!"

I stare until I forget to blink.

"Hey, did you eat my pizza?" Courtney shouts from the kitchen.

I wipe the cheese off my chin and point at the television. "What's that about?"

"What?"

"The auditions for . . . something?"

Courtney flops down with her big bowl of popcorn. "Oh yes! I'm so there! Joe and I are going out for it. We've been planning for months."

I'm confused. "You are?"

"Yeah. They've been doing auditions all around the country. But . . ." She sees the wheels turning in my head. "Don't get any ideas, Nell. Trust me. If you think *Millionaire Bachelor* is cheese, *Million Dollar Marriage* will probably make your head spin."

"Why?"

"Because people—normal, everyday people who don't have sticks up their butts—like cheese. They gobble it up. So I guarantee this will be more of the same. I mean, it's a new show, but word is the premise is totally out there."

She doesn't elaborate.

"Out there as in . . ." She doesn't fill in. "What do you mean? The top prize is a million dollars. I've got debt. I'd probably sell my soul for that."

She laughs, long and hard. "Uh, no. Nell. No. It's really not for you. Remember? It said it's only for the adventurous."

"And?"

"And?" She gives me a look like it's obvious. "Nell. You think a wild time is organizing the medicine cabinet in the bathroom."

My jaw drops. "I do not." Okay. Well, maybe I do. One time I found a couple of pills I'd never seen before. "Besides, what are you? Indiana Jones? You're not exactly Miss High Adventure either. And it asked for unique personalities."

She shrugs. "Well, that you definitely have. But still . . . you'd be on television and let everyone into your business?"

"For a million dollars, I guess. Come on. Can't I go with you guys?" I give her my puppy-dog eyes.

"Uh . . ." She looks at the television. "May fifteenth. You know that's the day of your graduation?"

Right. "Okay, but it's noon to five. Graduation's not until seven. What would it hurt if I just went and checked it out with you?"

She gives me a doubtful look.

I don't get why she's being so reluctant. She's usually all for these things. "Come on, Nee. Please. I need that money." I called her Nee once because I thought it both cute and funny, and Courtney laughed so hard with me that it's stuck. So we're Nee and Nell.

"Okay. I guess you can come. But if you roll your eyes or tell me how stupid it is one time, I'm going to kick you to the curb."

"Yay!" I hug her. "I can't wait."

"Oh, girl," she says, patting my head like I'm a Labrador. "You can. Trust me. You have no idea what you're in for."

Luke

All I have to say is this: Bring it. I'm up for anything.

—Luke's Confessional, Day 1

Tim's Bar is hopping, standing room only, every eye plastered on the television screens in the corners of the room.

By the looks of this crowd, you'd think my little place was doing pretty damn well.

But looks are deceiving.

Everyone is here to cheer on Jimmy Rowan, the legend, as he debuts his brand-new stunt on YouTube. This is where he got his start. His following. Where he made his mark. Where he also met Elizabeth Banks, the rich girl he's been dating for the past six months.

Jimmy does all his business out of my bar, so much so that one booth in the back is his designated "office." He's been sitting in that office for the past hour, doing hell knows what with her. I launch a plastic straw at him from over the bar, and he turns.

"You ready?" I call.

He slides out of the seat, never dropping Lizzy's hand. She grins at me. "It's James. He was born ready." She looks at him. "Isn't that what you always say?"

He gives her a grin and nods. "Yeah. Ready." He rubs his hands together. "Hey, you okay?"

I nod. Fan-fucking-tastic.

He turns to the audience and clears his throat. "Everyone. Here it is. The world premiere of my latest stunt, which will debut on my channel this weekend. Filmed down in Oahu."

Jimmy hasn't changed a whole hell of a lot since he started dating Lizzy. He has, though, gotten the capital he needed to expand his YouTube channel to a lot more exotic locales. I can't say I'm not a bit jealous. Before Lizzy, Jimmy and I were on the same track: raised on the toughest streets of Atlanta and destined to live the rest of our lives and die here. Now Jimmy spends every other week on an adventure, when I've never so much as been out of the state. But he and Lizzy? As different as they are, she's so damn good for him it almost makes me think love exists.

Almost.

I press play on the Blu-ray player, and the black screen cuts to a shot of Jimmy, standing on the edge of a volcano, in a crash helmet.

Everyone cheers for the man. He's the neighborhood hero.

A guy I've never seen before gets my attention. "You call this a whiskey? What do you do, water down shit?"

I give him a hard look. "Go somewhere else."

"Yeah, I will, but I'm not paying for this shit."

It's because of the phone call I'd gotten earlier that afternoon that my temper flares. I grab the shot glass I'm polishing and slam it on the bar. It shatters in my fist.

Jimmy whirls to look at me, stunned. Lizzy too.

Jimmy gets in the guy's face. "You are gonna fucking pay for that, aren't you?"

"Hey," I say, holding up a hand. I don't need him to fight my battles. And the last thing I need is Jimmy breaking any more of my furniture, which he's prone to do. "It's fine."

Jimmy narrows his eyes. "No, it's not. He complains about the drink, but he drained the whole damn thing."

The guy, reconsidering, opens his wallet, throws a ten down, and hurries out the door.

"And don't come back, asshole!" Jimmy shouts after him. Then he leans on the bar. "Mind telling me what that was all about?"

"Nothing," I mutter.

"But your hand!" Lizzy points at it. It's covered in blood.

"No big deal." I wrap a clean dishrag around it. They're still studying me, waiting for me to say more. "Look. This is your night. Have fun. We'll talk later."

"Later" ends up being at three in the morning. I announce last call at two, but the bar doesn't fully clear out until an hour later. Jimmy helps me round up the last of the stragglers. By then, Lizzy's curled up in his "office," sleeping on the bench under one of his flannel shirts.

"So why you been giving everyone that look?" he asks me as I pour two tequilas. "That *I want to rip off your head and shit down your neck* look?"

I toss back the entire glass in one gulp. "I'm broke."

"All right. Well, you've run into hard times before, and—"

"This ain't like before. I've been getting more and more in the red for years. The bank's done. They told me I got a whole shitload of mortgages I didn't even know my grandfather took out on this place, and I need to pay up in full by the end of the year. Which ain't gonna happen, 'cause I gotta pay Gran's nursing home bills."

"How much?"

"Five hundred thousand dollars."

Jimmy chokes and looks around. "No offense, Luke, but this place ain't worth half a mil."

"I know. My place upstairs is an even bigger shithole than down here."

"Hell. This place has been in your family for years."

I don't want to think about that. My granddad was the "Tim" of Tim's Bar. To have his legacy end with me blows hardcore.

"That place your grandmother's in is like the Ritz."

I nod. "And she's gonna stay there. She has friends there. She plays mah-jongg with them and shit. She's happy."

Jimmy looks over toward his office, where his girlfriend is sleeping soundly, and I know exactly what's on his mind. "Well, Lizzy has a soft spot for this—"

"No. Don't tell her. I know Lizzy. I know she'll give me the money in a heartbeat. I don't want it from her. I don't want to be in debt to anyone."

He looks at me like I'm crazy, but he nods anyway. "All right. Then what?"

"Pray for a miracle?" I shrug. "Hell if I know."

He leans on the bar, thinking. "No. You don't need a miracle. I've got your answer right here." He goes over to his office and pulls a sheet of paper off the messy pile on the table. "These guys wanted to put an ad on my channel. They're holding tryouts for a new reality TV show in this area tomorrow. The top prize is a million dollars."

I stare at the sheet. "*Million Dollar Marriage*? I don't watch that reality shit. What is it?"

He shrugs. "I don't know. It says contestants must be between the ages of twenty-five and forty-nine, in good physical shape, and up for adventure. That's all. That's you, man."

I laugh. "That's *you*."

"Yeah. But I don't need the money. And you've got a face for the camera, man. The ladies'll lap you up."

"All right, all right," I say, scratching my chin. "I'll think about it."

I close up the bar, say good night to my friends, and go upstairs to my two-bedroom shithole. I used to live up here with my grandparents until he died and she suffered the first of many strokes that put her in the nursing home. Back when we were living together up here, Gran had made it homey, with curtains and candles and womanly touches. But I don't do that shit. I'm barely home to take care of it.

Even the bar downstairs is falling apart in my hands. At first I'd had this sense of pride. Owning my own place at twenty-three, taking care of business. It was a complete one-eighty from where I'd been just five short years before. I'd felt like a success for the first time in my life. A poster child for all those addicts out there who think it's not possible to pull out of the hole.

But it hasn't been easy. And now? I feel like shit.

Like I'm digging myself another hole. I'm ruining Gran's place, little by little.

I strip down to my boxers and sit on the edge of the mattress, looking at the scars on my inner arm. All those nights lying slumped in my own piss in the dark alleyways in downtown Atlanta, strung out on whatever juice I could find cheap—I thought I'd be dead by my twenties.

Everything I've made for myself since then? It's all hanging in the balance. I'm going to lose this place. And I'm going to lose Gran soon too. And then what'll I have? I live every fucking day knowing those two things are at the top of the very short list of Things Preventing Me from Being a Junkie Again.

Without them . . . really. What the fuck else do I have?

I reach over onto the dresser and unfold the flyer Jimmy gave me. As I lie back on my mattress, I think about it more than I should. Reality TV? I never thought I'd consider it. But the more I think about it, the more I think it might be my only shot at saving my bar . . . and saving my ass in the process.

THE AUDITION

Nell

I suppose if this is more of a cerebral challenge, I might do well. But if it involves any hand-eye coordination, I'm in trouble. I'm a bit uncoordinated.

—Nell's Confessional, Day 1

Turns out, Courtney is right.

I really had no idea what I was in for.

It's ten in the morning, and the Atlanta Convention Center is mobbed. You'd think they were playing the Super Bowl here. We found a parking spot about a mile away from the end of a line that snaked endlessly toward the front doors of the center. When we got there and I could barely see the huge arena from where we stood, I started to pout.

Now I'm just miserable.

"You're right, Nee. This was stupid," I mumble to her as she leans on Joe for support. Joe is the perfect boyfriend who treats her like a queen. He finished undergrad the same time we both did, went out and got a good job, and now he's making six figures. He takes Courtney out to expensive meals and does the adulting thing really well.

Unlike some people I know.

"What did I tell you about that?" Courtney says, nudging me back upright as I try to lean on her. My feet hurt. "We don't need Negative Nelly. Negative Nelly can go take a hike."

I sigh and check my watch. We've been here only fifteen minutes, and we've moved about . . . three feet. Sigh. I stand on my tiptoes to see if I can spot the convention center any better. "Is all of Atlanta here?"

"Hey. Zip it," Courtney says, zipping her fingers over her lips.

"Fine." I wish I had someone to lean on. I squat, then sit, but the second I do, the line starts to move again. Story of my life. I push my glasses up on the bridge of my nose and scramble into place.

"What are you reading?" Joe asks me.

"*A Compendium of Ancient Chinese Philosophy*," I say, not looking up because if I lose my spot one more time, I might go crazy.

"Riveting," he says.

"It is." The line moves again. This time I don't get up. I crawl with it, my nose buried in the book.

I try to read more, but the people in front of me are talking too loudly. The big topic of conversation is what the hell the premise of this *Million Dollar Marriage* show is actually going to be. The craziest rumors are flying around. The bouncy blonde girls in front of me with their surfer-dude boyfriends seem to think that they're going to offer people a million dollars to get married to their respective partners on live television.

Which sucks for me, because the only partner I have with me is my giant textbook.

"You know what I think?" Courtney says to me, leaning on Joe's shoulder. "They said adventure. I think they're going to split teams up into men and women and send them through an obstacle course. And whoever wins has to get married on live television or else forfeit the money."

I stare at her. All the more reason for me to get the eff out of here. I am not athletic. I am beyond two left feet. I am all soft and squishy curves, and I'm happy that way. The only reason I'd run is if something were chasing me. And marry a complete stranger? No to the thousandth power.

I look longingly in the direction of where Joe parked his Jeep.

"They wouldn't do that, would they? Force strangers to marry?" I ask, alarmed.

She shrugs. Oh god. They would. "Haven't you ever seen *Married at First Sight*?"

Married at what? She does know who she's talking to, doesn't she? "So wait . . . you'd get married to a stranger, even though you're dating Joe?"

She nods. "For a million dollars, yeah. He'd do the same."

Joe wraps an arm around her and says, "Hell yes."

Who are these people? Romance is truly dead in this world.

A bit later, a woman in a polo shirt with a name tag that says "*MDM*—Hi, I'm Eve!" comes by. She has a very official-looking headset on and is murmuring into it.

"Excuse me," I say to her. "Can you tell me if the contestants will be required to marry?"

She just looks at me and laughs like I'm an idiot.

Oh god.

She's handing out sheets of paper and pens. "Please fill out this survey and have it ready for when you approach the check-in table. Thank you!"

Check-in table? I stretch out my neck, trying to see anything other than Siberian wasteland. Just as I do, Courtney laughs. "Oh my god, these questions are a riot."

I look down at my paper. Besides all the regular info, it has this:

Please indicate on a scale of one to five (one being "fits me perfectly" to five being "does not fit me at all") how well each of these statements fits you:
I love to meet new people.
I like being alone.

I have a huge social circle . . .

And on and on. I page through it and realize there are more than five hundred of these personality questions, on everything from sociability to athleticism to intelligence.

Well, happy day. I love taking tests.

I get right down to it, using my book as a desk, filling out ovals excitedly. For some reason, this has always relaxed me. I actually loved taking the SAT and the GRE. I smile the whole time, or at least until Nee nudges me.

"Anyone ever tell you that you look like a serial killer when you take tests?"

I smack her.

The thing that takes me longest is listing all my degrees and awards, but I still finish before everyone else. As I do, I sense someone's presence hovering over my shoulder. "Shit, you did that fast."

I turn and look up, up, way up at the dirtiest hunk of man I've ever seen. All his ripped muscles look like they're fighting to escape from an inadequately small T-shirt. He has tattoos—I'd say way too many, but one is too many for me. He's hairy, too, unshaven, with a mess of brown hair falling over his eyes. I detect a whiff of tobacco. He's a . . . thug.

And his eyes are on me. Beautiful, sparkly green eyes that don't fit with the rest of him. Penetrating to my core.

Ohhhkay. I stiffen and face my back to him, hoping that if I ignore him, he'll go away. I pretend to be really interested in what Courtney's doing.

That's when Joe says, "Holy shit. Aren't you Jimmy Rowan?" to the men behind me.

"Yep," the dirty guy's friend says.

"Shit! That's crazy. You going out for this thing?"

Oh no.

Behind me, Jimmy says, "Nah. Just here to support my friend."

"Really? They'd probably pick you in a second. They'd totally want a celebrity," Joe gushes. Courtney's ears prick up at the mention of the word *celebrity*. She stands up and stares closely at him as Joe says, "He's a famous YouTube star."

Courtney's jaw drops. I roll my eyes. What the hell is a YouTube star, and why do my goofy friends find it so appealing? The guys behind me are thugs.

Joe starts to go through his backpack. "Can I have an autograph?"

Oh god. I stand on my tiptoes and try to see if the line is moving, then cross my arms, completely not willing to turn around and engage. Courtney yanks on my sleeve, but I tear it away and give her a death look.

"Nell," she murmurs in my ear, dazed. "He's famous. And did you see his friend?"

She fans her face. Is she insinuating what I think she's insinuating? "I don't care," I singsong.

"You should care. Flex your flirting muscles for once in your life. Maybe then you'd get Gerald the Goofball out of your head."

"Um. One, I don't have flirting muscles. Two, I don't have Gerald in my head. And three, even if I did, that thug isn't going to get him out of it. He's like . . . an animal."

"A dirty, hot animal. Mmm."

"Nee! Put your tongue back in!"

Joe gets the autograph and stares at it like it's his most prized possession as he continues to talk the dirty guys' ears off. I try to walk as close as I can to the people in front of me so that I can get as far away from the thugs as possible. I open my book and read.

"That's a mighty big book for a little girl like you." The voice comes over my shoulder, breath tickling my ear.

I nearly jump.

He smells good. Why does he smell good? I grit my teeth and push my glasses up on my nose. "I'm not *that* little."

I'm really not. I'm almost five seven. Compared to him, though, I guess I am. He's a beast.

"You studying for some test or something?"

I roll my eyes. "No. Just reading for fun."

He laughs. "You find reading fun?"

Ugh. Yes, I do find reading fun, as opposed to what he must find fun, like shooting up or biting the heads off chickens. I decide I won't answer and maybe he'll get the picture that I'm not interested in talking to him.

I don't know how I manage it, but I ignore him the rest of the time. Two hours later, we make it to the check-in desk, take numbers, and then we're ushered into a part of the convention center with tables where we can sit. I try to sit as far away as possible from the yeti and his famous friend, but unfortunately, Joe drags us so that we're sitting at the same table, all the while acting like the YouTube star's groupie.

A voice over the loudspeaker says, "Number 4,322." I look at mine. 5,696.

Blah.

An older man in a baseball cap waves his number and runs toward the stage. A woman in an *MDM* polo nods at him, and he follows her out the door.

A second later he appears again, looking kind of angry. I guess he didn't get chosen. He says something to his girlfriend, and the two of them leave, giving the woman at the door the middle finger.

Nice.

She ignores them and calls the next number.

At least they're moving fast.

"I'll be pissed," Courtney says with a sigh, "if I spend all day here just to be in with them for only five seconds!"

"Yeah," I mutter. I'm kind of embarrassed to be here to begin with. Did I really think this was going to be my ticket? I'm not unique. And I'm not adventurous. I'm sure as hell not going to get married to just any old guy for television ratings. And Courtney's right. This totally isn't my scene. The people here probably have a collective IQ of ten. When I leave here an hour from now, completely empty handed, I'm going to have to get real and get a normal job, like everyone else in the world.

Which is probably why I haven't left.

I bury my nose in the textbook and try to ignore the conversations going on around me. People are still theorizing about what this *Million Dollar Marriage* show is, and the whole place is on the verge of explosion from curiosity.

When I look up across the table, the yeti's eyes are on me. Penetrating, dark, possessive.

Okay, I see what Courtney means. He is attractive, in a bad-boy way. If I liked those things, I'd probably be interested. But I don't. I like clean. Intelligent. Cultured.

So why do I feel heat between my legs?

I swallow and lower my eyes to my book, but I wind up reading the same sentence about a hundred times.

I look up again. He's still staring at me, his gaze as heavy as a brick, trapping me. I've never been stared at like this before.

"What?" I snap.

He shakes his head almost imperceptibly. "I just like looking at you."

Great.

I grab my book off the table and turn away from him, propping it up on my knees. *So you can just like looking at the back of my head.*

I do manage to finish the chapter on Mencius, still feeling prickles on my neck from where I think his eyes may be boring into me. God, he has crazy, hot eyes, unblinking, like he's marked his prey and is readying to pounce. But eventually I hear him talking to his friend the "star," so I relax a little.

The loudspeaker goes off again, and Courtney jumps up and waves her page. "It's time! It's time! Wish me luck!"

She bounds excitedly over to the door as I trade glances with Joe. "She's been talking about this nonstop. What do you think her chances are?"

"Good," I say. She's beautiful, bubbly, and people love to be around her. Even though there's a lot of competition, she's just the type of person you'd find on a reality show. The cameras would love her. "Really good."

But a second later the door opens, and she comes in, head down. There are tears in her eyes. "They didn't want me," she moans as Joe pulls her into his arms.

Then they call his number, and he kisses her head and says, "Well, they sure as hell aren't going to want me, then."

But he goes anyway. When she slumps down next to me, she says, "That was brutal. They didn't even ask me a single question. They just looked at me and said I wasn't what they're looking for. The end."

"Really? What are they looking for?"

"Who the hell knows?" she mumbles as the door at the far end of the room opens and Joe comes in, his arms raised in victory. Courtney's eyes widen. "You got through?"

"Hell no. They took one look at me and told me not to let the door hit me in the ass."

Courtney sighs. "Well, at least it's not just me."

Joe piles up both of their numbers and rips them in half. He puts a hand on my shoulder. "Help us, Obi-Wan. You're our only hope."

The words are still hanging in the air when my number is announced.

All right. Well. I don't feel so bad, now, if they're just going to look at me and tell me to get lost. I shove my book under my arm and wave my number at the woman. "Hello."

She looks at her clipboard. "Hi. Name?"

"Penelope Carpenter. People call me Nell."

"Penelope Carpenter. Right this way." She leads me down a dark, narrow hallway toward a set of double doors flanked by two security guards, one male, one female. "No questions. Please do not speak unless spoken to. If you are asked to leave, you must leave immediately. As part of your application, you signed a waiver that states you will not discuss the audition process with anyone," she reads in a dull monotone. "Is that understood?"

"Okay," I say, thinking, *Can I just get my no so I can go home?*

"This way, miss," the male guard says, leading me through a metal detector like they have in airports. I have to surrender my purse and book as I walk through it. They hand them back to me, and the woman nods at me to go inside. Who the heck am I meeting with, the pope?

I take a deep breath and go inside.

It's a large wood-paneled room, with a giant table in the center. There are three people seated at the far end of it, a woman and two men, and they look restless. The men are probably just a little older than me, but the woman looks about fifty. There are Coke cans and an open pizza box in front of them, all but one slice devoured. The man with the mustache is chewing on his pen, looking at me like I killed his family.

"Hi," I say, giving a half wave.

"Next," he says gruffly.

Thank the lord.

I spin on my heel.

"Wait, wait, wait," the woman says. "What is that book you're reading?"

I show them the title.

The mustached guy who hates me lets out a little "Ah." I don't figure him for a philosopher, but . . . "Do you wear those glasses all the time?"

I push them up on my nose, on instinct. I've worn glasses since I was three and am one step away from being legally blind. Contacts have always been a hassle, and glasses, to me, have always been my little insulation from the outside world. "Yes . . ."

I expect that's my cue to leave. After all, I've already been in here a hundred times longer than Joe and Courtney combined. The woman says, "You look young. How old are you?"

"I just turned twenty-five."

She looks down at a paper. I realize it must be the survey I filled out and handed in at check-in. "It says here you're a doctor."

"Yes," I say. "I graduate with my doctorate in comparative literature tonight."

"You have quite a long educational history here," the other, completely bald man with the hipster glasses says. "I'm interested to know why you're here. Watch a lot of reality television, do you?"

I shake my head. "I don't watch television at all. It's not sufficiently stimulating to me. I'm here because my friend was coming, and I need the money to pay off my student loans."

"So . . . sufficiently stimulating, to you, would be . . ."

"I play the harp in my spare time, so I love music that moves me. Mozart. Mussorgsky. Mahler. I'm very interested in theater and art—and obviously good literature . . ." I stop when I realize they're way more interested in my life than anyone ever has been. They're suddenly hanging on my every word.

Why, again?

"And your pet peeves?"

This is definitely not happening. "Ah. Well, normal things. Ignorance. Laziness. People who overindulge. People who don't read or think sports are a religion or eat fast food all the time. All those things, I think, are the downfalls of modern society."

"Hmm. Do you consider yourself athletic?"

I looked down at myself. "What do you think? I've never even *watched* a sport before. Like I said, it's not sufficiently stimulating to my mind. I think the human body is a work of art for the mind alone."

The woman looks down at her sheet. "Interesting, Penelope. And are you seeing anyone right now?"

For a second, I think of Gerald. "Nell. And no."

Hipster guy motions me forward. "Can you come closer? Take your hair down from that ponytail and spin around?"

I don't want to, but I do. I walk toward the table, pull my dishwater-blonde hair out of the tie, and do a little catwalk turn, nearly falling over on my ass. I grasp the edge of the table before I topple down.

When I look up, they're all smiling at each other and nodding.

The woman reaches under her clipboard and pulls out a black folder. She motions me forward and says brightly, "Congratulations. You've made it to our first round. I'm Eloise Barker, the executive producer. This folder contains everything you need to know."

I stare at her. This isn't happening. "First round?"

She nods and shakes my hand. "Yes, you are one of fifty contestants plus five alternates who will be selected for the filming of the first season of *Million Dollar Marriage*, which will begin filming this September! There are several rounds, but you've taken a very big step toward one million dollars."

No, this really isn't happening. I'm dreaming. "But—what? Aren't you even going to tell me what the show is about? Like, the marriage part?"

The mustached man shakes my hand. Now he seems to love me. "I'm Vic Warner, the showrunner." He points to the bald hipster. "And that's Will Wang, famous television personality and our host."

I stare at him. Famous? Never seen him before in my life. "Uh . . . about the show?"

Eloise shakes her head. "Everything you need to know is right in the folder. Please call us should you have any questions. I'm afraid not everything is answered in there because we want to keep a certain air of mystery, but it'll all be divulged in due time."

I shake my head. Air of mystery? Oh, that is so not me. "Actually, I—"

She opens the first page and points to something that says "Prize Schedule." I squint to read it. "As you'll see, though we can't tell you what you'll be doing, contestants who do show up for the first day of taping will receive twenty thousand dollars. That's yours to keep, whether or not you decide to continue on."

Twenty thousand dollars.

For just showing up.

My throat closes, but before it completely seals, I manage to squeak out an "Okay."

Then I'm ushered out the door to a totally different place from where I'd been before. I spend a good half hour wandering about before I find Courtney and Joe sitting in the front of the convention center.

She runs to me as soon as she sees me. "Well? Where were you?"

I hold up the folder with the *MDM* logo on it, still dazed. "I'm in."

Luke

My strategy is this: make everyone love me. It ain't hard.

—Luke's Confessional, Day 1

Cutie doesn't like me.

It's become my new favorite pastime, staring at her, watching the blush crawl across her cheeks, which are snow white except for a few freckles over the bridge of her nose, magnified by those glasses.

Not like I have anything better to do. Jimmy's in deep conversation with one of his fans, and so there's hours and hours of nothing. And . . . her. She's cute. Looks younger than twenty-five, that's for sure.

And she brought a fucking textbook to the auditions. What kind of girl brings a textbook to these things?

She's one of those smart girls. Well bred. Maybe not a virgin, but I bet she doesn't fuck. She doesn't even make love. She probably does it making sure there's as little bodily contact as possible. I saw when she was filling out her survey that she doesn't like to drink, party, smoke . . . hell, she *could* be a virgin. She's just so *clean*.

They've been whipping through auditions, one after another. They finally get done with Cutie's two friends, and then it's her turn.

I watch her as she walks away. She's wearing mom jeans, like she wants to cover up the fact that she has a nice ass.

A really nice one.

After she leaves, I watch the clock on the wall as I sit next to Jimmy, who's texting with his little brother.

Cutie doesn't come back. Interesting.

It's about twenty minutes before they call my number.

The woman looks at her clipboard and says, "Luke Cross?"

"Yeah."

I follow her through security as she gives me a long rundown of the rules. I don't listen. "Good luck," she says to me.

"Right, baby."

I go inside. This is easily the shit-stupidest thing I've ever done. How did I let Jimmy talk me into this? Maybe I should give up Tim's Bar. Gran always says I work too hard. She'd understand.

No, fuck that. If I lose that, it's just a blink away from getting my breakfasts from trash cans and sleeping in alleys again.

There is a woman and two men at the end of a table. They study me closely as I enter. "How you guys doing?"

The woman just says, "Him. Definitely. Him."

I'm confused. "What do you want me for, baby?"

She gives me a wink and leans over and starts to whisper with a guy with a mustache. Mustached guy nods and says, "You look like a man who can hold your own in a fight, Mr. . . ."

"No *Mr.*," I say. "Just Luke. Luke Cross. I do okay."

"Twenty-eight, six three, and two hundred pounds, huh? Grew up downtown Atlanta. So, you a Falcons fan?" the bald guy says, reading what I wrote on the survey.

"Damn straight."

"Says here you like to have fun. What's that to you?"

I shrug. "Have a few beers. Watch the game. You know. Kick back."

"Drugs?"

"Nah. I don't do that shit anymore."

"But you were in rehab? For addiction?"

"Yeah. When I was eighteen. Got myself clean and never looked back."

"You obviously work out," the woman says, her eyes lingering appreciatively on my biceps.

I flex them for her, give her the full show. Why the hell not? I reach for my shirt. "Want to see my six-pack?"

The woman nods, but Mustache shakes his head. "It says on your application that you were incarcerated for a period of time?"

"Yeah. Ancient history. About a decade ago. Breaking and entering. I did a lot of stupid shit when I was young. For drug money."

"And as far as schooling?"

"Dropped out of high school when I was sixteen. My parents kicked me off our farm outside of Atlanta, and I haven't seen them since. Spent two years on the streets until my grandfather caught up with me and took me in. Got me to rehab, got me off the streets, and taught me how to tend bar. He's kind of my hero."

The woman swabs at her eyes. What, is she crying? "That's sweet."

"Hmmm," the man says. "And what do you do for work?"

"I bartend at my place. I own a bar. Was my grandfather's until he died five years ago."

"And with the money, you'll . . ."

"Pay off all the mortgages I have on it. Then blow the rest on beer and an entourage."

The cougar's looking at me like she wants to take a bite of me. Tapping her pen to her bottom lip. I think she likes me. We have a connection.

I grin at her. "Kidding. About the last part, at least."

"I want him," she says suddenly, like she can't hold it in anymore.

"But he's—" The mustached pecker puts his hand in front of his mouth so I can't lip-read the rest. Probably something about me being a wild card who's destined to give them trouble. Damn right about that.

"I don't care! He's perfect. Look at that face. Those eyes. He's the perfect hunk. Our target demographic will go wild for that face."

The target demographic. Women.

Mustache throws up his hands. "Fine."

"So we all in agreement?" the woman asks.

The two men nod reluctantly. Assholes.

"Wow, two in a row!" She grins wolfishly at me. "Okay, handsome. Get on over here and get your welcome packet. Welcome to round one. All the information you need is in this folder."

I pump my fist. "Fuck yeah."

"You'll have to tone down your language for television."

I pump my fist again. "Then, hell yeah. Better?"

"Good enough." She introduces herself as Eloise something, her hand lingering in mine, and tells me she's the executive producer of the show. I wink at her. If this shit is rigged, I have a pretty solid in with the executive producer in my pocket.

Then she introduces the two men, but I forget their names. "Please call us with any questions. I look forward to seeing you next season for the start of a great adventure."

I shake their hands. "Yeah. Fuck yeah. Looking forward to . . ." I realize I have no fucking clue what I'm in for. But I don't care. I'm up for anything. I've made it through the hard part. That money is already mine. "Whatever the fuck you're going to make us do."

She smiles at me. "You'll see. I'm sure you'll do well, Luke."

I know I will. Everyone else who got a black folder might as well line up and kiss my ass. Because that cool million is all mine.

I'm led outside, and I find Jimmy out there waiting for me. He scans the folder under my arm. "Well, shit. What did I tell you? You're gonna be a star."

"Fuck yeah," I tell him, since I'm not on television yet. "Let's go celebrate. I can taste that million already. I'm buying."

PANIC

Nell

> *What is my ideal mate? I don't know. Yes, I do want to get married, ideally before I'm thirty. I like classical music and art and the finer things in life, so I guess that's what I'd love. Someone cultured, classy, refined. A doctor, maybe . . .*
>
> —*Nell's Confessional, Day 1*

Four months after the audition, early in the morning, I'm sitting in the front seat of Courtney's car, pointing all the air vents right at my face because I think I might throw up.

"I can't believe I'm doing this. I can't believe I'm doing this. I can't believe I'm . . ."

She snaps her fingers at me. "Nell? You're doing this."

I nod. As I do, my teeth chatter.

She pulls on her seatbelt and gives me a look from the driver's side. "Come on, girl. You're a doctor now. Dr. Badass. You can do anything. And this is your moment. You were chosen from over ten thousand applicants. You're going to do something great."

I try to let the pep talk sink in and hope the nausea will go away. "Yes. Right."

The past month has been, in a word, insane. I read the paperwork over again and again. Most of it was legal junk, papers that needed to be signed. I had to have a physical and get a waiver from my physician. I also had to take a drug test, fill out a personality test of about two thousand more questions, and get a psychiatric evaluation. Two weeks ago, a photographer and stylist came to my house and took portraits of me that gave me flashbacks to my elementary school photos.

And now it's the first day of filming. It's a closed set, being filmed at the rec center at Georgia Tech. Since I don't have a car, Courtney volunteered to drive me, but she's bummed because she can't come watch. No, this first episode, where the fifty contestants are introduced and find out what the show is really about, is very hush-hush. When filming is done today, we'll be whisked off to an undisclosed location where the race will resume. It's all very secretive.

I guess it's good that it's private. I can wait until later to embarrass myself in front of millions.

As we drive, Courtney's spouting off random tips. "You can act smart. But don't be a know-it-all. And for god's sake, don't lecture people or roll your eyes."

"I never do that."

"You *always* do that."

I shrug. "I can't help it if I find people tiresome."

"Okay, okay. Do your best not to, Nell. Really. If this is anything like *Survivor*, before you can win, you've got to get people to like you. Bond with you."

I cringe. People don't do that with me. They avoid me.

"So even if you hate someone, pretend they're your favorite thing in this world." She thinks for a moment. "Like, pretend they're all the Sunday *New York Times* crossword."

I stare at her. "Saturday is a bit more challenging, actually."

"Okay, okay . . . pretend they're the Saturday crossword. Whatever. Just don't go off on them for their ignorance. Okay? I don't want you blowing your shot by being socially inept. The social inepts always get voted off the island first."

I can't argue with her. I am socially awkward, I know. "First, I've only seen one episode of *Survivor*, when you watched it, and it scarred me for life. They ate centipedes. Secondly, how do you know that this'll be anything like *Survivor*?"

"I don't. I'm just warning you."

"Well, if I have to eat a centipede, I'm out. Anything else?"

"Yeah. Smile. Relax. Look like you're having fun. Try to make alliances with the most likeable, social people. Don't think about the money or else you'll start looking constipated, and . . ."

"I'll get voted off the island. And?"

"And if there is a challenge that involves swimming . . . offer to do the smallest part of it. Actually, any physical challenge. Just . . . don't."

"I'm an okay swimmer."

She snorts. "Nell. You look like a drowning insect, flailing." She moves her arms wildly in the air for a second before fastening her hands back on the steering wheel.

"Fine. But . . . Courtney." I suck in a breath.

"What? I can tell there's something really bothering you. Spill it."

"It's just that . . . remember how you said that you wanted to watch *Millionaire Bachelor* so we could make fun of the contestants? Does that mean people will be watching and making fun of me?"

She gives me a sympathetic look. "Aw, hon. You're not going to please everyone. Sure, there will be people who make fun, but there will be people rooting for you too. The producers chose you out of thousands for a reason."

I sink down in my seat and stare straight ahead. My voice is quiet. "Do you think . . . Gerald will be watching?"

She closes her eyes, like she can't bear to look at someone as pathetic as me. I guess holding a torch for a guy who told you absolutely no nine months ago is kind of sad. "Yeah. He probably will."

When we used to double date, Gerald was always talking with Joe about reality television. Gerald was a big fan and always saw himself as a contestant on *Survivor*. While I was studying, he was in the other room, his eyes glued to the television screen. I'm sure if he wasn't so busy as a resident, I might have seen him in the audition line. I cringe. He'll be watching me potentially make a fool of myself?

Maybe that was part of the reason I agreed to this in the first place. I wanted to get in front of him again any way I could, even if I look pathetic doing so.

"Don't focus on him. Do your thing. Just be you."

Right. Be me. I can do this. "Minus the eye rolling and the lecturing and the social ineptitude. Right?"

She nods. "Right. And swimming. Don't forget. No swimming."

Ugh. "Are you done?"

She's not. She starts saying more, but at that moment we pull into the lot for the rec center. It's packed. There are at least twenty trucks there with camera crews, and a massive eighteen-wheeler is parked out back with **MILLION DOLLAR MARRIAGE** on the side, along with a picture of the bald guy I met, Will Wang.

I start to shake again.

She pulls up to the front doors and lets out a sigh as I look at the entrance.

"I am so jealous. This is going to be life changing for you!" I know. Good or bad, I don't know, though. "You have everything?"

I run through the checklist on my lap again. "I think so."

I reach into the back and pull out my giant heavy-duty backpack. Then I hug her. "They say we can't be in contact with anyone during the filming, and we can't use our phones. I put you down as my emergency contact. So, bye. I'll miss you."

"I'll miss you too," she says. "Give 'em hell!"

This is it. This is really it.

I put my hand on the handle and push open the door. The second I step onto the curb, I'm accosted by a woman with a microphone. Where the hell did she come from?

"Excuse me, are you one of the contestants for *Million Dollar Marriage*? Do you know what this show is about? Is there anything you can tell us about the filming happening today?"

I stare at her, mute.

Actually, I can't tell her anything. They've really kept us in the dark. And one of the clauses in the contract said not to divulge anything in the folder to anyone. But the camera's in my face and I can't even seem to remember how to walk, or talk, or breathe.

Suddenly someone snakes a hand around my waist and yanks me toward the door. I let out a shriek in confusion as a male voice says, "No comment. Get the fuck away."

I look down and see a massive tan hand splayed on my midsection.

Up, and there's a hairy beast of a man. The yeti. I get my voice back in a hurry and pound on his hand with my fist. "Let me go!"

He pulls me through the doors and deposits me roughly on the ground. "As you wish, sweetheart," he says, grinning at me. "You know, if you're actually gonna win this, you'd better start getting more comfortable around cameras."

I scowl at him. "What are you doing here? This is just for contestants."

He reaches into the pocket of his jeans and pulls out a folded piece of paper. When he unfolds it, I realize it's the contestant paperwork.

Oh no. No no no no. "You're a contestant?"

"Hell yes," he says. "And I'm going to clean the floor with your ass."

My scowl deepens. Courtney wants me to be nice to everyone? Forget that. I heft the bag onto my shoulder. "We'll see about that. Leave me alone."

I stomp off toward check-in, but he follows right behind me. "What, you didn't bring your massive textbook with you?"

I pat my bag. I have a lot of reading with me. Then I realize he doesn't need to know. "That's no business of yours."

He's still trying to talk to me as I hand my registration papers to the woman at check-in. I decide to ignore, ignore, ignore.

"Welcome," the woman says to me, reading my name on the paper.

I swear, the guy is right on my heels, breathing down my neck. I reach for my ponytail and smooth it, flicking him in the pecs.

His superhard Superman pecs.

"Penelope Carpenter. We're happy to have you as a contestant. The rest of the contestants are getting ready for filming, through those doors over there."

"Thank you."

I walk through the doors, my teeth chattering again. They told us to wear and bring athletic-type clothing. I didn't have any, so I went to Target and put $200 worth of workout bras, spandex capris, T-shirts, and a pair of sneakers on my credit card. When I get inside, I realize that "athletic clothing" means different things to different people. There's one insanely muscular woman in nothing but a bikini top and tiny boy shorts. Another beautiful woman with a long braid down her back is wearing an entire bikini. One man is in a pair of tight bike shorts, muscles bulging. A lot of people, actually, are baring way too much skin. Aren't they afraid of a boob or some other body part slipping out on film?

I know I am, as I've packed the baggiest T-shirts I could find.

I skulk along the outskirts of the room as I watch the men flexing and the women preening in front of a floor-to-ceiling mirror.

I am so in the wrong place.

As I'm wondering whether the $20,000 is worth this, I trip over the foot of a girl who's sitting on a bench. She's dark skinned and is wearing a sari over shorts, plus sneakers. Her boobs are fully undercover.

"Hi," she says, scooting over to make room for me.

I sit beside her, my heart beating like mad. "Hi. Are you a contestant?"

She nods. "I am so, so, so nervous," she says, in a tiny and very soft voice. "I have no idea why they picked me for this!"

I smile. "Me neither."

She extends her hand. "Shveta Patel," she says. "From New Jersey. I'm trying to earn money to send back to my parents in India so that they can get a surgery for my younger brother."

Oh. That sounds noble. Much more worthwhile than the stupid mess I'm in. I shake her hand. "Nell Carpenter. From right here in Atlanta."

"I've been looking around," she says, "and I think they tried to get people as different from one another as possible. I mean, it's a real cross section of America. You've got young and old, all races, athletic and non, all walks of life. It's very interesting."

I look around and see what she means. Still, one thing most of them have in common? Their private body parts are all in a precarious position.

Just then, I catch sight of the yeti. He's wearing a tight T-shirt and cargo shorts. He doesn't need to preen or flex—he clearly knows he's all that. He's talking with two other beautiful people, laughing like they've been friends forever. The blonde with barely any clothes is clearly enamored with him, as is the tattooed older woman in a leather bustier who's sitting on a bench, watching. Actually, all the women are staring at him. And as he tells his story, using hand motions and talking animatedly, more people take notice, gravitating to him.

I can almost hear Courtney's voice in my head: *He's the one. Form an alliance with him.*

Good thing she's not here. Because I refuse to go anywhere *near* that guy.

Besides, Shveta's much more my type. We talk a little, and I find out that she's an epidemiologist. She tells me she's a slave to reality television and knows everything about it, since growing up in India she wasn't allowed to watch TV at all. She's a huge fan of *Millionaire*

Bachelor, Survivor, The Amazing Race . . . all these shows I know nothing about. I won't hold that against her. Since she knows so much, I decide that she might be a valuable ally to have.

But I can't stop looking at the yeti, at the way he effortlessly works the room, making every single person turn toward him like flowers to the sun. They love him. Why?

As I'm contemplating, he stops talking midsentence, and his eyes settle on me. Those raw, pure emerald, unnervingly sexy eyes. He winks.

Everyone in the vicinity turns to look at me.

My face heats. My skin prickles with awareness.

He goes back to his story. I want the bench to swallow me up. Then I hear someone with a bullhorn yelling names. "Penelope Carpenter. Please report to the red door for your confessional."

I look at Shveta. "Confession? I'm not religious . . ."

"No, no. I just did mine. Don't worry. It's not scary. They just lock you in a room and film you answering questions. Like, why you're here. What your initial impressions are. What you think the premise of the show is about. Who you think your biggest competition is."

Not scary. And yet, I'd completely freaked when that lady thrust the camera in my face outside.

I go, my knees wobbling a little, but it turns out it's not so bad. The woman behind the camera is nice and is able to pull answers from me pretty easily. At the end of it, she says, "You'll be expected to do confessional twice a day, as long as you're still in the competition. Good luck, Nell!"

Feeling a little better, I go out to the locker room, where I realize everyone is lining up, women on one side, men on the other. I get to the very end of the line, and we're taken out into a dark hallway and then into an empty basketball court. Will Wang is there, in his suit with no tie, waving at us. "Ready for your official class photograph?" he says.

The woman—Eloise Barker, the executive producer—is there. She's scrutinizing each person. "Can you remove your shirt?" she says to one man. Then she shouts out, "For publicity purposes it would be really helpful if you wear as little as possible, since this is going on the billboards and we want to get people's attention. So get naked, people! Within reason! Especially you, Luke!"

People start ripping off clothes, like it's no big deal. All the men are shirtless. The women aren't much better. The girl in the bikini top is rolling her boy shorts down to bare her flat tummy.

I cringe. I look down. I am already wearing tight capris and a big T-shirt over my workout bra. I don't want to lose anything else, or my dignity will be next to go.

Thankfully, when Eloise's eyes scrape over me, she doesn't ask me to take the T-shirt off. I push my glasses up on my nose and wonder if I'm really that repellent that people would rather have me clothed.

The staff members start to line us up, alternating the men and women. As I climb to the second row of the bleachers by an Asian man, I realize who's going to be on my other side.

The yeti bounds up.

I can't look.

Because holy chest.

He's all smooth, tanned, rigid muscle. Tattoos galore. A massive six-pack. For someone I thought was so dirty, he smells really good.

And the thoughts he conjures up in my head? Beyond dirty. I can't help it. He looks like something I'd want to eat with a spoon.

He snakes an arm around me. All that hardness ends up wrapped around me in a tight little package. "Fancy meeting you here, Penny."

Every pore on my skin seems to rejoice from his touch, pricking with arousal.

I refuse to let that continue.

I scowl at him as the rest of the people line up. "Don't call me that. No one ever calls me that."

I try to nudge him away, but that's impossible without actually touching him, which I've sworn not to do. The staff members seem intent on squeezing us together like sardines. They keep motioning us to squish closer. His arm drapes over me, and I press against his hard pectoral. I feel the heat of his bare chest, even through my T-shirt.

The photographer is looking through his viewfinder. "You know, all of you, kind of turn to the side a little so we all fit."

We do. Now he's behind me. The heat from his body is making me dizzy. "I'm Luke," he whispers in my ear, and I do my best not to concentrate on every inch of hard, naked flesh . . .

Don't care. Don't care. Don't . . . oh my god. I suddenly feel something twitch behind me.

Is that his cock, pressing against the small of my back?

I shove forward into the Asian dude in front of me and let out a gasp as I lose my balance and nearly tumble off the riser. Two massive hands grasp my arms, hauling me back onto steady ground before I can make the plunge and knock everyone else down like bowling pins.

"Steady." I look up, and he's giving me this cocky grin. Eyes almost feral and catlike, with thick, dark lashes. He has very white, straight teeth for a man so dirty. I wiggle my arm so he'll release it, and he does, but slowly, his fingers lingering there.

My knees weaken. I feel this odd sensation, like he's branded me. No man's touch has ever done that to me.

But he's him. And I'm me.

And never should the two of us come together. It's insane. It'd totally upset the laws of the universe.

Finally, the photographer snaps the pictures he needs. I hold my breath almost the whole time.

"Now, I'm warning you all," Eloise calls to everyone as we step down from the risers. "Don't wear anything that doesn't wash well. The first challenge is going to be a little dirty."

Dirty? Ugh. I hate dirty.

But then I look at Luke, walking away from me. No, strutting away from me, like he knows he owns the whole damn room. With a spring in his step, he reaches down and picks up his shirt. I can't stop staring at the way the tattoos dance across his perfect, tan, muscle-bound back.

And I think I might not hate dirty as much as I once did.

Luke

My ideal woman? Shit, who knows? All I know is I haven't met her yet. I ain't met a single girl who's made me say, "Yeah, I want to have that in my life forever." Haven't even come close.

—*Luke's Confessional, Day 1*

I don't know if alliances are important in this thing, but I've got them.

I've always been good at making friends. Filming hasn't even started, and I've already got an understanding with Ivy, the blonde bodybuilder; one with Michael, the IT kid; and in a foursome with a bunch of athletic guys who look like the "cool kids." We've made a pledge to help each other out until the end. Add that to my in with the executive producer, and I think I'm in pretty good shape. I'll add a few more.

Like Penny.

Or . . . not.

She likes to run in the opposite direction now. But when I was close to her a minute ago, she couldn't hide the way her body reacted to mine any more than I could hide the way my cock thickened for her. The little girl had goose bumps everywhere, even on those cute little freckles of hers.

We line up again to go into the next room, girls on one side, guys on the other. "All right," one of the staff members announces, walking up and down the aisle. "This isn't live television, but we're shooting it all in one take, so no language. No nudity. Keep it clean, folks. We're going to start filming with Will Wang walking backward toward those doors. The camera will be on him, and I want you all to lean in and give a wave or high five as he goes past you, and introduce yourself to the camera. Then when he announces 'This is *Million Dollar Marriage!*' you'll all run through those double doors and line up on the marks on the floor. Do you understand?"

We all clap and cheer, pumped. I give a wolf whistle as Ivy rolls her eyes and claps her hands. "Let's go, let's go, let's go!" she growls.

She's a fucking beast. If anyone's my competition, it's her. There are a few more seriously athletic people out there, but I've made friends with all of them. I'm ready to rule.

"And three . . . two . . . one . . . camera's on," the director says.

"Hello, coming direct to you from the Georgia Tech rec center, welcome to the first season of the newest sensation to sweep the country! Tonight, we have fifty contestants who have absolutely no idea what they're going to have to do to achieve our prize. The one thing they all have in common is that they're raring to win this season's top prize of ONE MILLION DOLLARS! This. Is. *MILLION. DOLLAR. MARRIAGE!*"

He runs backward as he talks, introducing some of the contestants, then shoves open the door. I clench my fists and follow the leader.

I can't believe I'm here, doing this. That I gave Jimmy and another friend of mine named Flynn the reins at Tim's for the next three weeks and told them to do their best to check in on Gran. Before I left, I told Gran that I was going away for a while to be on television and that for the next three weeks I'd have no idea where I'd be or what the hell I'd be doing. And I still don't know. All I know is it'll be played out for the entire country to see.

I'm game.

I run through the doors, and it's like it's the big game and we're the home team. People are screaming from packed bleachers—they must be actors because they look way too excited about this. They're screaming and trying to touch us as I run through, and *HOLY SHIT*.

I nearly stop in my tracks when I see what's in front of me.

It's an Olympic-size swimming pool.

It looks like it's full of balloons.

One of the contestants behind me nudges me, so I find my mark, an *X* on the ground that has "LCROSS" on it. I stand there and wave at my fake fans. Blow a few of the cute girls kisses. They cheer louder.

"All right, here's the name of the game!" Will Wang shouts when we're all assembled. He climbs to a podium overlooking the pool, and there's a cameraman there, filming us from above. I've counted at least ten cameras. I look for Penny and see her way on the other side of the pool. She looks terrified. "We have loaded this massive pool full of balloons. There are nearly one million of them. When the whistle sounds, your job is to dive in and find the balloon with your name on it. Simple, right?"

I scan the balloons. I notice two first off that have writing on them in Sharpie. I look up and note that one of my biggest threats—this shaved-head dude called Ace, who's tattooed and pierced within an inch of his life—is doing the same thing.

He looks up at me, and a snarl appears on his face.

Oh, he's fucking going down.

"There is *one* catch!" Will Wang smiles. "If someone finds your balloon first, they might choose to hand it over to you, out of the goodness of their hearts."

I almost laugh at that. I haven't met a hell of a lot of people who are that good when it comes to sharing a million dollars.

"Or you can pop it, in which case that contestant is out of the game for good."

Several people gasp.

Hell no. That isn't happening to me. I've come too far to be here. And I have my alliances.

I'm ready.

"If your balloon is popped, only one thing can save you, but we'll get to that later. However, keep in mind before you go around popping everyone's balloons . . . you might need these people later. It's up to you how to proceed."

I wipe my chin and get ready to dive in. Name of the game: find my balloon. No popping.

"At the end of this round, we will narrow it down to eighteen contestants. Yes, over half of you will be eliminated. The first to find their balloons will advance to the next round." He takes a breath and raises a hand. "Any questions?"

We all shake our heads.

"On your mark! Get set! Go!"

All at once we jump in, some shitty canned music playing overhead. It's havoc. Balloons of all colors are flying everywhere.

And then it hits me when I feel it squishing through my toes. It's not just balloons in this pool.

It feels like . . . jelly.

I take a whiff as I push through. And then I see it. Sticky, sweet, lime Jell-O.

Screaming. Shouting. Fights break out, and overhead Wang shouts, "No fighting!" And there's the sounds of latex sliding together, Jell-O sloshing, and the even more jarring sound of balloons popping. All over.

I grab for the two balloons I saw before and notice the first one says "SHVETA PATEL." I wade over to the other one and grab it before the kid on my foursome, Silas Chen, can. I grin when I see the name on it. "PENELOPE CARPENTER."

"Whose are those?" he asks me, sifting frantically through the balloons and handfuls of lime shit.

"Not yours."

"You'll give me mine if you see it, right?"

"Yeah."

I whirl in a different direction and dive through a sea of lime and latex as a woman throws herself at me. She's crying, tears running down her face, a glob of jelly between her tits. "This is so nasty!"

"Fuck you!" someone screams behind me, and more balloons pop. "Give me that fucking balloon! You asshole!"

So much for keeping it clean.

"Our first contestant, Greta Waltz," Will says solemnly, "has been eliminated."

I can't see any more balloons with writing on them from my vantage point, so I straighten and look for Penny. She's all the way on the other end of the pool, slowly and carefully going through each balloon. I start to wade toward her, sloshing through Jell-O as I go. As I do, I run across a girl in a sari who's practically buried to the nose in balloons and trying to keep her head above them. "Shveta?"

She almost doesn't hear me, the noise is so loud. "Yes?"

I hand her her balloon.

"Are you serious?" She lifts it up and stares at it. "Oh my god. Thank you."

I keep wading through the chaos to get to Penny as Will Wang announces, "We've found our first contestant, ladies and gentlemen! Shveta Patel from New Jersey!"

He proceeds to give a long rundown on Shveta's background. All the while, I've got my eye on the balloons around me as I make my way across the pool.

Five more people are disqualified, one from my athletic foursome, who I see stalking to the edge of the wall with the rest of the losers, muttering curses under his breath. Then I see Ace. I watch as he squeezes a balloon in his hands, popping it.

"And yet another one bites the dust!" Will Wang cries. "Ace Moulder is on a tear, people. He's already sent three people to their doom. The rest of the contestants better hope that their balloons don't end up in his hands!"

Fuck. But I'm still in it. As I get closer, I notice Penny is looking a little more worried. She's still methodically checking each balloon, but there's a little crease on her forehead, and she keeps looking up at the losers' wall, as if she can see herself there.

"Penny!" I shout.

She doesn't look up.

Right. She doesn't go by that name.

"Penelope Carpenter!"

She looks up this time, and her eyes light when she sees the red balloon in my hands.

Just then, out of nowhere, Ace comes up behind me and makes a dive for the balloon in my hands. I yank it away in the nick of time, but I lose my grip on it and it floats into the air. I grab for it, but it's just out of my reach. It floats aloft, toward Ace.

Who's grinning at it.

He holds his hands up for it, and it floats right to his fingertips.

Shit.

Clenching my fists, I run for him and dive onto his shoulders, taking him down under the waves of latex and lime. Away from the eye of the cameras, I deliver a punch to his throat that makes him choke out all the air in his lungs. When I surface, there's a spotlight on me.

Will Wang's annoying voice blares: "Would you look at that, people. That's Luke Cross, playing Prince Charming to Penelope Carpenter. Ladies, isn't he a dream?"

Wiping globs of green shit from my eyes, I grab the balloon solidly in my hands. By now, Penny is in front of me. "Are you going to pop it on me?" she asks, worried.

"Nah." I hand it to her. "Who do you think I am?"

"I guess I don't know," she murmurs, pushing her glasses up on her nose. "Thank you."

She starts to climb out of the pool as Will Wang announces, "Our next contestant through to round two—Penelope Carpenter!"

She looks back at me and smiles broadly.

Well, well, well. So she can smile. Maybe she's not so uptight as I thought.

"Hey. Pussy boy," a voice calls behind me.

I turn.

Ace is holding a yellow balloon. I can see "LUKE" written on it.

Shit.

Before I can think to do anything else, he squeezes it between his palms, and it bursts, leaving me looking at nothing but his ugly-ass satisfied smile.

SURVIVING ROUND ONE

Nell

> *What is my strategy? I don't know. I suppose I'll use my brain,*
> *since I'm not very athletic. I once nearly drowned in two feet*
> *of water.*

> *—Nell's Confessional, Day 1*

Even though my entire lower half is covered in lime jelly, I stride to the winners' risers, feeling like I could float on air.

I can't believe it. I survived round one.

Thanks to him. My dirty boy who can't stop looking at me.

Courtney and I joked that I'd probably be the first one eliminated. We'd bet that I'd probably be home snug in my bed by the end of day one of filming.

But not only am I not eliminated . . . I'm not one of fifty anymore. I'm one of eighteen.

I have the prize schedule from the black folder tattooed on my brain, so I know what each of the eighteen will get. Fifty thousand dollars.

Fifty thousand dollars!

And I barely had to lift a finger. I just got the right balloon, and . . .

"Our next elimination—and ladies, I'm sorry about this one, I know it's gotta hurt—Luke Cross. I'm sure our entire female audience is crying out right now. The knight in shining armor is no more. I really thought he'd get a lot farther in this competition," Will Wang says, a note of sympathy in his voice.

I look up in horror in time to see Luke, covered in a head-to-toe glaze of gelatin, heading to the other wall. The losers' wall.

No. No.

Did I do that? Is it my fault?

I hold the balloon in my hands, the one with my name on it that Luke rescued for me. And I can't help feeling that it should be his. That he should be here instead of me.

Shveta comes over and hugs me. "I can't believe this! We're going to the next round!"

My heartbeat is thudding in my ears as I watch Luke standing there, against the wall, a mildly pissed-off expression on his face. He's probably ruing the day he ever helped an incompetent like me. He crosses his arms, and his eyes stay trained on the ground.

And I. Feel. Like. Crap.

Another ten minutes go by, and that's all it takes for the rest of the balloons to be either popped or found. When everyone has exited the pool and is standing on either the winners' or losers' side, Will Wang says, "Well, here we are. We have seventeen people who have found their balloons. Thirty-three who have had their dreams crushed in the first moments of *Million Dollar Marriage*. But as I mentioned before, there is still a chance for those who don't have a balloon to be put back in the game."

He comes down from the podium and walks to Shveta. He smiles at her. "Our first winner. And now we get to what *Million Dollar Marriage* is all about. You're going to be divided into teams now. On the count of three, I'd like you to pop your balloon and find the sheet of paper inside."

He counts, and the second he reaches three, Shveta squeezes and pops the balloon. A piece of paper falls to her feet. She reaches down and opens it.

"Please read the name for the audience," Will Wang says.

She wrinkles her nose. "Ace Moulder."

The crowd cheers. "Come on over here, Ace!" the announcer says. Ace struts from farther down the winners' side over to them, looking warily at Shveta. Will Wang takes his balloon, pops it, and pulls out the name Shveta Patel. "You two are partners and must work together!"

Ace lets out an audible "Fuck," and Shveta looks nothing less than horrified. Will motions them over to a set of bleachers, where Ace is positioned behind Shveta. They both look utterly thrilled.

Then Will Wang looks at me. "Our number two, the lovely and brilliant Dr. Penelope Carpenter."

There's mild applause as I suddenly realize that I'm going to be paired with one of these men. Will looks down at my balloon. I struggle to pop it, squeezing my eyes shut as it does. Will picks up the paper and looks down at it. "As we mentioned, there is still a chance for our people from the losers' wall. And now one lucky loser is about to come back into the game, courtesy of our fair doctor." He hands me the paper. "Please read the name aloud."

I look at it, and for the first time, I'm glad. Because for the first time, I think I might be in good hands.

"Luke Cross."

Luke

My strategy? I have the same strategy in life. Be good to people, and the rest'll take care of itself.

—Luke's Confessional, Day 1

"Luke Cross has been saved by the shy but very lovely Dr. Carpenter!" Will Wang shouts. "Come on over here, you big lug!"

Will Wang has already begun to annoy me, but fuck it.

I'm going to round two. Fifty thousand dollars.

I pump my fist and break free of the losers' wall, then give him a hug, waving to the cheering audience of fake fans. "Don't thank me—thank your girl," he says.

I advance on her to give her a hug, but she takes a step back, almost falling into the pool again. She has that deer-in-the-headlights look on her face, I think from all the cameras. I give her a thumbs-up.

"Is he my partner?" she mumbles softly, looking shell-shocked.

"Indeed he is! But we'll get to that part in a minute!" Will says, so brightly I wonder if he had crack for breakfast. "Let's meet our next seven couples!"

Will goes down the line, pairing off couples. Next is Ivy, my bodybuilder alliance, and Cody, this slight Asian guy I don't know. I stand next to Penny on the platform, and I can almost feel her shaking.

"You okay?" I ask her.

"I—I can't believe I made it this far," she says.

"Yeah? Well, I'm going all the way," I tell her. "You can come with me."

She raises an eyebrow. "You're not going to clean the floor with my ass?"

"Hell no. Not now that you're on my team."

She's quiet for a minute as the applause from the next announced couple—one of my athletics, Brad, and an older, badass motorcycle woman in a leather bustier and piercings by the name of Natalie—dies down. "I think I'm going to weigh you down."

I laugh. "How much can a little thing like you weigh?"

"I'm just saying . . . if you want to win, I think you'd be better off with—" She points to the others. "Any one of them."

"Maybe. But I have you. I'm good."

The rest of the teams are decided, bringing us up to nine couples. Will Wang says, "Here they are, people! Your original *Million Dollar*

Marriage teams! Each individual here is guaranteed a minimum of fifty thousand dollars!"

We all cheer. Fuck yeah.

"But, losers . . . there's still a chance that you can get into the game, and we're going to go over that right now."

The lights dim, and some intense music plays overhead.

Will Wang says, "Teams, you have the choice to participate in the next challenge. If you decide to, you'll receive a minimum of seventy thousand dollars! All you have to do is say YES!"

I shrug and call out, "Hell YES!"

Will laughs. "Hold on, buckaroo. There's a catch you might want to know about. And that brings us to the main premise of the show. John Phillips, are you out there? Please, join me on the podium."

A man in a suit stands up, and the crowd parts to let him through. He jogs up to the podium, shakes Will's hand, and stands beside him.

"John is here for a very special reason. A very special ceremony, if you will."

The cameras are focused on our faces, and I know something is up.

"Yes, in fact, John happens to be a justice of the peace."

The crowd gasps. Next to me, Penny's body stiffens.

"Yes. In order to participate in the next challenge and any challenges going forward, you and your partner must be man and wife!"

Louder gasp. The screens overhead focus in on the shock of the contestants. Penny's trembling. Ivy looks pissed. Ace is hurling out f-bombs into the air. The Indian girl has sunk to the ground and is covering her face in her palms. It's chaos.

Me? I'm calm as can be.

It's called *Million Dollar Marriage*. Did they think *marriage* wouldn't factor in?

I'm in.

"You will need to spend the rest of the time living with your partner as a unit. You'll do everything together for the duration of the contest.

There will be challenges that test your endurance, your strength, and your ability to work together as a couple. If you win, you'll each get two hundred and fifty thousand dollars and the opportunity to have the marriage annulled, should you choose. BUT, if you decide to stay together as lawfully married, you'll together receive the grand prize of ONE MILLION DOLLARS and an all-expenses-paid honeymoon package!"

I look around. All the couples are yin and yang. It's like they ran our personality tests through a machine and picked out the person we'd be *least* compatible with.

"Now, we understand this is a big commitment on your part, so we'll give you and your partner five minutes to talk things out and decide what you'd like to do. Please note that once your decision is made, it is final, and you will be married here, on the spot, before you board a flight to where the *real* competition will begin." He winks at the losers' wall. "If you drop out now, you'll go home with fifty thousand dollars, but if you decide to continue on, you'll earn seventy thousand and the chance to compete for even more! Time starts . . . now!"

I turn to Penny. She's hugging herself and won't look at me. "Hey. I'm in."

She doesn't say anything.

I wave a hand in front of her face.

"Are you crazy?" she finally says, staring at me. "I'd never marry you."

"Fine. Forget the marriage. This is about the money. And I need the money."

She sighs. "But . . . my parents . . ."

"Fuck your parents. Fuck everyone. Who cares? After we win, we'll get it annulled. But I need the money, and you do, too, right? Think of all the people you beat out so far to be here, standing on this stage. Let's fucking do this."

She stares at the ground. "We won't win."

"Hell yeah we will, girl. You've got the brains, right? I've got the brawn. Whatever challenges there are, we can handle them. Trust me. We'll kick ass."

She wipes her hair from her face and stares at the countdown clock, which shows we have less than two minutes to come to a final decision.

I nudge her. "What are you afraid of?"

"I . . . I don't know," she says, her voice quiet. "That I'll make a fool of myself on national television?"

"I won't let that happen. Anything else?"

She looks up at me with those big blue eyes, and it gets me. Right there. In the heart, in my cock. I want to pry open those big soft lips with my tongue and have my way with her.

"That you'll fall in love with me?" I grin at her.

Her eyes widen more, and her face reddens. "No. Not that."

"Good. Then what's your answer?"

She stares at her hand, and at first I don't get it. But then I do. That's where the ring is supposed to be. "It's just that . . . all my life, I've dreamed of a romantic wedding. With an actual ring, a white dress, and a church and cake and the man I'm in love with. Not this. This is cheesy and gimmicky and just . . ."

Just then, the buzzer above us sounds.

"Time's up!" Will Wang says, dragging his microphone down the line of contestants. "So, we come to Shveta and Ace. Before you let us know your final decision, please tell us, have you enjoyed your time on *Million Dollar Marriage* thus far?"

Ace frowns. Shveta says, "Yes. Up until now."

"Ah. All right. So now, what is your final decision? We do, or no way?"

Shveta leans into the microphone. "I've decided . . . no way. I will not be continuing on. Thank you."

The crowd starts to murmur. "Ah. And why have you decided to give up the chance of winning a million?"

"I can't," Shveta says as Ace scowls at her. "In my culture, we are very strict about marriage."

"Okay, okay." He thrusts the microphone at Ace. "And how does it feel for you?"

"It fucking sucks. But I didn't want to marry this bitch anyway."

Will shifts uncomfortably because Ace looks like he's about to punch the nearest thing, which could be his head. "Don't worry, sir, there's a chance for you to get back in the running later on. If fewer than nine couples decide to be married for the next challenge, we'll draw straws from the remaining contestants to fill the open spaces."

I lean toward Penny's ear, and she stiffens. Hell, is she always going to stiffen around me? "Look. Ace is out. Our chances are getting better and better by the minute."

And I know it. I know from the way she won't look at me. The way she tenses whenever I'm near. Her body may react to me, but she's got that big brain of hers telling her no, telling her to run as far and fast as she can in the other direction.

She's probably better off that way.

Her answer is going to be no.

"Now, couple number two!" Will Wang says, moving toward us. "Prince Charming and the lovely doctor. Talk about a striking couple! Dr. Carpenter, what about you? Have you had fun here so far?"

She swallows and nods.

"All right. So, let's not keep the people waiting. What say you? Are you going on for the million, or does your journey end here tonight? We do, or no way?"

She looks in my direction for a blink, brings her mouth close to the mic, and says, "We do."

And I swear I could hug her. If I knew she wouldn't flinch away.

WE DO

Nell

No, I did not think they'd make us marry right then. I thought possibly the winners might have to do that, because that's the name of the show, but I figured I'd be long gone by that time. It's fine. I mean, obviously my parents are probably thinking I've lost my mind. But we're obviously going to get it annulled the moment we get eliminated.

—Nell's Confessional, Day 2

Ten minutes later, we're all standing on a podium. There are nine couples total now; after several of the contestants decided not to marry while others were rescued from the loser pool, the winners were put in a pool and had their names chosen and paired at random until we got up to nine teams. We're listening to the justice of the peace spout out the basic marriage vows, "for richer, for poorer," and all that. But he's doing it in a game-show-host voice, the spotlight is making me sweat, and I look like crap after that last challenge. Plus, I'm wearing workout capris, my sneakers are full of lime Jell-O, and I have a cheesy white veil on my head that has an *MDM* clip in rhinestones.

If my parents could see me now . . .

Well, hopefully by the time they see me, this'll be over and I'll already have the marriage annulled.

"Now, brides, take your husband-to-be's hand in your own, gaze deeply into his eyes, and repeat after me . . ."

I swallow. Luke's hand is like twice the size of mine, calloused and rough, but warm. Mine is slick with sweat. I look up into those green eyes of his. In this light, I can see the amber flecks within them.

We are toe to toe. Hand in hand. So close I can feel the heat from his body. His skin is glistening, and I bet it tastes like lime and sweat.

God, he's beautiful. So beautiful it almost drowns out the cheesy justice's voice. So beautiful I almost forget the cameras and spotlight and that we're here in the Georgia Tech rec center, about to compete on a game show.

I manage to choke out the "I do."

Then the justice turns to the men and asks them the same. Luke says, his voice a low tremor, "I do," even as the words "till death do you part" are still hanging in the air. The rings we exchange are gold tone, but plastic, and say *MDM* on them; they really spared all expense with that detail.

"I now pronounce you man and wife," the justice says.

And just like that, Luke Cross and I are married.

I'm married. Married to the dirty yeti who can't stop staring at me.

"You may now kiss the bride."

My eyes widen. I turn to the justice in shock.

Luke doesn't even attempt it. We just stand there awkwardly. Behind me, I hear the sounds of a scuffle and whirl to look. Ace—who managed to get back in the game because his number was drawn to pair with a dark-haired beauty named Marta—just got slapped. "No touch me!" she shrieks.

I look back up at Luke. "Don't worry, sweetheart. Not going to try."

"Thanks," I mumble.

"Now," Will Wang says, striding down the podium and grinning big, "take a look at your nine happy couples. They're getting ready to embark on a honeymoon, if you will. But this is no ordinary honeymoon! First, a few ground rules!"

Will starts to explain the details of the game. When we arrive at the first stop, we'll be given $5,000, which we'll need to budget for travel to the locations we'll be visiting. For the most part, flights will be booked for us to keep an air of mystery as to the next location, but we have to secure most of the ground transportation and lodging. At most stops, there will be challenges that will test our ability to work as a couple. Places will be determined based on how we fare on those challenges and how soon we arrive at each check-in. The last couple to arrive at the final outpost or check-in during each leg of the journey will be eliminated, though there will be several stops along the way that are non-elimination rounds. I listen to all this, feeling dizzy and overwhelmed. "Sounds like *The Amazing Race*," someone says. I shrug dumbly. Now I kind of wish I'd watched that show. Maybe then I'd have some idea what to expect.

A staff member urges us off the risers and rushes us out of the room as Wang is still talking. I catch, "Right now, they're going to be shuttled off to an undisclosed location in the United States, where the hardest test of their relationship will begin! Who will learn to work together? Who will be torn—"

The doors close, and then they're running us down the hallway we entered through. Outside is a big tour bus. They load us all on, telling us that our packs are already loaded and that we need to sit with our spouses.

My spouse.

Oh my god, I'm married.

To this hot, dirty, completely-wrong-for-me hunk.

Still sticky with Jell-O, we sit down, all eighteen of us, and I look out the window as the Georgia Tech rec center disappears from view. "Where are they taking us?" I ask after a few minutes.

"Airport," he says.

He's right. We're heading south down I-85, toward the Atlanta International Airport. "You think it's going to get a lot more intense? Dangerous?"

He nods. "I think they're gonna fuck with us as much as they can."

I cringe.

He notes it with some amusement. "What? You don't like the word *fuck*?"

I cringe again.

"Or is it the action you have a problem with?"

"I don't approve of that kind of talk, actually. I find it low class."

"Oh. Well, I'm sorry, Mrs. Cross. I'll try to tone it down—"

"No. Not Mrs. Cross." He gives me a confused look, and I explain. "I'm going to keep my name when I get married. I'm not even going to hyphenate. And I earned my title. I'll always be *Dr.* Carpenter, thanks."

He squints. "You're bullshitting me."

I cringe again.

"All right, *Dr.* Carpenter. So before we get on the plane, let's get a few things straight so we can win this." He lowers his voice and leans toward my ear. "Ace and Marta are the ones to look out for. I don't know about Marta, but as we've already seen, Ace is gonna play dirty."

He peeks between the seats to make sure no one is looking.

"Ivy's strong and competitive, but she can't beat me, and her partner, Cody, is about as weak as they come. Brad's tough. He and Natalie are going to be a hard team to beat too. He's athletic, and she's a badass."

I stare at him. I barely know these people's names. I've been so busy just making sure I don't trip and fall flat on my face. How has he sized up the competition so quickly?

"The others are no problem. So. Number one, I want you to trust me. Completely. And I will trust you. We are each other's first and most unbreakable alliance. You got that?"

I'm surprised by how serious he sounds. He's definitely in it to win it. Which sucks for him, since I'm probably going to let him down

59

big-time. Hell, I was out of breath from that tiny run from the arena to the bus. "Fine."

"Number two, you have to chill out. Stop worrying about every-thing and just relax. Do as I tell you and everything will be fine."

Is he serious? "I never said I was worried."

"Your body says it enough for you," he says, running his finger down my bare arm, which is a sea of Jell-O–covered goose bumps. I shudder, not so much from the touch but because it feels unnaturally good. Like I could use a whole lot more of that. "Jeez. Fuck. Are you always this uptight?"

"No. Just when I get married to complete strangers."

He laughs. Is this all just a game to him?

"What? You don't care that you're now wedded to someone you just met and would never even consider marrying otherwise?" I demand.

He shrugs. "It's not real."

"Yes, it is. As cheesy as it was, we have an official license with our name on it. So we basically just spit in the face of a time-honored tra-dition that should be treated with respect. I sullied my dreams for the future with a husband I love. People will look at me when I get married for real and think I'm a fraud because I married you. For what? Money? I feel . . . dirty."

He considers this. "Hell, when you put it that way . . . All I know is, it don't go against my dreams for the future. I never planned on mar-riage at all. That ain't my thing."

He's so gross. "By *that* you mean commitment? Love? Monogamy?"

He gives me a look of disgust. "Yeah. All that shit. Maybe you just need to relax and not worry about what other people think so much."

"I can't help how I act. And yes, I'm normally high-strung. It's an asset, actually. I'm organized, focused, and competitive, even if I'm not athletic. That's why I graduated summa cum laude with all my degrees."

"Don't know what that means. All I know is you're uptight as hell. You'd be hot as fuck if you weren't so wired, maybe lost those glasses you're hiding behind. Take it easy, baby."

I scowl at him. I don't care about being *hot*. Even though he's probably right. People have called me an uptight stick-in-the-mud all my life. "Don't call me *baby*."

"Whatever, sweetheart. Number three, you seem to be down on yourself a lot," he says, his eyes not leaving mine. "And there're going to be a lot of physical challenges in this. I don't want to hear *I can't* from you, even once. If you're having trouble, tell me. I'll help you through. And I'll be asking you if there's a puzzle or anything that involves more brain cells than I got. I don't know a lot, but I'm never gonna tell you I can't. Got it?"

I don't really care for his manner. He's acting like those vows we took means he owns me. "Anything else?"

He scratches the scruff on his chin. "Don't think so."

"All right. Well, I've got something. Absolutely no touching me. And no, we do not sleep in the same bed. And if they make us share a room, I get the bed and you get . . . something else, preferably in another room. Also, don't think that because I'm your wife on paper that it entitles you to any of the normal things wives do for their husbands. Think of this as a business arrangement. Nothing more. Okay?"

The corners of his mouth twist up in amusement. "Yes, ma'am."

I nod, satisfied that he's actually gotten it through his brain. I glimpse the airport in the distance and exhale.

Then I hear him say, under his breath, "But I expect you to change your mind on that."

I swing my head to look at him. "Under no circumstances will I change my mind!"

He shrugs. "If you say so, baby."

"I know so! And do not call me *baby* or *sweetheart* or any of those things, because I'm not amused!" I cross my arms and pretend he's dead for the rest of the trip.

Which isn't very long. The next moment, the bus pulls to a stop. I look at him, and he reaches over and gently touches my cheek.

And he brings his fingertip to his tongue and licks it. "Damn. You taste sweet."

I nearly die right there.

The touch is as light as a feather, but it rockets straight to my core.

"Did you listen to a single thing I said?" I demand as my temperature skyrockets. "No touching?"

He stares at me for a long time, then licks his lips. "Yeah. I heard. But I have a thing against following directions. Especially from someone as lickable as you."

My jaw drops. My mind whirls.

I can think of nothing.

Except that he just called me lickable. *Me.* Lickable?

One of the staff members walks down the aisle handing out black cloths to us. "When you board the airplane, please be seated with your spouse. You will be instructed to put on your blindfold after the flight takes off."

Blindfold? Great. Being *blindfolded* next to my *spouse* is probably a recipe for disaster, considering the fact that he just. Tasted. Me.

We get our bags and board a jet. I take out my book, and I'm struggling to load my backpack into the overhead bin when Luke effortlessly shoves it in.

"Thanks." As I sit next to Luke, I notice his hands tighten on the armrests. He has his earbuds in, as they let us keep our phones, but they blocked data, Wi-Fi, texting, and calling. I decide I'll put mine in, and maybe we won't have to talk. But then curiosity gets the best of me. "You don't like flying?"

He smirks at me. "Never done it before."

"Seriously?" Somehow that makes me feel better. Braver. "It's nothing to worry about."

"Never said I was worried."

"Your body says it enough for you," I say, mimicking his voice as I point out his grip on the armrest. I'm careful not to touch him.

His fingers loosen. He starts to twist the plastic *MDM* ring on his finger. "You fly a lot?"

I nod. "I'm from Cape Cod." Not that I go back there much.

"Where's that?"

"Massachusetts."

"What's a Yank like you doing down south?"

I smile. "Wanted to get away from my family, I guess. Came down here and had no interest in ever going back. I've lived here eight years, getting my undergraduate degree, my master's, and my doctorate."

"Holy shit. You're smart."

"I suppose. I also have a very good memory. That helps."

"Jeez. Fuck. My parents disowned me when I was sixteen. That's when I dropped out of school. Thought about going back for my GED, but fuck it. I hate tests. Never was good at school. But you? You're every parent's wet dream. You're seriously telling me your family gives you shit? For what?"

"My father wanted me to go to Harvard Law and follow in his footsteps. But it never interested me. He basically told me that if I wanted to follow him, he'd pay for it all. If I didn't, I was on my own."

He stares at me, impressed. "That takes some balls, girl."

I shrug, though I feel a surge of pride. The tough guy thinks I have balls. "Well. I'm either brave or stupid, because I have a lot of student loans. But you have to be true to yourself. Right?"

The plane starts to taxi down the runway. He cranes his neck over me to see out the oval window. He's not saying it, but I think he might be nervous.

"What about you?"

"I own a bar. Or . . . the bank owns a bar. I need the money to pay it off."

"Oh. Which one?"

"You don't know it. I doubt a sweet, pure thing like you'd ever go to my neighborhood. It's a dive." He touches the book on my lap. "You get a lot of stuff in your big old brain from books?"

I nod. "I love Baudelaire."

"Baude who?" He takes the book from my hands and flips the pages. "Holy shit. It's in another language."

"French."

"And you can read that?"

I nod. "I spent my summers in Paris when I was growing up."

"Holy . . . fuck." He clears his throat. He's still absently paging through the book. "I mean, holy . . . *fudge*. That's strange as hell. I haven't even picked up a book in . . . who the hell knows?"

I shrug. *"Le bou est toujours bizarre."*

He gives me a look. "Le what?"

"The beautiful is always strange."

"Ah." He points to my earbuds. "What're you listening to?"

"Mussorgsky. *Pictures at an Exhibition*. You?"

He pulls out an earbud and hands it to me to have a listen. I'm not sure I want to trade, considering that seems almost intimate, sharing something that's been in his ear. But I take it, then hand him one of mine.

All I hear is a headache-inducing bang of drums from some rock band whose lead singer sounds like he's screaming in pain. I wince and hand his back to him.

When I look up at him, he's so close I can see the amber flecks in his green eyes, which are piercing me. He's still listening to mine, his lips curved in amusement over the fact that I clearly didn't like his. "You're a classy girl, aren't you?"

"I appreciate classical music," I say, tugging the earbud away from him and returning it to my ear.

He's gazing at me like I'm some mythical creature. I think all this conversation has done is prove that we are about as night and day as two people can get. I don't think the *Million Dollar Marriage* crew could've picked a couple that is more wrong for each other. But maybe that's just what they wanted.

I almost laugh as I realize the knuckles of his one hand are white on the armrest. "And by the way, you can have mercy on the armrests. We've already taken off."

His eyes move to the window, where the plane is climbing into the sky, leaving Atlanta as a patchwork beneath us. He leans over me. He has small sideburns, stubble on his caramel skin, and a shock of dark hair falling over his eyes that I just want to reach out and sweep back. I get a whiff of his smell, masculine, deep, and . . . delicious, enough to make my insides twist. "Wow. Would you look at that?"

"Would you like to switch seats?" I ask, wondering if he knows what he's doing to me.

He turns his head a little, and now he's just inches away. His eyes practically undress me, glinting with mischief. "Nah. I think the view is better right where I am."

Luke

> *Sure, it was a surprise. I never saw myself as married or set-tled down. Especially not to someone like her. I'm easygoing. Whatever works, you know? But Penny . . . she's another story.*

> —*Luke's Confessional, Day 2*

I survived my first flight. We're sitting blindfolded on the runway, ready to get off the plane and go . . . who knows where.

"Where do you think we are?" Penny whispers to me. "We were only in the air three hours. So based on that and the wind shear and the location of the airport as we were taking off . . . I'd guess that we're in . . ."

"Philadelphia."

"How do you . . ."

"I'm peeking."

She nudges me. "Well, don't. You know they're filming us at all times. Even now. Don't get us disqualified."

I like that she's thinking about the game. "Yes, ma'am."

A staff member escorts us onto another bus, and we end up driving for another hour. By then, it's dark. I'm ready to hit the hay.

Which might be exactly where I end up sleeping, knowing Penny's rules.

"All right, guys!" Will Wang announces from the front of the bus after it stops. "We are at your first outpost. You may remove your blindfolds."

I pull mine down around my neck. It's dark outside. I scan all the windows. Hell, we might really be in the middle of nowhere. "What the fuck is this?" Ace says behind me.

We all file off the bus and form a circle around Will in some rutted, muddy field. It's cold as fuck; I can see my breath. I stuff my hands deep into the pockets of my shorts.

"The time is now nine p.m. Go right to your quarters, where you may freshen up, eat something, and rest. When the siren sounds, you must all converge here for the instructions on your next challenge. From here on out, you and your spouse will be traveling independently from other contestants. Whoever arrives at the next outpost first will be given an advantage in the next leg of the journey. Any questions?"

Charity, a model with enormous tits the cameramen are clearly in love with, says, "I don't see any quarters here?"

With that, a floodlight switches on, illuminating a handful of small tents.

Then I see Penny's horrified expression.

Fuck. I'm sleeping on the ground, outside of the tent. In the cold.

We find the tent with our names on it. It's even smaller up close. The producers are definitely fucking with us. I motion for her to go in first.

She climbs in and lets out a whimper. "I *hate* camping. God, it's cold."

I go in and see that there's only one sleeping bag. I think the producers are trying to get us as uncomfortable with our new spouses as possible. It's a two-person bag, but I don't think I'll be lucky enough to use it. I twist on a lantern on a small pack, and it casts a circle of light on Penny's huddled shape.

"Hell yeah!" I shout when I open the pack and find a container of Cheez-Its and Cokes. I pass one to her.

She plops down on the bag and shakes her head. "I don't eat that stuff." She looks at her sneakers. "I'm all sticky, too, from that Jell-O."

"So you got a thing against junk food, nature . . . anything else?"

She pulls her knees up to her chest and hugs herself, shivering, as I tear through the pack of snacks. I haven't eaten all day, so I easily clean it all up. I could go for a beer, but I settle for the Coke. She rummages through her bag.

She pulls out a toothbrush and toothpaste.

Is she crazy? "I think you're shit outta luck there, girl. This ain't the Four Seasons."

She wrinkles her nose. "I have to brush my teeth."

"Good luck." I pull off my shoes and start to lie down on the bag as she stands up, going for the tent flap.

She's half out of the tent when she turns around and sees me lying there. "What do you think you're doing?"

I close my eyes. The bag ain't much, but it's sure as hell better than nothing. "You were serious about that?"

She nods. "Dead."

I sit up, put my shoes on again. I'm just getting ready to go find another place to sleep when she comes back, a sour expression on her face. "I think I've scarred myself for life."

"What? No spa?"

She shakes her head. "Porta-potties. So gross."

She climbs in past me, and I smell mint—so she must've gotten her teeth brushed after all. That, and her. I think it's her shampoo, but maybe it's the lime Jell-O. I smelled it on the plane, and I couldn't stop leaning into it.

What I wouldn't give to curl up in a sleeping bag with that and feast on it all night long.

She sits down on the sleeping bag and unties her sneakers, slipping out of them. Then she crawls to the top of the bag and slips inside. She winds her hair up on top of her head and pulls off her glasses, setting them atop her backpack.

Then she looks up at me.

And fucking hell. She's beautiful. She wears those too-big glasses to hide her face, and it works. I blink twice in the dim light, trying to see more of the girl she keeps trying to hide.

"What?" she mutters.

"Nothing," I say.

I go outside and close the flaps on the tent. The temperature has gone down, even in the last hour since we got here. I look around for someplace to rest and wind up tripping over another form on the ground. It's Brad, one of the original members of my athletic foursome. He's lying on the ground, along with a couple of other people I can't make out.

"Your *wife* kick you out too?" I ask him, finding a spot I can lay out. It's muddy earth and dried patches of grass. It fucking sucks.

He shakes his head, bundled up in his North Face jacket. "No. She wanted me to stay. But she's older than my mother. So . . . yeah. I told her I'd sleep outside."

Oh. Fuck. Well, at least I have company out here.

Not the company I'd prefer, though.

In the darkness I make out a wiry, kind of weaselly-looking guy named Steven, who must've been kicked to the curb by his wife, Erica, who's one of those type-A, business-suit types and reminds me a little of Lizzy, Jimmy's girlfriend, except that Erica is all bitch. She's loud and abrasive and would drive me batshit. He leans over and shakes my hand.

Then I meet Elliott, who's probably over four hundred pounds. He's paired with a hot girl named Jen, who supposedly makes workout videos for a living.

There's Zach, who's forty-five, divorced twice with three kids, who seems like a bit of a shyster. He is paired with Cara, a twenty-five-year-old ballet dancer.

There are others out here too. "So all the guys are out here?"

Brad grins. "Not Ace." He points to a tent. "Listen."

I listen and hear it. A definite moan.

Zach shakes his head. "They wasted no time in consummating their marriage."

I raise an eyebrow. "Are you fucking kidding me? Ace and Marta? The beauty queen who can't speak English?"

To think, that could've been me and Penny. If she'd just let loose a little and relax.

He shrugs. "She didn't look like the sharpest tool in the drawer."

"He's a piece of work," Steven says.

"Yeah," Brad says, sitting up and cracking his knuckles. "I think that if we can find a way to slow him down, we should try. Work together, you know?"

Steven and Elliott nod. Steven says, "I'm in."

I shrug. "I don't know, man."

That ain't the strategy I'd told myself I would use going in. Even if Ace is an asshole, I want to win this clean. I'm all for helping each other, but I'm not going to try to bring anyone down. I got too much on my mind to think about that.

We talk a little more, but eventually we're all so tired that we drift to sleep. The sky is clear and filled with stars, and I'm so beat, I don't dream. It feels like a blink, and suddenly a siren wails overhead. "Contestants up!" someone shouts. "Get ready!"

I sit bolt upright and look around. It's even darker than before because clouds have moved in, covering the moon. And also because . . .

"No wonder I feel like I hardly slept," Zach, the older guy, says, rubbing his hand through his receding hairline and looking at his watch. "It's three in the morning."

LOST IN A CORNFIELD

Nell

> *How do I feel? I think I slept on seven different rocks for a total of twelve minutes. I haven't eaten anything since breakfast yesterday. And I'm covered in Jell-O. I guess I'm not very happy?*

> —*Nell's Confessional, Day 2*

Scraping my hair back into a ponytail and putting my glasses on, I stumble out of the tent but struggle to see anything but darkness. What time is it?

Will Wang's annoyingly peppy voice is coming through a bullhorn, so I follow that, along with the other contestants.

"We are coming to you from Lancaster County, Pennsylvania, where the *Million Dollar Marriage* contestants are about to embark on their first challenge. It's three in the morning, so it's time to get this underway!"

I have no idea what I look like, but I feel like death. I keep blinking to try to stay awake. I'm still wearing the same lime-crusted, smelly clothes, and I didn't have a chance to wash up this morning. This is cruel and unusual.

I make my way through the crowd and see Luke standing there, arms crossed. For someone who slept in the mud, he looks darn good. He spots me and gives me a grin. "Sleep well?"

I almost feel guilty for not sharing the tent with him. But it was a small tent. What was I supposed to do? Sleep on top of him?

My pulse skitters at the thought.

"Yes. You?"

"No complaints. You pumped?"

I nod. "Totally."

"Brush your teeth?" He winks at me. "I hear that's important."

I frown at him. "Shut up."

"How's everyone doing this morning?" Will holds the mic up for our answer.

As tired as we all are, we manage to scream pretty loudly in reply. It's freaking cold out, and I don't see any trace of the sun getting ready to rise. I dig my hands into the pockets of my black ski jacket and jump up and down in my sneakers.

"Welcome, our nine couples, to the start of your *Million Dollar Marriage* race to the finish! At the end of each leg, you will reach a check-in or outpost, where you can rest and refuel for the next day's activities. Do not stop until you've reached that check-in, or you will lose valuable time. The last couple to show up at each check-in will be eliminated, unless it is a non-elimination round. The order in which you arrive at each check-in will determine your starting time for the next leg of the journey.

"You are going to set off on the first part of the journey in three groupings of three. The order in which you set out will be determined by Marriage Test Number One."

Marriage Test? That doesn't sound good. I manage a look at Luke. His brow is low, his eyes focused. Total game face.

"What is a Marriage Test, you ask?" Will says, striding back and forth in front of us. "Well, you'll have several of them throughout the journey, and they will award you crucial bonuses like earlier start times. You remember filling out your personal questionnaire before the show began? The Marriage Test will see how well your partner knows you and can answer your questions. First, women. Please step forward."

I take a tentative step forward. I'm flanked by the older woman in leather and Marta, who can't stop looking at one of her broken finger-nails. A staff member comes along and hands us each what looks like an electronic wipe board.

"Ladies, you will have twenty seconds to write down how you think your spouse would complete this sentence: *If I were stranded on a desert island, the one thing I'd take with me would be . . .*" He pauses for effect, and my stomach drops. My mind goes blank. "And . . . go!"

I turn and look back at Luke, who's staring at me, trying to transmit the answer telepathically to me. "Don't help, men! Let your wives do it on their own!" Will chides. "Ten seconds!"

I think I've got it anyway. I quickly scribble down the answer.

A buzzer sounds somewhere in the darkness, and Will says, "All right, let's see how the couples did on Marriage Test Number One!"

He starts with Marta. Amazingly, though I'm not really sure Marta can speak English, she knows the p-word, the slang, vulgar word for a woman's sexual parts, and it turns out, that's just what Ace said. So one point for them.

Natalie, next to me, says, "Protein shakes!" which, weirdly enough, happens to be Brad's answer. They also get a point.

Then Will comes to me. I gnaw on my lip. "Okay, Dr. Carpenter. What do you think Luke Cross can't live without if stranded on a desert island?"

I flip over my board and show the answer. "A woman?" I ask.

People start to laugh. Luke lets out a muffled curse behind me. So, I'm wrong? That same annoying buzzer sounds, and Will says, "Sorry, Dr. Carpenter. The answer we were going for was a penknife. A penknife."

I whirl around to look at Luke, who's squinting at me. *A woman?* he mouths, like I'm insane. I shrug.

Turns out, he doesn't do much better at answering my questions either. We end up going zero for six, which puts us in group three, the last group, which will end up leaving ten minutes after group one. Of course, Ace and Marta are in that group. I can already tell by the way Luke's muttering that he hates them.

"Our first challenge is taking place at the Riverview Farm in Lancaster County, site of the largest and most challenging corn maze in the entire world. This corn maze is not like any other. There are miles and miles of paths, and one wrong turn can put you off track for hours. There are also underground tunnels that you might have to go through. As you go along, you will be collecting numbers to show that you are on the correct path. There are dozens of paths through the maze, but you must collect the numbers one through ten, in your color, on your journey. On your way, there will be various challenges and riddles for you to solve.

"Also, be aware that there are several 'ghosts' hunting you in the maze. If you see one, run. If it manages to catch you, you will need to go back to the beginning of the maze and will lose valuable time. Any questions?"

I look at Luke. Do we have any questions? He doesn't; he's in ready stance, like he can't wait to plunge in.

"Oh, I almost forgot. Because we really want to encourage couples to work together, you'll be tied to each other, front to front."

Everyone collectively lets out a sigh.

But I can't even bring myself to do that. I'm just plain . . . horrified.

I have to spend the next few hours pressed up against Luke Cross? I thought that was why I kicked him out of the sleeping bag. To avoid such a thing!

The teams leaving earlier get tied up and sent on their way. We watch them, and all the while my heart is racing. Most of them don't seem at all bothered by the proximity. But right now, I can't think of anything other than being so close to Luke Cross that I will be able to feel his every breath, and he will feel mine.

A few minutes after the second group goes, it's our turn.

Blushing furiously, I manage a peek at him as the staff members come around with thick lengths of rope. He has one hand fisted on his hip, one hand working through the even darker scruff on his jaw. His eyes are on me. "You okay with this?"

I like that he's asking me. But it doesn't matter. "Do I have a choice?"

The staff member instructs us to stand close together. Luke spreads his feet, and I step between his, and we lift our arms as they coil the rope around our waists. Then the rope is tightened, pushing us impossibly close to one another. My breasts squish against his hard chest.

We drop our hands down, and I feel embarrassed looking at him, so I just stare right ahead, at his chest.

A moment later, I feel it. His cock hardening against my abdomen. I blush. Oh god. This is not happening.

I shift my stance. "Can you not . . . do that?"

He lets out a low chuckle. "Can you not . . . have tits? Can you not . . . smell that good? Can you not . . . feel so soft?"

I tense. "What?"

"I'm a man. You stop turning me on, baby, and maybe I'll stop being turned on."

I'm . . . turning him on? Me?

Change the subject. "So, what is the strategy for this?"

"Same strategy as always. Win. Just follow my lead."

"How can I follow you when I'm facing you?" I snap.

"You know what I mean."

With a struggle, we manage to stumble to the starting line. It's nearly impossible to walk because I'm going backward. I can't take the lead because I can't see beyond Luke's massive chest, so . . . sucks for me. Meanwhile, his cock is growing into a redwood tree between us, pulsing and alive, poking my already roiling tummy. I try to concentrate on the challenge so I won't think about how it's turning me on too. Or wonder what it would feel like if he dipped his head down and kissed me.

"On your mark!" Will Wang shouts.

"You ready?" he mumbles to me.

I nod.

"Get set!"

He whispers, "When he says go, I want you to lift your legs up and wrap them around me, okay?"

He didn't just say that, did he?

"Wait . . . what?"

"Go!"

It all happens so fast. He hoists me into the air, wrapping my thighs around his hips, my arms around his neck, so that he's cradling my ass. And carrying me, ahead of the other two couples, he races into the maze.

Luke

> *It wasn't hard. She weighs, like, ninety pounds soaking wet. What was hard was the rain. It was like ice, and sloshing through ankle-deep icy mud sucked. We don't get weather like that down south.*

> *—Luke's Confessional, Day 2*

"Go left! For the last time, go left!" she screams at me.

My timid little church-mouse wife is the worst back seat driver.

But I can't deny, she has some incredible tits. I've gotten very close to them, so I know them intimately. Her nipples are hard against me. What I wouldn't give to feel her, bare, against me, skin against skin.

And I also can't deny that I'm rock hard for her. For some reason, the more she screams at me which way to go, the more I want to throw her down in the mud and have my way with her.

It started pouring about two hours into the maze, and it hasn't let up since. I haven't seen another soul in about that long. We've made it through five of the markers, and we're looking for number six.

I ignore her screaming to go left, and it bites me in the ass, because five seconds later I run into a dead end.

Shit. I let out a growl.

"What?" Even before knowing what the problem is—she can't really see shit, her face buried in my chest—she says, "Told you we should've gone left."

"You're fucking brilliant." I spin to move, and that's when I see it, about fifty yards away and closing in.

A ghost.

Well, really, a guy in an all-blue outfit, slowly lumbering toward me. It's the first one we've seen.

Fuck.

"Hold tight," I tell her, racing forward and taking a quick left like she told me to, running at top speed. Mud is flying everywhere, the rain blurs my vision, and everything bleeds together as I careen left, then right, then left again, trying to lose the ghost. It'd really blow if we had to start from the beginning after all this.

I see the blue number six up ahead and race for it. She grabs it, tucking it in my jacket, between us. "Number six! Yay!" she shouts.

"Shh," I tell her, peering through the dried corn husk wall as I stop to catch my breath. "Think we lost that ghost."

"We did? Then let's keep going."

"Give me a second," I say, still breathing hard.

She lets out an annoyed sigh. "Just so you know, my favorite pastime is not filling in ovals. I actually am a very good harpist."

I let out a laugh. The Marriage Test was more than two hours ago. So that's what she's been stewing about all this time? "You're going to give me shit about my answers when you didn't get any of them right yourself? What was that shit about me bringing a woman on an island?"

"Well," she says, into my T-shirt. "Clearly you like women."

So she got my cock's message? "Yeah, but I like being alive a little more. So, penknife."

I start to pick up the pace as she says, "If you think my answer was dumb, what about yours? A bottle opener? Why would I need a bottle opener on a desert island?"

I shake my head and mutter under my breath, "It auto-corrected. I didn't know how to spell it."

"What?"

"Bottle . . . whatever. That French guy." I lean against a wall of corn. "Can we just rest for two seconds?"

She's quiet for a little bit. She'd answered *books* for that question. So in a way, I was right. But I'm not going to say that. I'm shit-stupid compared to her.

"Oh." She unwraps her legs from around me and lowers them to the ground, loosening her grip around my neck. I guess that's the closest she's going to come to admitting it. And the closest I am. "Sorry. Better?"

No. "Yeah."

I reach between us and adjust my cock through my cargo shorts, but nothing I do is going to stop this raging hard-on. Nothing short of stripping her down and fucking her here, and I know there are cameras. Lots of cameras. There are drones overhead, and the ropes that tie us together are equipped with cameras and voice recorders too.

"I'm good. Up you go." I lift her into the place that feels right. Complete.

I don't know if I've gotten past the point of pain or if my body just wants her that bad, but whatever it is, I don't have to drop her again.

Over the next hour, we manage to get the last four markers, still not seeing anyone else in the maze. Either we're doing really well or really shitty.

"Hold on—I see the exit," I say to her, sprinting forward.

Her body tightens around me as we explode through the gates. Camera crews are there, as is Will Wang, waiting for us.

"Are we first?" I ask him.

"You're not done yet!" Will says as we're quickly untied from each other. I look over at Penny. The lime shit is gone; now she's covered from head to toe in mud. I bet I don't look much better. "This van will take you to your next challenge."

I'm breathing hard. Penny looks absolutely exhausted. "Next?"

He nods.

Fuck.

We load up into the van, soaked and shivering in the heat being pumped through the vents. A single cameraman comes with us, sitting in the front of the van, filming everything. The driver pulls away, and I say, "Hey. Can you tell us where we're going?"

He shakes his head. "Sorry."

I punch the seat and sit back. Penny is shaking, drenched, her clothes sticking to her skin. I put my arm around her. "You mind?"

She shakes her head and leans into me. She smells like earth and rain, and as my lips graze the top of her head, I nearly kiss her there. My cock is still hard for her, so I can't get comfortable.

She drops her head on my shoulder, like she doesn't mind being near me at all.

And somehow, just like that, we fall asleep.

FIRST OUTPOST

Nell

I'm tired, yeah. But I think with a shower and a good night's sleep, we'll be fine. No, of course we'll be doing both separately! The vows matter nothing to me. He's not really my husband. Who do you think I am?

—*Nell's Confessional, Day 2*

We are so close.

After making it to the airport, the driver gave us our bags and an envelope that wasn't to be opened until we landed. We cleaned up a little in the airport restrooms, and then we, and the other contestants, were flown off on a three-hour flight to another undisclosed location. Then we were separated and had to decide whether to take a cab or an airport shuttle to our next location, someplace in the mountains.

Almost the second we got there, I started throwing up.

Altitude sickness. Great. I'd had the same problem during a family trip to Switzerland when I was younger, but I'd thought I'd outgrown it.

Now it's almost nighttime again. We were blindfolded again by one of the accompanying crewmen, but I think we're in the Rocky Mountains, because there's a thick fog over the massive peaks around us. It's damp and gray. We're in front of a large wrought-iron fence with nine colored gates. If I look through, I can see the sign that says **OUTPOST. REST HERE.**

Beyond that, it looks like cabins. Real cabins, with beds and indoor plumbing and all that good stuff.

I can almost taste it.

But really, all I can taste now is the bile in the back of my throat. My stomach roils as I sink to the ground and clutch my knees to my chest. I sip some water, hoping that it won't come back up. My clothes are stuck to my body with dried mud, and I can't stop shivering from the dampness.

Luke runs back with another set of keys. There is an old mine car at the front entrance that's filled with thousands and thousands of keys of all different colors. The rules are that you can try only one key at a time.

We've been trying for hours, pulling blue keys from the car one after another. Or, at least, Luke has. It's probably a football field's length to the entrance where the mine car is, and he's made at least a hundred and fifty trips. There are hundreds of blue keys scattered at our feet.

Even the cameraman filming this whole fiasco seems annoyed with us.

I've just been slowly dying.

"You okay?" Luke asks as he runs forward, shoving the key into the padlock.

I nod.

"Shit." I look up when I see a bright-red droplet fall on the ground at his feet. His hands are bleeding. It doesn't slow him down, though. He keeps right on powering through, like a machine.

When we got here, we had the lead, miraculously. They'd let us leave the airport in the order we'd left the cornfield, so we must've been first. But I keep scanning the road in the distance, waiting for the next group to show up. I know they'll be here soon. Meanwhile, our lead is shrinking.

Luke shows up again with another key. He tries it as I struggle to my feet. "Shit!"

"Let me go," I say, handing him my water bottle.

He gives me a doubtful look.

"Come on. You've done enough. I can do this a few times. Just catch your breath."

I start to run, which slows to a lumber when I grow dizzy and realize I might throw up again. I dig deep into the pile of keys and pull out a blue one. Then I run back to see Luke pacing back and forth. He uncaps the bottle of water and sucks down a big gulp as I try the key.

Fail.

"Look," he says.

I peer over my shoulder to see the lights of a taxi coming nearer. Our lead is almost gone.

I start to run for another one, but he charges ahead of me. I can sense the frustration in his voice as he says, "I'm faster than you. You took too long."

I should probably be angry at him, but I'm just too tired. Everything's starting to blur. I lean over and throw up some more— nothing but water and bile. My head hurts. When I look up, the taxi stops and out comes Ace and Marta.

Great.

Luke shows up just then, cursing under his breath about "that asshole." He tries the lock just as Ace sings over to him, "Hey, pussy boy! Looks like you've got company! Stand aside and we'll show you how it's done."

Luke is pretending to ignore his trash talk, but I can see his facade crumbling. "Fuck!" he mutters under his breath.

"Let me go next," I tell him, rushing back before he can argue. I reach into the giant mine car again and pull out another key, thinking how impossible this is. We could be here all night and then never have a chance to experience the nirvana that waits for us behind this gate. I choke back a sob at the thought. I am so, so, so sick. Tired. Weak.

I limp up to the door, and he takes the key, trying it. He shakes his head and rounds off to head back to the mine car.

As he does, Marta lets out a whoop. "Would you look at that!" Ace says, pushing open his door. "First try!"

Of all the dumb luck.

The two of them waltz in, all over each other. They pause on the other side of the fence to wave at us, and then Ace grabs Marta's ass and starts to make out with her as they throw their bags down on the outpost platform. "First place!" they scream. Will Wang and a camera crew appear out of nowhere and film the celebration from the other side of the fence as confetti flutters through the air.

Luke glares at them darkly.

I pull on his sleeve. "Look."

He does. Sure enough, there are three more cars cutting through the darkness, on their way here.

He's just standing there, jaw working, so I go back to the mine car. When I come back, he's yelling at me to go faster.

"What the fuck? Do you have molasses in your veins?"

I stare at him as I try the key. "I'm sorry if I'm not as fast as you."

"We should've found this key by now." The key doesn't twist, so he yanks it out from my hands. "Okay. We shouldn't panic."

He's trying to be calm. But he's panicking.

Then he looks at the key I brought and growls. "This isn't blue! It's purple!"

I push my glasses up on my nose and squint at it. "I'm sorry! It's getting dark, so—"

He points to the ground. "Why don't you just sit there and do nothing. We'll go faster that way."

And then he leaves.

And I have just about had it.

So I do as the wise master says. I sit on the ground, and I don't even look at him. I look at my nails. I stare at the sky. I sip my water. When he asks for help, I tell him to take a long walk off a short pier.

"Are you serious?" he says to me. "You're going to sit there and do nothing?"

"I'm doing exactly what you told me to, remember?"

He stares at me, breathing hard, nostrils flaring.

"Fucking stupid goddamn idiotic challenge!" he shouts at the lock when he tries another key that doesn't work. He kicks the ground with his boot, grabs ahold of the bars, and starts to shake the whole gate. Meanwhile, the second and third couples—Brad and Natalie with Ivy and Cody—waltz right through.

"I think you need to calm down," I tell him.

"I think you need to get more riled up," he snaps as another couple—Cara the dancer and Zach the father—gets through easily. "I hate losing."

"Obviously."

"I mean, what the fuck? I thought you were lucky, Penny."

I scowl at him. "Maybe I'm not because my name is *Nell*!" I almost scream it at him.

We are definitely losing control. I've never been so riled up as this man has made me. And until now he always seemed so calm, so relaxed. I'm shaking so hard, I just want to claw his eyes out. And I've never felt like that before, toward anyone.

We don't find our key until nearly midnight, after almost four hours of trying. Despite our early lead, we end up coming in sixth place, which I can tell Luke isn't happy with. But when we stumble into our cabin, his mood magically improves.

"Fuck yes," he says as he throws his pack down and looks around. "I mean, fudge yes."

I survey the room. It's small and dark and has one bed.

One bed. Sure, it's a double, but . . .

"Steven and Erica just got through after us. So either Webb and Daphne or Jen and Elliott are going to be eliminated."

He's still talking game. He knows the teams so intimately, but they're just names to me. I don't say anything.

"But we're way behind Ace and Marta. We have some serious ground to make up." He scrapes his hands over his face but then stops and looks at his bloody palms. "I am so fucking spent."

I peek into the bathroom. It's a stall shower, a toilet, and a sink. Very rustic. A daddy-long-legs skitters near the drain. I cringe.

"I'll let you have the shower first," I say, my voice clipped. "Then you should go to medical and get your hands looked at." *So you can get away from me.*

He gets the hint. "Wait. Are you mad at me?"

I give him a look, like, *What do you think?*

"Why?"

I cross my arms. "I'll give you a hint: 'Why don't you sit there and do nothing?'" I mimic, dropping my voice an octave.

He shrugs. "I was frustrated. That asshole Ace's trash talk was getting to me."

"But you don't take it out on me!" I shout at him.

He sucks in a breath and lets it out slowly. Stretches his arms up over his head. "You know what the problem is with you?"

"I'm sure you're going to tell me."

"You don't appreciate shit," he growls, storming to his bag and unzipping it. "I ran about ten miles today carrying your ass so that we could end up in first place, and what do I get in return? A thank-you?"

My jaw drops. "A thank-you? Are you kidding me? Like I wanted your thingy jammed between my legs all day!"

He laughs. "My *thingy?*" He shakes his head like he can't believe he's having this conversation with me, a grown adult who can't seem to say the word in front of him. "Sweetheart, you'd be lucky to have my *thingy* jammed between your legs. Maybe it'd give you a sorely needed dose of chill-the-fuck-out."

I stare at him, so angry I'm shaking again. All witty retorts have flown clear out of my head.

He kicks off his shoes, shrugs out of his jacket, and rips his shirt off before I can remind myself to look away. Once I capture a single eyeful of those glorious tattooed pecs, it's like my eyes become glued to him. I can't look away.

And then he goes for his cargo pants. It's only when he smirks that I realize I'm transfixed. "See anything you like?"

I whirl away from him. "Sorry!"

Then I realize it's all his fault for being such an exhibitionist.

"You know, you could get naked in the bathroom and spare me the embarrassment."

He shrugs. "Can't sell if you don't advertise, baby. And it's nothing to be embarrassed about. If you see anything you want to sample, just let me know."

How about . . . all of it?

I curse my greedy little brain, zip up my jacket, and do my best to face away from him as I skirt to the door. "Don't make me sicker than I already am. I'm going to go to the mess hall. I need saltines for my stomach."

"I don't want anything, sweetheart. Thanks for asking," he calls after me as I slam the door.

I make it to the mess hall, cursing him. He's hot, there might be a marriage certificate with our names on it, and obviously we were really close today, but that doesn't mean he can treat me like that. All we do is bicker like an old married couple. And stripping naked in front of me? What does he think I'm going to do, jump on him?

I'm sure most women would. But I am *not* most women. And I'm sure I'm not the kind of woman he's used to. They probably love his tattoos and his dirty mouth and his blatant talk of sex.

Not. Me.

There are a few couples dining in the mess hall. Natalie, the biker woman . . . and Brad? Ivy, the body builder, and Cooper? I can't remember. They actually all seem to be getting along swimmingly compared to me and Luke. They don't look at me, so I don't speak to them. I grab my saltines and go back, since I'm dying to get in the shower.

When I open the door, the first thing I see is Luke's sculpted, naked ass. He's standing by the bed, scrubbing a towel through his wet hair. He turns and I shriek. I squeeze my eyes closed and drop my saltines. "Put some clothes on!"

"Shit, girl. I sleep au naturel. If you have a problem with it, you can go somewhere else."

I'm standing there in the door, eyes cemented closed, afraid to open them for what I might see.

"Your saltines?"

When I do open an eye, he's holding them out to me. Wearing boxer briefs. "My *thingy's* all covered now, sweetheart."

I let out a sigh and snatch the crackers from his hands. There are water droplets on his shoulders and chest, and the smell of him is thick in the postshower haze. His wet hair is falling in his face, and he's looking at me with a predatory gleam in his eye. "Don't do that to me."

"Do what?"

"Make fun of me. Or . . . look at me like that. Like you want to . . . devour me."

"Baby, if I wanted to devour you, it already would've happened. Since I'd rather do women on a desert island than actually, you know . . . live." He slips on a T-shirt and cargo pants and leaves as I sit on the edge of the bed.

Trembling at the thought of . . . *sampling*. What would I sample first? His lips? Yes, of course. He has nice lips. But my mind trails to his hard chest, with all those tattoos, and lower, to his thingy. To his *cock*. I'm surprised that I like the dirtiness of that word. I've felt his cock pressed against me, but I closed my eyes before getting a good look at it a few seconds ago. I imagine it, imagine touching it, taking it into my mouth.

Oh god. I've never sucked cock before. Gerald wanted me to, but there is no way I can compare Luke with Gerald. Gerald was cute, but Luke is . . . a man. Hard, masculine, every part of his body big and sculpted and . . . almost too much to think about.

When Luke's gone, I take a heavenly shower, watching as caked-on mud that I wasn't able to get off in the airport bathroom turns the drain at my feet black. I think about Gerald, wonder if he'll be watching the show, but only for a moment, because my mind soon finds its way back to Luke. His ass. He has those little dimples on the sides. I bet you could bounce a quarter on each cheek. I find my hands lingering near my sex and force myself to do what I came into the shower to do.

When the water runs clear, I step out, slip into my pajamas, towel-dry my hair, and settle down in the center of the big bed. Au naturel? If he thinks he's going to bring his au naturel ass into this bed, he's sorely mistaken.

As perfect and hard and amazing as it is, no.

Just no.

A minute later, I hear it. A banging noise coming from the cabin next door.

I scoot to the edge of the bed, open the door, and peer out.

It's coming from Marta and Ace's cabin. Are they . . . having sex in there? Oh my god. Gross. They've barely known each other for two days.

I go back to bed, pull the covers to my chin, and try to sleep through the noise as a thought occurs to me: Whatever chemistry they have, it's working for them. They aced the Marriage Test, and they're in first place.

But it doesn't mean I'm about to do the same with Luke. If that's what it takes to win, no thanks. Sure, we worked together all right in the corn maze, but then it all fell apart after that.

We're just too different.

Case in point: I can't wait to curl into bed and go to sleep. Him? He never comes back to the cabin. He stays out all night long.

I thought that would've made me happy. But I was wrong.

Luke

The lock challenge was a killer. It was made worse because it was pure luck, hitting upon the right key. We weren't lucky. I thought with her brains and my brawn we'd have something, but I guess you don't got nothin' unless you got luck. I need a drink.

—*Luke's Confessional, Day 2*

I rub my hands over my face and look down through bloodshot eyes at my hands. My fingers are raw and sting from turning those keys.

But it'd been a good night. Once I lost Dr. Carpenter, Her Royal Bitchiness, I found a watering hole behind the mess hall, stocked with a full bar. Tim's doesn't close until two, so I rarely haul my ass to bed until four. I found myself downing tequila shots with Ivy, Brad, Zach, and Charity.

We talked a little about the game. I learned that Webb and Daphne had been eliminated. Webb, a swimmer and one of my athletic alliance, had looked like a threat, but his coupling with Daphne had damn near been suicide. The rumor was, the second it started to get a little muddy, she asked to leave.

After that, we bitched about our spouses. It was good to hear that everyone was having the same problems.

Then we bitched about Ace and Marta. Brad, the most. Brad hated Ace since he'd very nearly had his balloon burst by him too. "I think," I'd said as I lit a cigarette, "we're all just jealous that that asshole is having all the luck."

"Why?" Charity asked me. Charity is a bikini model—blonde, skinny, big tits. Where I was chosen to pick up the female audience, I get the feeling Charity was picked to get the guys. She'd been paired with Tony, a rocket scientist. "Aren't you happy with your *wife?*"

I'd shrugged, motioning to the camera filming behind the bar. "She's all right."

She didn't seem to get the picture. She leaned in closer, pressing her tits into me, and said, "I can't even understand a thing Tony says half the time."

Zach begged off early, and then there was just the four of us. Then Ivy and Brad, the two serious athletes who obviously didn't give a shit about their "spouses," went off together, to who knows where, probably to compare muscles. That left me with Charity.

And I could tell what was on her mind. I spun on my chair and told her I had to go. She followed me down to the back of the mess hall and wrapped her arms around me.

She was hot, sure. After the cocktease I'd been through with Penny, I wanted release. She gave me those puppy-dog eyes that said, *Take me.* "You know, there's a place over there we could be alone."

I didn't follow where she pointed.

She tried to kiss me, but I pulled away. "Come on. Stop it."

"Why? We're not really married. You like that fake wife of yours? Is that it?"

I shoved her aside, gritting my teeth. "Cameras," I muttered.

But there were other reasons. First, I was married to Penny. Even if it was a fucking sham, even if she hated me, I'd meant what I said. We were each other's first and best alliance. I didn't need anything or anyone to interfere with that.

I spent the next hour trying to get sober. Now I'm sitting on a bench outside the cabin where Penny's sleeping, watching Will Wang giving Ace and Marta their marching orders for the next leg of the journey. Because they found their key first, they get to start out before us.

In a few more hours, when it's our time, we'll get to leave.

A little while later, the door opens behind me and Penny pokes her head out. She sees me, pulls her hood over her head, and stomps past me to the mess hall.

Fuck. She's still mad.

It won't be good if we have to complete another challenge still pissed at each other.

I push off the bench and go after her. "Hey. What's the problem?"

"You," she mutters, throwing open the door and stalking inside.

She gets in the line and grabs a tray, then starts loading it up with fruit, cottage cheese, eggs. I follow, doing the same. "And why am I on your shit list today?"

She whirls to me, about to unleash, then looks around for the cameras. "Where were you?" she whispers.

"What do you mean? You didn't—"

"Oh my god. Were you . . . drinking?" she says incredulously. "You smell like a brewery! Are you drunk now?"

"No. I had a few drinks. I'm—"

"You're disgusting."

"What? You don't—"

"No. I don't. I don't drink myself silly. I don't smoke. And I don't do any of the things that you seem to find appealing. That's why you disgust me."

I let out a low laugh. "You didn't look so disgusted last night when you were sneaking looks at my *thingy*."

Her jaw drops. Her face reddens as her eyes scan to the camera that's filming close by. Instead of answering, she storms past me, shoving

Katy Evans

into me and upending my tray. Fruit scatters everywhere. She doesn't stick around to help clean it up.

Ten minutes later, I go out to the eating area. The remaining contestants who haven't yet left are talking together at one table. But Penny is sitting all by herself, reading her French poetry shit. I push my tray on the table. She slowly raises her head and scowls at me.

I sit down across from her. "Look," I say in a low voice. "There are cameras all over us. Can you just pretend to be civil to me?"

She ignores me.

"Today's a new day. Can't we forget about what happened yesterday?"

Nothing.

"Come on. I still want to win this, and I know you do too. We can't do that if we're pissed at each other." I offer her my hand. "Truce?"

She eyes it warily and then shakes just the tips of my fingers. "Fine. But only because I want to win."

"Fine." I glance down at my tray, then start to shovel eggs and toast into my mouth. "You psyched for today?"

She shrugs. "I guess."

"Why aren't you sitting with the others?"

She looks at them for a moment and hitches her shoulder. "I'm not social."

"So what are you trying to say?" I ask, bringing my coffee to my lips. "I've got the strength game, the cunning game, the intelligence game, and the stamina game . . . and now you want me to have the social game too?"

She looks up at me, and I see the scowl starting to form.

"Kidding," I finish quickly. "Geez. I thought if you slept well, you wouldn't wake up on the bitch side of the bed."

Her fingers tighten on her fork. I think she may be thinking of launching it at me. Instead, she smiles. "I think I would like you so much better if we didn't talk. Even better, go away."

I hold up my hands in surrender. I know when I'm beaten. I go over to the other table and hang with them—having enjoyable conversation for a change—until it's time for us to set out. I'm surprised that even though Ivy and Brad keep giving each other *We hooked up* looks over the table, they both seem to be getting along better with their respective jilted spouses than I'm getting along with Penny. Charity's talking to Tony like she didn't just make a pass at me. We're the most fucked-up group of married people ever.

No. What's most fucked up is that I feel the need to be faithful to a woman who clearly hates my guts.

We meet Will Wang at our scheduled time, and before he gives us our envelope, he has to taunt us with memories of the shit we went through yesterday. "So, Luke, you were getting frustrated last night, huh?"

"Yeah." *Give me the damn envelope, asshole.*

"And, Nell, did you worry your husband had blown a gasket?"

She huffs. "I don't worry about anything where he is concerned. He is not my problem. The only thing I'm focused on is winning."

Will grins. "You didn't seem to do very well on the first Marriage Test. And I noticed you spent last night separated. Trouble in paradise?"

"No," I say flatly.

He gets the message and hands us our envelope. "All right, guys, good luck. You are on your way!"

Penny tears open the envelope and reads it out loud. "Proceed northward on Ravine Trail to the stables to be matched with your horses. Oh."

"Horseback riding?" I say. "Kick ass."

"You ever been?" she asks as we take off, finding the trailhead.

"I'm a southern boy. May have grown up on the outskirts of a big city, but I lived on my parents' farm before they kicked me off it."

She raises an eyebrow. "Why did they do that?"

"You don't want to know. They teach you how to ride horses in Paris?"

She shakes her head. "Back home."

"Let me guess. Your daddy gave you a pony for your tenth birthday."

She frowns. "Eleventh, actually. Brownie. Haven't ridden him in ten years, though."

"Yeah. I haven't ridden in a long time either. Bet it's like riding a bike. We might be able to make up some time on the others if they don't know riding."

"Hope so. But if so . . . oh my gosh. I think this may be a physical challenge I can actually do. Who'd have thought?"

I give her a sidelong glance. "Don't get cocky."

The path is steep, but we make it to the stables while the sun is in the sky. We're given our two horses—I get a big black one called Maximus, and she gets a girl named Sweet Pea—and a map, and told that we need to get to the top of Frank's Summit.

She reads the map. "There's a roundabout route that looks less steep, but the direct route would probably save us time."

I look down the trails. One definitely looks rough. Knowing Ace, that's the one he took. Ace doesn't look like the type to know shit about horses, though. "What do you think?"

She looks surprised. "You're actually asking me? Wow. I didn't know you were capable of that."

Maximus whinnies and tosses his head as if to tell us to cut it out. "Well, that route looks steep. I don't want you getting halfway up and chickening out."

She snorts. "I won't."

She snaps the reins and flies ahead of me, fearless, up the steep trail.

That answers that question.

I catch up to her, and she doesn't waste time. She leads her horse easily up the rocky path, fearless. She doesn't turn around or hesitate. I get to spend the next hour looking at her perfect ass in those jeans.

When we get to the top of the hill and dismount, we're met by a couple of park rangers, who point our way through trees. I can tell she's feeling good about herself by the rare smile she's sporting—she doesn't smile nearly as much as she should, but when she does, it lights up her whole face.

This confident Penny is sexy as hell.

She walks ahead of me toward a clearing, then stops dead in her tracks.

We're at the edge of a steep drop, and there, ahead of us, is a long wire, stretching down as far as the eye can see. It's a zip line.

I pump my fist. "Fuck yeah. I've always wanted to try this."

"Welcome to the Heart Attack, one of the longest, steepest, and scariest zip lines in the world!" the guide says.

This is right up my alley. I run up to it, and the view is insane. I've spent my whole life around Atlanta. In all my years on the farm or on the streets downtown or tending bar, I never thought I'd ever be here. Six months ago, I was jealous of Jimmy for jet-setting all over the place, and now look at me. I take in the entire vista, breathing the mountain air, and feel like that loser on the *Titanic*, screaming "I'm the king of the world!"

Then I look back at Penny. She's frozen, green in the face.

This ain't good.

I nudge her closer to the guide. The guide says, "Welcome, travelers. You have an important choice to make. You can either mount your horses and take Switchback Trail to your destination, which on average will take you three hours, or take the Heart Attack, which will get you there in three minutes. The choice is yours."

She gets a sheepish look in her eyes, and I know what she's gonna say before she opens her mouth. Her voice is soft. "I'm afraid of heights."

"Yeah. But think of all the time we'll save. We were sixth at the last outpost. We can't afford to come in much later."

"I know. But I can't."

"You can. All you need to do is hold on." I look at the guide. "We do it in tandem, right? Together?"

He nods.

"Yeah, see? It ain't nothing. You hold on to me like you did in the corn maze and we'll be down before you know it."

"But . . ."

"You can be behind me this time, okay?"

She inhales a sharp breath. "I can close my eyes?"

"Yeah. Remember, Penny? I told you to trust me. I ain't gonna let nothing happen to you."

She's trembling. "That's a double negative. That means you're going to let me die!" she whines, covering her face in her hands.

"Look," I tell her, getting down to her level and peering in her eyes. "This is all you. All your choice. You know what I wanna do, but I want you to decide. I'll do what you want."

She gives me a look, and I swear I see a trace of gratefulness. She walks to the edge and peers carefully over the side, and then her eyes follow the path of the zip line to the point where it disappears among the pine trees.

She sets her jaw, rips the glasses from her face, and tucks them into her pack. Then she nods at the guide. "Set us up for this thing."

I don't want to say anything to make her change her mind, but I'm so pumped I could kiss her. I was never one to follow Jimmy on his stunts because the stuff he does risks serious injury, but I've dreamed of doing shit like this all my life. The guide gets us into helmets and harnesses and sets us up on the platform. He attaches us to the tandem zip and shows us where to hold on. "I'm just going to give you a little push, and you'll be off. Easy ride," the guide says.

I can't see her behind me, but I can almost hear her heart beating. "You okay?" I call to her.

"I can't believe I'm doing this! I must be insane!" she cries. "Tell me when it's over."

She must have her eyes closed. She's going to miss one hell of a view. The guide calls, "One, two, three . . ."

And before he gives us the push, she's already screaming in fear. Loud.

We careen toward the trees below, and it's steep. At first it almost feels like we're falling. Everything's rushing by in a blur. But somewhere along the way something changes.

She stops screaming in fear and starts squealing in delight.

"Oh my god! This is awesome!" she shouts, laughing. I see the tops of her feet as she kicks out wildly, and I start laughing too.

We break through the trees, and the landing platform comes up fast and furious. I put my feet out for the landing, and a guide is there to slow us down. He unclips the carabiners and I jump out, feeling like I already have that million dollars in my hands. I rip off the helmet, and when Penny gets loose, she bounds over to me, wrapping her arms around me.

And I kiss her. Tongue and teeth, hands and hair. Crush her lips with mine and devour her mouth like she's my last meal.

The weirdest thing? She lets me. She groans and kisses me back, tangling her hands in my hair and thrusting that little tongue of hers into me like she can't get enough.

And the cameras capture every last beautiful minute of it.

FRENCH IN THE DARK

Nell

> *Sure, I kissed him. It was an amazing experience. No, it doesn't mean anything. We were both just high on adrenaline. There's nothing to read into, believe me.*

> —*Nell's Confessional, Day 3*

I kissed him.

Oh god, I kissed him.

That's what keeps cycling through my mind as we hike to the next outpost. Luke doesn't mention it. Doesn't touch me again, even just offering a hand to help me scale the rocks on the trail. But I can still feel his heat, and my lips feel raw from his stubble. I know I've never been kissed like that. Never in a million years did I think I could be kissed like that.

What does it mean?

Nothing, of course. That's what happens when you overload on adrenaline.

We don't talk much. The sun is fading in the sky, and we need to get to the outpost. Feeling brave and a little reckless after the zip-lining experience, I do pretty well keeping up with him, even though the trail is steep. A crew member gave us each a pack with hiking gear, food, and other necessities, but Luke didn't bother with any of it, so neither did I.

On the way up, we pass Ivy and Cody, who are resting, but we don't see anyone else. Then, though Luke assures me Ivy's part of his alliance, we spend the next hour trying to race each other to get the best position.

We end up coming in about ten seconds ahead of them.

When we throw our stuff down on the platform, Will Wang announces that we're third.

Third!

"Holy cow!" I shout as he pumps his fist and pulls me in for a quick, clinical hug.

I read into that, of course. It's a hug a person would give his sister, one that says he's regretting the kiss.

It makes my stomach twist.

The guide leads us into a clearing. It's dark by now, and all I see are trees, until I look up. And what I thought was the moon and the stars is actually the moonlight reflecting on the windows of tiny treehouses. "Welcome to your next outpost, where you'll be spending the night among the trees. Enjoy."

We have to climb a rickety ladder to get to the front porch. I'm a little worried, since the last place we stayed wasn't so great, but when I flip on the lights, I'm charmed. It's adorable and clean, and there is a fireplace going.

Of course, there are some drawbacks. The big one is that it's romantic. Like I need romance right now, especially with all the thoughts of that kiss still going through my head. One bed, of course. No running water.

I'm not as bone tired as I was before, so we decide to go down to the campfire to have some food. That's where we find out that Ace and Marta once again came in first, followed by Brad and Natalie. As we grab our barbecue and sit down at the fire, Ace and Marta get up and leave.

"Something we said?" Luke says, grinning at me.

Katy Evans

And it's that grin that makes my insides turn to mush. Or maybe it's the "we." Whatever it is, I feel like I'm more than just an obstacle in his way. For the first time, I feel like I'm truly *in this* with him.

Luke clearly knows Brad; I can tell they must have allied sometime during the filming. They talk like old friends. Natalie, the motorcycle chick who is on the older edge of things, is quiet but nice. We actually end up laughing together as we talk about our experiences. I've never fit into a group like that; Courtney is the only real friend I've ever had. But I can tell Luke just effortlessly gets along with everyone, and he manages to draw me out and add me to the conversation, so I feel like I belong. It makes me feel so warm and squishy and . . . yearning to have this kind of life back home.

It makes me almost dread going back to my boring apartment with no boyfriend, no social life, no job, no future.

After the rest of the couples show up, we learn that Jen, the workout-video and weight-loss guru, and Elliott, her "husband," who was a rather large guy, were eliminated.

It's pretty late by the time we head up to the treehouse. "I'm beat," Luke says as we climb the ladder.

I don't say anything, but he must misinterpret my silence because a second later he says, "Don't worry. I'll sleep on the floor."

I hadn't been thinking about that at all. "Actually," I say, "do you think they're filming inside the rooms?"

"Nah. It's against the contract. But the rooms are probably bugged for sound."

"Oh. The bed is bigger than at the other place. It wouldn't be terrible if you slept on the bed with me. If you stay on top of the sheets. Right?"

He gives me a raised eyebrow. "You're the boss."

"Oh. And you have to wear clothes."

"If you say so."

We go inside, and I take my pajamas out of my bag. He pulls off his shirt. I motion for him to turn around, and I pull on my tank and boxers. "I'm done," I say, slipping under the covers.

He sits down and pulls off his cargo pants, then lies beside me in his boxer briefs.

After the kiss, it feels strangely intimate. Everything he does now feels intimate. Like we should be doing more.

I reach over and turn out the light. The second the light is out, I know I'm going to have trouble sleeping. It has everything to do with his naked body, inches from mine. "Do you want to . . . practice? For the Marriage Test, I mean?"

His laugh is low. "Didn't think you'd want to practice anything else, sweetheart."

I'm glad it's dark so he can't see the way I blush. I try to think of some of the questions they asked on the test. "What's my favorite food?"

He rolls over onto his elbow, staring at me in the firelight. "Let me guess. Slim Jims."

"No. Beef Wellington. I also like brussels sprouts."

"You're just fucking with me, right?"

I ignore the question. "Yours is . . . Slim Jims?"

"Bingo."

I smile. "Um . . . who inspires you?"

"Easy one. My grandfather. You?"

I shake my head, and now I'm really blushing. "I don't . . . really have anyone. I left that question blank."

"Why's that?"

"Because I don't need anyone to inspire me. I rely on myself."

He nods like he understands, then says, "Huh."

I look over at him. "Huh, what?"

"Nothing. Just . . . sounds kind of lonely."

"Says the man who doesn't want to get married."

"I don't. But I love surrounding myself with others. The more, the better. What can I say? I like people. Most of them."

I cringe. "I guess I . . . don't. I mean, I might. I'd rather just surround myself with a few close people who I know have my back. And one of them will be my husband. Maybe he'll inspire me."

"Shit, girl. You're going about it the wrong way. You won't meet him if you hide away from everyone and don't give 'em a chance. You know?"

He's probably right. But that's . . . terrifying. "I just don't think those people like me all that much. I'm too different from them."

"No, you ain't. They would like you. You just don't give them a chance."

I guess that's true.

A moment later, he says, "Penny?"

"Nell."

"Right, whatever. Say something in French to me."

I laugh. "What? Why?"

"Because I don't sleep so good. And maybe it'll keep my mind off the game so I can."

"Okay." I think for a little while before saying:

Comme deux anges que torture
Une implacable calenture
Dans le bleu cristal du matin
Suivons le mirage lointain

I open my eyes. In the firelight, he's rolled over onto one elbow, looking at me. The shadows of the flames dance across his tattooed skin, a pleasant blur with my poor eyesight. "Fuck. What did you just say?"

"It's Baudelaire. Basically that we should go to sleep."

"Hell. Is that all? Everything in French sounds so hot. I could've sworn you wanted me to climb under the covers with you."

I press my lips together and shake my head. "No more French."

He falls onto his back and puts his arm over his eyes. "Damn."

102

"Um. Why would you want to?"

He pulls his hand off his head. "Why? You're shitting me, right?"

"Well. I'm not exactly your type, am I?" I say lightly, pulling the covers up to my chin. "I mean, boys don't make passes at girls who wear glasses, right? And the women on the other teams seem like—"

"You felt my cock. You don't think you got all the right equipment to turn a guy on?"

"I don't . . ."

"I happen to find those Coke bottles you hide your face with sexy as fuck," he says. "And I sure ain't the only one. You're not a virgin?"

"Oh no!" I find myself tittering. Why are we even discussing this? Am I insane?

"All right. Then you gotta know, right? You have a boyfriend? You ever get him hot?"

"Well." I trace my finger over the sheet, picking at a loose thread on the blanket. "I've only had one. And he isn't really the type to . . ."

He closes his eyes. "Wait. Let me get this straight. You've only been with one guy in your whole life?"

I nod. Is it getting warm in here? "Gerald. He's a doctor. He's . . . brilliant, handsome, kind . . ."

"And a shitty lover."

"What? No. How can you . . ."

"Are you still dating this asshole?"

"He's not an asshole!" I say, not sure why I'm defending him. "We broke up almost nine months ago."

"Okay. So . . . this guy has taught you everything you know about sex. And yet the woman I see before me hasn't had sex in almost a year, blushes whenever she looks at something she really wants, doesn't want anyone to touch her, and can't even say the words *fuck* or *cock*." He shrugs. "He made you frigid. So, in my book? Asshole. Shitty lover."

I gape at him. "I'm not frigid!"

"Hey. It ain't your fault."

I want to smack him, but I can't bear to have contact with his naked parts. Oh god, maybe he's right.

I flip on the light and sit up in bed. "I kissed you, didn't I? Was that terrible?"

"No. That was fucking hot as hell. But I think you'll need about a thousand more of those to undo the number that that asshole did on you."

I stare at him, scowling. "You know," I say, pulling the covers up to my chest, "I think you'd better sleep on the floor."

He grins lazily at me and starts to pull the blanket off the bed. I tug it back, and he just laughs at me. "Whatever you say, sweetheart."

He lies down on the floor with just a pillow and doesn't make another sound the rest of the night. I try to fall asleep, but I can't.

Because I have a very strong feeling that he might be right. About Gerald, but most of all, about me.

Luke

> *Penny's shocked we got this far. I'm not. I always said I was in it to win it. And yeah, she can't stand me. We're different. But somehow, we're making it work. Who knows, though. This might be the end of the road for us.*

> *—Luke's Confessional, Day 7*

We've been in the game for a week.

After Colorado, we traveled down to Texas, where Erica, the type A, and Steven, the weaselly guy, were eliminated after a challenge where one of us had to build the biggest haystack, and the other had to carry hay bales across a farm. Supposedly, Steven didn't want to do either, and Erica was all-out screaming at him to choose one, so he just told her to screw off and walked away from the set.

We did okay on that one because we didn't need to be near each other.

Then we went to Charleston, South Carolina, where we had to spend the night at a haunted plantation. We stayed on opposite sides of the mansion and ended up getting our fucking wires crossed, each thinking the other had gone and made the sweetgrass basket we were supposed to make. After that, a second Marriage Test, where—surprise surprise—we again got all three questions wrong about each other. Like I was supposed to know her favorite way to relax was going to fucking art museums? I'd said shopping, because I thought all women loved shopping. I thought it was ingrained in their heads. I might as well have called her a cannibal, from the eye daggers she gave me.

My favorite way to relax, according to her? Vegging on the couch. My favorite way to spend a night? Hitting on women. My favorite place to hang out? A strip club. I can tell she thinks I'm a dumb, horny asshole.

The result of that shit? We nearly came in dead last.

The only people who screwed up worse than us were Cara, the dancer, and Zach, the father, who missed their flight. So they got eliminated.

And now we're the last of the five remaining couples.

We're in pea-soup fog, up on a pier near a lighthouse in cold-as-hell Lubec, Maine, which is supposedly the easternmost point of the United States.

The only thing colder is Penny.

The girl can hold a grudge. Ever since we had that talk in the tree-house in Colorado, she's been closed off and barely says two words to me at a time. I've spent most of my nights getting drunk with my alliance, and she's pissed off about that too. All the other couples have an understanding. They may not be a love connection, but they appreciate and tolerate each other for the sake of the game. Penny won't even look at me.

I'd thought that after the kiss, we'd just get closer and closer.

But instead, we ended up veering completely apart. Any more and we'll lose.

And at this point, I don't give a shit. I'm thinking about the game and how we can salvage things and somehow pull ahead, even though we're on the brink of elimination.

Maybe we can't. Part of me thinks that we can do everything in our power, but if we aren't working together, it won't be enough.

But I'm done.

If she's happy in her lily-white prison and she don't want to face facts, there ain't nothing I can do.

Still, every once in a while I'll catch a glimpse of her, and I'll think, *Hell, it's such a damn shame.*

She's beautiful and has no idea how beautiful she is. She closes herself off to the rest of the world because she thinks the only thing she has to offer is that big brain of hers. She has absolutely no confidence in herself otherwise. I don't know why she feels that way, but I see those cracks. Every so often, I'll see that person she's trying so hard to hide, the hot, sweet, sexy Penny she's keeping underneath . . . if only she'd pry that fucking stick out of her butt. Trapped in a fucking cage she doesn't want to leave.

She pulls her coat around her body, zips it up to her chin, and looks down at the frothing black water. She's wearing these orange rubber waders, and she still makes my cock twitch. I think about that night, lying next to her in bed, how much I wanted to touch her, to strip her bare, to claim her mouth and the rest of her body. How can she possibly think that she doesn't make men hot?

"This is your thing, right?" I say to her as Will Wang strolls by in his parka and earmuffs. "'Cause you grew up around here?"

She pushes up her glasses and gives me a look that screams *Get away.* "No."

The fishing boat coasts up to the pier, full of grizzled old guys who look like they've lived their entire lives on the sea. Will Wang says,

"These men are going to give you a little lesson on pulling in lobster traps. Then you'll have to pull in one hundred lobsters. If you catch a rare blue lobster, you'll get a special reward at the end of the day when you arrive at your next outpost. Ready?"

I climb onto the boat, offer her my hand. She doesn't take it.

She spends most of the time talking to the lobstermen, learning what needs to be done. So, ignoring me. The wind whistles through our ears, and the fog is so thick it settles between us as I'm working the left side of the boat and she's working the right. I don't see her as we start pulling in the traps. All I hear is the lobstermen calling: "Three here." "Six."

They're counting up to one hundred, but I'm keeping score.

I want to get more than she does.

I don't know what proving I can bring in more lobsters even means. But I get it in my head that if I do, things between us might change. She might actually think I'm worthy of talking to. Or maybe, just maybe, she might be so excited by me that she'll jump into my arms and kiss me again.

Yeah. Snowball's chance in hell.

We're neck and neck; I have fifty, and she has forty-eight. I pull in a trap to find it empty, and then I hear her squeal excitedly.

I look over at her trap. She has three.

One of them is blue.

Fuck it. I lost. We're on the same team, but I feel like I lost.

As we go back to the shore, she's smiling. It ain't from anything I did, but still, I'll take what I can get.

"You did good," I offer, taking advantage of her rare good mood.

"Thank goodness for Dramamine," she says, rubbing her gloved hands together. "What do you think the blue lobster will get us?"

I shrug. "Maybe we'll get lucky and won't get eliminated."

She sighs. "You think we're close?"

We'd shown up to the outpost last night in Lubec, at this bed-and-breakfast, thinking we were at the end of the line. We'd only learned we were still alive when we found out that Cara and Zach hadn't yet checked in, since they'd missed their flight.

We pull up to the dock and leave the boat. All the other teams must've gone out before us, so I'm sure hoping that we can make up some time. As much as she drives me crazy and makes me want to throw up my hands and go back to Atlanta . . . I don't want to leave the game. As crazy as it is, I don't even want to leave her. No, I just want to take some time and figure her out.

But time is something we don't have.

Will is at the end of the pier to hand us our next envelope. She opens it and reads. "Boston. The Freedom Trail. *This* I know."

"Does it say what we got to do?"

She shakes her head. "It just says to meet at the head of the Freedom Trail."

We take a taxi to the airport, where we board a prop plane to Portland, and then we take a train down to Boston. By then, it's evening.

This is her turf, so she knows just how to get there. We get out of North Station, and she takes off running. I follow behind her, weaving through all the crowds, until we see the platform. Will Wang is already there, waiting. Somehow, no matter how fast we go, he always seems to get there faster.

We come to a stop.

"Welcome, travelers," Will says. Is it me, or does he not seem as happy as usual? "You've arrived at the Freedom Trail in Boston. Unfortunately, you are the last remaining team to arrive."

Shit. It's over.

I look at Penny, whose eyes widen. This is it. The end. Now there's nothing left to go back to in Atlanta, and . . .

And what, exactly?

Fuck. Just then it hits me how much this sucks. How much I'd do anything to stay in the game. I think about all the times we could've worked together and cut our time and . . .

FUCK.

"But there is good news," Will says. "This is a non-elimination round. You two are still in the game. You will start out last tomorrow. But for tonight, you can rest assured that you will be continuing on."

I stare at him. My mind's so full of thoughts of my bar and how I'm going to have to sell it that for a minute it doesn't sink in.

"Not only that, but because you two were the only team to find a rare blue lobster, you two will be treated to a dinner unlike any other, at the world-famous Chart House on the pier. Head on up to your room and get on some clean clothes, because you're going to have a night to remember in the great city of Boston, with all the lobster you can eat!"

I look at Penny, who looks like she's going to cry, her lower lip trembling. She grabs my arm, and I pull her into a hug, one she doesn't seem to want to step away from.

And I fucking breathe it in. She hasn't touched me in days, so I bask in this rare opportunity. I smooth her hair, dip my head down, and inhale her scent as I take her against my chest and let the calm settle over us.

"I can't believe it," she says, looking up at me, and now there are tears in her eyes.

Arms entwined, we grab our bags and start to follow the guide to the hotel, but then Penny suddenly slows to a dead stop. I follow her line of vision. A gray-haired man in a black coat and suit.

"Oh my god." She swallows and loosens her arm from mine. "One second."

Then she goes to the man.

He has her eyes. Her chin. And I can tell from the way he's talking *at* her, making her shrink smaller and smaller with every passing second. It's her fucking dad.

She touches his arm tentatively and says something to him, motioning to me.

Will Wang says, "I'm sorry, but speaking with—"

I grab his arm. "Give her a minute."

I can see his face better than hers because he's faced my way. It's red, twisted. I can make out the words. "*This* is what you're doing with your life now? Running around with cameras on you? And this loser? What *for*? Jesus, Penelope, I thought we raised you better than this."

She shakes her head and whispers something, but I can't make it out.

He says something to her, something curt, like a warning, and she hangs her head.

Then she nods and goes to give him a hug. But the goddamn bastard just stands there, stiff, with his hands in his pockets. His eyes are on me, cold.

Fuck you too, man.

Then she runs over to me. Will Wang starts to remind her that talking with any family or friends during the game is strictly forbidden, but I move her down the street and into the hotel lobby as fast as I can, so we lose him.

She's still frowning as we step into the elevator, her brow wrinkled with worry. "I get the feeling he wasn't here to welcome me to the family."

She doesn't even smile.

"You okay?" I ask her.

She's silent for a long time, watching the numbers above the door climb. Then she nods. "But I'm not in the mood for lobster."

I shrug. I've never had lobster, so I don't give a shit either way. "That's all right. If you want to—"

"I'm in the mood to get drunk," she says, not looking at me. "Are you in?"

I almost choke. I stare at her, wondering if she's really okay. Either way, there's no way I can turn down an invitation like that.

"Yeah. I'm in."

"LOBSTER" REWARD

Nell

> *Yes. It was a very nice night. We went out for . . . lobster. It was a nice reward.*

> —*Nell's Confessional, Day 7*

My father.

My annoying, absent, never-impressed father actually showed up at the taping of my show.

He treats my mother like crap. He spent eight years ignoring me. Didn't come to a single one of my graduations because he thinks my degrees are worthless. And yet somehow, when I least want him in my life, he's there.

It's just my luck. He works in downtown Boston. I'd thought the town was big enough that I'd safely escape him. Apparently not.

He was so angry. Expecting me to explain myself? I'm an adult! Why should I have to?

I'm still fuming about it when I go to my bag to pull out a fresh change of clothes. Part of me wants to just hide in my bed, but I know that's what my dad wants. To keep me out of the public eye and not embarrass him.

So I'm going out, hoping I get my plastered face plastered on the front of the damned *Boston Globe*.

But when I peek into my bag I realize that most of my clothes are not there. Just a bra top, a T-shirt, a bathing suit, and a few pairs of socks. I'd been running short of clean clothes last night, so I'd washed them in the sink and hung them out to dry on the line over the bathtub at the bed-and-breakfast in Maine. But I was so tired . . . did I put them back in?

Oh god.

I left most of my clothes in Maine.

Like I need any more reasons to break down into tears right now.

My father's made me so furious, though, that it's spurred me out of my comfort zone. Natalie doesn't answer her door, so I end up knocking on Ivy's door. I tell her what happened, and she's more than accommodating. She gives me a fresh change of clothes and tells me to have fun tonight at my reward dinner.

I shower and put on the clothes. Actually, it's more like I have to pour myself into the clothes. The jeans are so tight, and the shirt is only half of a shirt—a little tank top with a plunging neckline. I look at myself in the mirror, and . . . Whatever. Maybe I'll get my boobs plastered on the front of the *Boston Globe* too.

I stalk out of the bathroom and grab my phone, wallet, and hotel card. "Ready?" I say, not looking at Luke, who's watching playoff baseball.

He's silent. That's when I realize he's actually looking at me and not the television. His mouth a little open.

"What?" I snap.

"Nothing, just—"

"I left my clothes in Lubec," I mutter. "These are Ivy's."

"Huh. You look . . ."

I cut him off. "Don't say it."

He holds up his hands in surrender but doesn't avert his gaze from my cleavage. Feeling naked, I pull the shirt up to cover myself a little better. Not that it helps much. I throw on my jacket. He follows me out onto Charles Street, and I look up and down the road. "Where to?" he says.

I shrug. "I don't know. It's not like I've gone out to . . . you know, before."

"You're telling me you've never gotten shitfaced before?"

I shake my head.

"Well. I live to be shitfaced. So . . ." He looks up and down. "Let's go."

I follow after him. "Where are we going?"

He shrugs and points behind him. "Somewhere without them."

I look over my shoulder and realize there are cameras following us, though on the other side of the street. He picks up the pace and grabs my arm suddenly and pulls me into an alley. "You seem to be awfully good at evading people," I note.

"Yeah. Well."

He doesn't say more. But funny, even if he is a thug, even if he's stolen from half the people in Atlanta, I still feel safe with him.

After we leave the alley, I don't know where we go—a bunch of rights and lefts—but eventually we look behind us and the cameras are gone. Straight ahead there's a tequila bar I've never seen before.

We go inside. It's a crowded, dark hole-in-the-wall. My pulse skitters as we sit at a long bar. "Is this like your bar? Back home?"

He smirks. "Shit, girl, this is the Ritz compared to my place. My bar's a dump. Tim's used to be a nice place when my grandparents were running it. But it's falling to shit now." He drums his fingers on the bar. "What'll it be?"

"Oh." I study all the liquor bottles, confused. "Margarita?"

"I thought you wanted to get shitfaced? None of the fruity shit."

"Then what?"

"Cuervo," he says. "Two."

The bartender pours two shot glasses for us. I lift it and stare at the amber liquid. I stick my tongue out to taste it as he watches me, a small, amused smile on his face.

"You ever do a shot?" he asks.

"No. Is it hard?"

He shakes his head, scans down the bar, and finds a couple of lime wedges and salt. "So just do what I do. Lick, sip, suck."

He licks his hand below his index finger, pours the salt there, and lets me do the same. Then he licks his hand, lifts the glass, drains it easily, and stuffs the lime wedge into his mouth. "Now you."

I lick the salt, but the liquid burns my tongue the second it touches, and it keeps burning all the way down. Somehow I manage to get it down, tears pouring down my face. He quickly hands me the lime, and I suck, feeling like I'm going to gag because my throat is on fire. "Oh god," I choke out when I catch my breath.

"Bad?"

"No. Different."

"Okay. You need to pace yourself. One is probably enough for you if you've never—"

I slam my fist down on the bar. "Bartender! Another round."

Luke stares at me. "Hey. Wait."

The bartender pauses, but I urge him on. "I don't want to wait."

The bartender pours the drink, and I hold it in my fist, feeling brazen now. "Why's your place not doing so well now, you think?"

He lifts the shot glass, contemplating that. "Part of it's that my grandfather mortgaged the place to the hilt and didn't tell anyone until the banks came knocking down my door six months ago. But a bigger part of it is that I'm just a shitty manager, probably. I was a high school dropout. Lots of shit goes right over my head. Even with my granddad's help, I don't know much of nothing."

Oh, gosh. He's so wrong. I rush to correct him on that.

"That's not true. A lot of what I learned in school is knowledge that'll never have any practical application outside the classroom. I think you have something better. You understand how things in the world work. You know how to talk to people. To make people like you. What do I have? A title and a bunch of worthless degrees. I'm not equipped to handle anything outside the walls of my university."

I motion for more lime wedges.

He gets them without removing his gaze from me. I can tell he's trying to figure me out. "This has to do with your old man, huh?"

I nod. I lick, sip, and suck. This time it doesn't burn nearly as much as it did the first time.

I motion for another.

"Hey. Doctor. I don't want you leaving here on a stretcher," he says, downing his drink without the lime this time. "What's the deal?"

"Oh, nothing. Same old thing. Haven't seen him in years, and is he happy to run into me? No, he accuses me of wasting my life. He tells me someone needs to talk some sense into me before I embarrass him. Can you believe that? *I'm* embarrassing *him*. Like he isn't doing that enough on his own, cavorting around with his secretary, a woman five years older than I am. He basically told me to get a real job and stop acting like a child."

"Yeah? I hope you told him to fuck himself."

"Not in those exact words. I told him that I don't care what he thinks. That it's my life, and if he doesn't like it, there's nothing he can do."

The bartender fills our glasses again. I'm feeling a little tingly, like I could tell my dad and Gerald and whoever else to go to hell.

"Fuck, girl. That's hardcore."

"I had to. I wish he would just be proud of me for once, but that's obviously never going to happen."

There's a new kind of appreciation in his eyes. "He should be. What I'm saying is that you've got balls. You come across as this mild-mannered little church mouse, but damn, you know what you want. And you go after it. And fuck your dad if he don't see that as a good thing."

I smile. I think I kind of love Luke Cross right now.

"He makes everything I do seem like a failure. All I've ever done is try to impress him, but it never works. And now I'm too scared to step out and leave school because I'm afraid I'm going to fail. Because in his eyes, I always fail. Always. So it's the only thing I can do."

"Some people you can't impress, no matter what you do."

He's trying to make me feel better. I admire that. "Really, what do you know about that? You impress everyone."

He laughs. "Not your dad."

I cringe. Did he hear the awful things my dad said about him?

"That's the thing! He doesn't even know you! He wants me to marry up. Marry a guy like him who treats his wife like crap? No thanks," I say miserably. "I've been thinking about it. And you're right. I *am* frigid. And Gerald is an asshole. You know, I dated him for six months, and five months into it I gave in and gave him my virginity. Because I was saving myself for real love, and I really did think that I loved him and he loved me. But I always felt like I was doing something wrong. 'Move that way.' 'Not there.' 'Do it this way.' All sex ever was was him barking orders at me. Of course I felt like I was doing something wrong. Everyone in my life except my best friend is constantly telling me what a screwup I am."

He's just staring at me. And I'm slightly aware it's TMI, but I can't stop. I look at my glass contemplatively.

"You know why he broke up with me? Probably because I wouldn't give him a blow job. I loved him, and he tossed me away because I wouldn't suck his thingy. But really, if a guy was always telling you that you weren't doing it right, would you want to give him a BJ?" I wag a finger at him. "Now, seriously, would you?"

He holds up his hands. "Fuck no. For more reasons than that."

"Yeah," I murmur. "You're right. He ruined me."

"Nah," he says. "You are far from ruined, girl. Some people just want to put you in a box. When people are like that to you, it's your goddamn duty to break out of it. Say, fuck them."

I lean on the bar, thinking.

"Yeah, right? Fuck them," I say finally, being like him and draining my glass without the lime. It's like water now. In fact, I can do this all day. I'm giddy at the thought.

He spins on the bar, so now my knees are between his legs. "Sweetheart? You've had three shots in fifteen minutes. Take it easy. Tequila'll hit you like a ton of bricks."

I give him a look and toss my ponytail wildly, like a sex kitten, something I never do. But I suddenly feel so free. Frisky and free and . . . hot. It might be that there are guys in the bar looking at my cleavage in this revealing pink top, or that I'm here with the hottest guy in the whole place. I put my hands on his thighs and lean forward so he can get a good look at my breasts, since I know he's been sneaking peeks since I put this shirt on. I've never actually used my tits, my ass . . . but from the way it's clearly mesmerizing Luke, I think I like it.

I notice there's a dance floor behind all the high-top tables. It's crowded. "Hey!" I shout. "Let's go!"

I manage to pull him with me, and a second later I'm dancing in the center of the crowd, moving with it, feeling like a part of it, so happy and sexy and alive. We're away from the cameras, and it's like the old Penelope Carpenter is gone. New clothes, new attitude . . . new sexy man that I could easily lick from head to toe.

Everyone's jumping with the throbbing of the music. Everyone but him. He's just gazing at me, his lips curved up in a smile like he likes what he sees.

He wants me.

And I want him.

I do.

I swing my hips as I come up close to him and touch his face. "Why are you not dancing?"

"Because I'm watching you."

I smile. "See anything you like? Anything you want to sample?"

"Yeah. All of it," he rasps.

Nice answer. I throw my arms around him and press myself up against his chest. He wraps his big arms around me, his hands massaging my ass, and I freaking die. Because every pore in my body wants him closer.

"Let's go, then," I whisper in his ear.

"No, Penny. The cameras . . ."

"I don't care about those," I tell him, giving him my best pout. "Let them see. Let everyone see. Fuck me right here."

"Penny." His voice is a warning.

He looks around, then takes my hand and leads me toward the door. The cold air hitting my bare skin is a shock, and now there's fog coming off the ocean and it's drizzling a little too. He dips his lips down and presses a soft kiss onto my hairline, sending shivers through my body. I waver on my feet.

He takes my hand and leads me down the street a little, toward the harbor. Away from the hotel. My body spikes with the thrill of the unknown as he suddenly swings me around to the side of one of the buildings into a closed-off, narrow alley.

He cages me in there, against the side of the building, one strong arm on either side of me. His mouth descends on mine, hard and rough, his teeth taking my bottom lip, scraping over it. His tongue slides between my teeth, his stubble rubbing my face red. It's all-consuming, not just a kiss anymore. This is thrusting, fighting, fucking with our mouths. It's raw and hard and exactly what I expect from someone like Luke Cross. We're in the middle of a busy city with all its distractions, but even so, there is nothing at that moment but his mouth and lips and tongue, taking me, making me his. His mouth is hot and hungry, making my breath shudder as his hands move down my bare arms.

I want him inside me. I want more than that. As if he feels that longing, his fingers trace a sweet, insane path to my breasts. He finds my nipple through the thin fabric of the tank with the pad of his thumb, already hard for him.

He tweaks it, and I writhe against the side of the building, my eyes rolling back in my head. I'm desperate for the feeling of his hot tongue on my bare breasts. I want to keep going. I want him to taste me. I want him to taste me everywhere.

He lets out a small groan, and his hands skim down the sides of my ribs. I let him slip his hands under my backside and scoop me up, wrapping my legs around him, feeling him, so hard against my aching sex.

I cry out as his tongue explores its way down my neck. I will never, ever get enough of this.

I want him to eat me up alive. I want to eat *him* up alive.

He pulls away suddenly.

"Penny?" he murmurs, running a finger down the side of my face.

"Mmm?" I lick my lips, studying his lips, red and wet and raw, the exact place I want to kiss again and again and again.

He's silent as he waits for me to force my gaze up—into his fiery, intense yeti eyes. "You wanted to forget your daddy. But this? You just right done lost your mind completely."

"Do you think I'm frigid?" I ask him, pleading.

He slowly drags a finger from my cheek to my lower lip, resting it there. My tongue slips out, tasting his finger. Salt and lime and him, yum. He lets out a ragged breath as I take his finger into my mouth, sucking lightly on it.

He groans. "No. Holy fuck, Penny, no," he mumbles, his body falling against me. "Now I'm losing it too."

I cast him a hooded gaze through my eyelashes. I don't know how to explain it, other than that Luke unleashes a side of me no one else can. With him, I'm only doing what feels right. Putting as much of my skin against his, tasting whatever I can of him, bathing in his essence . . . that feels right.

"Baby," he whispers, his voice low and throaty. "You keep doing that and there's gonna be trouble."

I suck on his finger more, dancing my tongue along the tip, sliding it along the sides, giving him a promise of what's to come.

Because right now? I want trouble.

Luke

Yeah, come to think of it, no. We didn't see the cameras. But we had a good night. Penny fell asleep on the cab ride back, so I carried her inside. We're ready, though. We've never felt better. We're gonna make up some ground.

Luke's Confessional, Day 8

I didn't sleep all night. Didn't even try. Sat out on the balcony and watched the sun rise over Boston Harbor before I went off for a quick morning confessional.

But Penny? She's another story. Out like a light from the moment I carried her inside.

I knew the second I laid her down in bed that I wouldn't be able to sleep. My mind was racing with thoughts of her, my cock hard as a rock for her. For this little girl who keeps opening herself up to me in the best of ways, like a Christmas present I get to unwrap every morning.

At six, I have to wake her up.

She's lying with her face under the pillow, her hair loose around her. When I tell her we have to go, she moans. "Oh, no no no. I'm dying."

"No, you're not," I tell her when she rips the pillow off her face and stares at me with bloodshot eyes. "What do you want? Hair of the dog? Grease? Or the old standby—water and ibuprofen? I got it all. Your choice."

She feels around for her glasses. I hand them to her. She puts them on and smooths her hair back as she blinks at the tray of bacon and eggs I brought up from the restaurant and the full minibar I have open for her. "Hair of the what?" She squeezes the bridge of her nose. "Forget it. Ibuprofen, please."

I hand her two and a bottle of water. She downs them. "Are we late?"

"We got about fifteen minutes to be downstairs."

She starts to pull off the covers and looks down at herself. At my T-shirt. And she goes from green to pale. "Why . . . what did we . . ."

She doesn't remember. Doesn't remember any of it. Doesn't remember that if she'd have had her way, we would've fucked in the street. I bet she doesn't even remember the way she licked my fingers and wrapped herself around me and told me she wanted to fuck.

"No. I couldn't find your pajamas."

Color floods her cheeks. "You . . . changed me?"

I nod. "Didn't peek. Much."

She looks around, almost accepting that, but then alarm fills her face. She rushes to the bathroom and starts puking her guts out. A minute later, I find her sprawled on the tile, her cheek pressed against the toilet seat. "I don't even have clean clothes for today," she whines.

I hand her the water. "You do. I told the producers, and they let me pick out some underwear for you at the gift shop. And Charity loaned you some of her shit."

She sips the water, then crawls over to the pile of clothing. She picks up the panties with a finger. "This is, like, dental floss. You really think I wear underwear like this?"

Back to the old Penny. "Just get changed, girl."

We wind up having to rent a car and drive through to Vermont. It's a good thing. Penny gets to sleep off her hangover in the passenger seat as I drive the four hours to our next challenge. But on the way there, I start sneezing. By the time we pull up at the Maple Run Sugar Shack, I'm blasting the heat but can't get warm.

I nudge Penny awake. "We're here."

I know it the second I step out of the car and my head feels like it's been hit by a ton of bricks. I'm fucking coming down with something.

Penny climbs out of the rental car and starts to walk toward the shack, wiggling her ass in a way that's half-funny, half-sexy. Charity's jeans are too long on her, so she has them rolled up at the cuff. They might not be her size, but her ass looks perfect in them. Even with a killer headache, I can't stop staring.

Then she goes and adjusts herself uncomfortably, reaching into the crack of her ass and pulling out the wedgie. "This underwear is the devil," she tells me, jumping around like she's got ants in her pants. "I can't believe people actually wear these on a regular basis."

Normally I'd tell her to suck it up, but my throat hurts. I blink and start to follow her in. She eyes me curiously.

"Are you okay? Your eyes look weird."

I nod and we go inside the sugar shack. A guy in flannel and overalls is there. "Welcome to Maple Run Farm, travelers," he says to us as he motions outside. "Today you and your partner will be harvesting maple sap from our trees. Maple Run Farm usually has anywhere from twenty to forty thousand taps running at a time in the spring when the snow thaws. However, because it's autumn, harvesting sap is a little trickier, though not impossible. I'm going to teach you how to tap a tree and harvest sap. You will be given all the tools to do this yourself."

He hands us a few liter jugs. "You can make up to five taps. All you need to do to win your next envelope is fill one container to the red line."

Penny nods excitedly, then follows him out the back door into the woods. I trail behind. It's cold, but the sun feels hot on my face. My vision bends. My throat feels thick.

Fucking hell. This was in the contract. *It's your duty to inform us if you develop any illnesses or conditions during filming so that you may be immediately evaluated by our in-house medical staff.* "Immediate evaluation" . . . to me, that means elimination.

And I'm sure as hell not going to be eliminated because of a little cold.

Or . . . whatever this is. Even a big one. Fuck that. I can get by. I *will* get by.

I kneel on the ground and watch the guy drill a hole in the tree, insert the spout. Or I try to. Penny follows along and does her own, and the man tells her she's got it, and leaves us alone. "You want to do one?" she asks me, handing me the drill.

"You're good. I'll just . . ." I fall back on my ass in a pile of dried leaves. "I just need a minute. Too much fun last night."

She sucks in a breath. "Luke. We're dead last. We need to make up time."

"I know." I try to get to my feet. After that, everything about the challenge happens in flashes. I haven't gotten high since I was eighteen, but I feel like I'm in a drug-induced haze. Operating on half a brain, only semiconscious. I help drill the rest of the holes for the taps, but I can't focus. By then, pain is screaming through my head like someone's drilling a tap into *me*. Somehow, we get the sap we need, get the next envelope.

"We've got to get to Burlington Airport," she says to me as she reads. "It says to be prepared for a long flight. I wonder what that means?"

We climb back in the car and make it to the airport in the early afternoon. I've come to hate flying in a cramped cabin with a bunch of people, but this time I'm fine with it. I get in my seat and, ignoring Penny's questions as to whether I'm okay, conk out. I awaken for the layover, buy a bottle of water for me and one for Penny, and nurse it while we wait to board. Feeling like shit. Aware of Penny eyeing me curiously. And once again, I conk out on our second flight.

The next thing I know, Penny's shaking me. "Luke. You will never believe where we are."

My blood feels like ice. I hope we're in some nice, warm paradise where I can lie in the sun and let it warm me.

I manage a look out the window, and all I see is darkness. "Where the fuck are we? Is it nighttime?"

"No. That's the weird thing—it's actually seven in the morning!" She nudges me to get up. "We're in Alaska!"

Fuck. Me.

SNOWBOUND

Nell

Yes, clearly we've been at the bottom of the pack for much of the race, and there have been a lot of times where we made it through by the skin of our teeth. We've experienced a few setbacks, but we're not giving up.

—Nell's Confessional, Day 9

The taxi takes us to some little town in the middle of nowhere, and meanwhile, I can't stop talking to the chatty cab driver.

First, I can't believe we're here in Alaska. Second, the more I talk to other people, the less I have to talk to Luke.

Not that he's talking much. I don't remember much of that night after the first shot of Cuervo. I remember his hand on my ass and me gyrating while he stood perfectly still and the room spun around me. I remember his mouth on mine. I remember asking him to fuck me on the dance floor.

After that . . . nothing. And if I think about it too much, I might die of embarrassment.

No wonder he's been practically ignoring me since then. I swear, he looks like he can't stand me. He's distant and removed, and it's like his whole attitude had changed. Before he was all gung-ho over the game. Now it looks like he's deliberately trying to lose so that he can get away from me. He barely lifted a finger during the syrup challenge. I want to grab him and shake him and tell him to get his act together.

I shouldn't have gotten drunk.

I shouldn't have thrown myself at him.

I shouldn't have acted like a total megaslut and turned him off. I even think I may have told him about Gerald and whined about my pathetic lack of bedroom skills.

Oh holy God. I'm a loser.

We're nearly halfway there. There are only five teams left in the running. This is serious. And what did I do? I went and . . . shook my boobs at him.

I might as well die here. Really, what was I thinking? I'm not sexy in the least. He must think I'm a total ass.

I'm tense and restless while Luke sits in the back of the cab, silent.

The driver drops us at the corner near a gas station. I climb out of the car, and wind whips against my face. I lift my hood over my head. The ground is covered in mounds of snow. I see Will Wang huddled with the camera crew in a nearby bus shelter.

"Hello, travelers!" he says to us as we arrive. "I hope you had a lot of sleep on the plane ride here, because you're about to get into your next challenge!"

I nod and rub my hands together excitedly as Will's helper hands us snow boots, bibs, extra-fluffy coats, and gloves and hats, all with the *MDM* logo on them. I start to kick off my shoes so I can pull on my snow bibs.

Then I look at Luke.

He's starting to worry me. He has his hands in his pockets, and his eyes are blearily staring at nothing in particular. I snap my fingers at him, motioning for him to get ready, and he startles. "You okay?" I mumble to him as he pulls on his snow bibs.

"Yeah. I'm good." His voice is rough but weak.

"This is not a challenge for the weak of heart," Will says, smiling at our coming agony. "Or the weak of body either. First, one of you will need to carry the other on a dogsled, a mile up that hill. Then you'll need to work together to construct an igloo out of snow, where you will have to spend the night. When the sun rises tomorrow, you and the other four teams will have one more challenge, where you will compete head-to-head to determine your placement for the last half of the adventure."

I peer through the darkness toward the hill. I can see the ruts in the snow of the contestants who came before us, which disappear into the darkness. Luke should have no problem pulling me. And building an igloo . . . that shouldn't be hard. But the last thing I want to do is spend the night in an igloo. Outside. Ice cold. Cramped. No running water.

Ugh.

I look at Luke for the pep talk. He's the one who galvanized me during the really intense challenges, like the run through the cornfield in the mud and the zip-lining thing. But he just looks . . . tired. His eyes are glassy and sunken and . . .

Oh god.

I realize something, right then.

He's my spirit. If he's lost it, then I have too.

"Come on," I say to him, pulling him toward the sled. "So, do you want me to pull or you?"

I meant it as a joke, but he doesn't even smile. "Sit your ass down."

He says it so abruptly, it's like an arrow to my heart. I wish he'd call me baby again. Call me baby and look at me with that hint of mischief that says he's undressing me with his eyes. Just once. Just a little.

But he's just surveying the hill up ahead, preparing for the climb. All business. Like I'd wanted. I wanted this to be a business transaction, and I got it.

I am such an idiot.

I sit. We pile our bags on my legs, and he starts to pull the sled through knee-deep snow. I expect the challenge to be easy for him, considering the way he dominated the corn maze with my weight wrapped around him. But he wavers on his feet, straining, breathing hard.

Something suddenly occurs to me.

Is he not feeling well?

I've been so preoccupied with how I made a fool of myself. But maybe this has nothing to do with the other night in Boston at all. I keep asking him if he's okay, and he keeps saying yes, but maybe he's just trying to hide from everyone that he's coming down with something. Because if the producers find out he's sick, he could be eliminated.

When he lets out a grunt and falls to his knees for the second time, I say, "Luke. Do you want to rest?"

"No," he grumbles, not looking back. "I just want to get there."

I look over my shoulder. We haven't gone far. I can still see the oily smirk on Will Wang's stupid, plastic face, the cameras pointed at us.

I bite on my lip. The rules are that one person has to sit on the sled the whole time. "You want me to pull it?"

"Get real."

I frown. "I may have no muscle, but I can still try. Maybe we can trade—"

"No." He turns to me, his cheeks red and wind-slapped. "You're half of me. You're not going to be able to pull me anywhere."

"Luke, I—"

"*Stop.*" The tone of his voice is heartbreakingly savage, silencing me at once. "I don't have the energy to argue with you right now."

He wraps his hands around the rope and hoists it over his thick shoulders. I watch his magnificent body, the wide span of his shoulders as he strains to pull the sled. It's not so much my weight as the snow in his way and the steep angle of the hill. He's right; I'd probably let go of the rope and send us slipping back down the hill.

The sun is up, but the day is overcast, so it doesn't bring any warmth. It's probably the worst thing I've ever seen, watching him try to pull the sled up the hill, only to have it slide back down every so often, as I sit there, helpless, weighing him down. He's in pain. The wind is whipping and working against him. And I can't do anything to help.

Finally, miraculously, we get to the camp. There are five large mounds there—the basis for our habitat for the evening. The four other couples are well on their way to constructing their igloos. The other teams barely look at us when we arrive, but Ace, whose structure is nearly complete, scoffs at us. "What's the matter, pussy boy? Your sled too heavy for you? Maybe you should go back to your playpen, little man."

Luke doesn't say anything, but his fists clench. I jump off the sled as soon as I can and step between them. "Don't listen to him. I'll start with the igloo. You just rest for a minute."

Unbelievably, he listens to me. He sits down on the sled for a minute, skullcap down low over his eyes, face down and out of the wind, as I start to walk around our shelter, taking little peeks at the others, trying to figure out where to start. They've given us tools to dig with, so I set to work, clearing a small hole in the snow. It's slow going.

When I turn back to see if Luke is okay, he's lying on his side, his eyes closed. Pulling off one of my gloves, I crawl over to him and start to lay my hand on his forehead, but even before I do, I feel the heat.

Oh my god. He's burning up.

"Luke," I whisper, grabbing his jacket and shaking him. "Luke! You have to get up."

His heavy lashes flicker open, and he focuses on me. "Hey."

"You're sick. Like, really sick. We have to tell the producers."

Now he's starting to stand up. He's insane. "No. We don't. Listen, we don't. I'm fine."

"You're going to get yourself killed. You can't—"

"No. We gotta win this."

I almost laugh. "Win? We've been practically dead last since that first day. It's only sheer luck that we've gotten this far."

"Right," he says, his voice gravelly. "And that's how we'll win. I brought my lucky Penny."

He reaches up and tucks a lock of hair behind my ear. And I almost break down right there. "I don't think I can make a shelter for us alone. Can you help me?"

"Yeah."

We're slow. Really slow. Luke takes a lot of time to rest. Night comes around by seven, and we end up working in the dark, with floodlights overhead. Everyone else ends up snuggled up in their igloos for hours as we work. And our igloo really leaves a lot to be desired. We only manage to carve out enough space for the two-person sleeping bag and our bodies.

But we finish it.

When we crawl inside, it's a struggle just to get comfortable. There is snow everywhere and I'm freezing, and I decide I will probably spend the whole night awake and shivering.

"Well, this sucks," he says.

And I laugh in total agreement.

That is, until Luke reaches out and pulls my body up against his, engulfing me in the warmest, most comforting hug. I don't know if it's that he's sick, but his body is the perfect furnace, even with the many layers of clothing between us. I breathe in his thick, masculine scent, and suddenly I would be perfectly happy staying in this insulated bubble with him forever.

"Come to think of it," he rasps out faintly in the absolute darkness, "this ain't so bad."

I giggle.

"I've been thinking about it, Penny . . . ," he says, his voice listless.

I expect him to talk competition strategy or tell me that he's feeling really bad and should go to medical after all. I suck in a breath.

But instead he says, "You shouldn't let your daddy or anyone tell you you're doing things wrong. You're good. You're damn good. You can do whatever you want and be damn good at it. I got no doubt about that."

He's babbling, probably half out of his mind, but I don't care.

Those are just the words I need to hear right now. He's warming me from head to toe, but those words? They warm me from the inside. I settle into them, and the more I think about them, the more I want to cry. Not from sadness. It's because I've been waiting twenty-five years to hear them.

He holds me tight, and that's how I fall asleep, my face buried in his chest, calmed by the steady thrum of his heartbeat.

Luke

I was a little under the weather there. I'm better now, and we're in it to win it. How we got through? That was all Penny.

—*Luke's Confessional, Day 10*

An air horn jolts me awake. I'm in pitch blackness, and it takes the smell of the snow and the feel of Penny's body against mine to remind me where the hell I am. She stirs, and I feel her eyelashes fluttering against my neck. Her skin is warm and dewy and smells sweet, like something I want to taste.

I find her glasses and help her put them on. "You don't feel as hot." Her voice is hopeful.

I tense my muscles, and they don't ache like last night. "I don't feel so shitty anymore."

"You don't?" Her arms tighten around me. Her nose bumps against my Adam's apple. Her breath is warm on my skin. Her lips move with the words "I'm so glad," feeling like a kiss.

I dip my head down to seek her lips out, and as I do, the air horn blares again.

Time to start the next leg of the race.

I help her push up and out of the small opening, hardly able to believe that this is what we made last night. I was half-delirious. When I slide out into the bracing Alaska cold, stand upright, and take a few breaths, I'm sure of it.

I'm ready to kick ass.

"What are you smiling about, pussy boy?" a voice calls from the igloo across from us. Fucking Ace. "You're dead last. This is gonna be your last challenge."

Next to me, Penny scowls, punching her open hand like a regular firecracker. "We'll just see about that, you . . . pierced-nosed . . . gross . . ." She trails off, lost.

I tug on her jacket, smiling at her. She ain't much of an expert when it comes to trash talk, but we need that spirit if we're ever going to come out on top of the rest of the teams.

"Hey, girl?"

She looks up at me.

"When you don't got anything good to say . . ." I point a middle finger at Ace. "This speaks volumes."

She tries it, but by then Ace isn't paying attention. Ace and Marta are still solidly on top, but Brad and Natalie have been giving them a run for their money, and Ivy and Cody and Tony and Charity have been working really well together too. It's anyone's game right now.

The staff members give us cereal bars and juice, and then we're called to assemble in front of a large log building. Will Wang is there. He says, "Hope you guys had restful sleep last night!"

He means it as a joke, because everyone's walking around looking like the living dead. But you know what? I did. I slept damn well.

"Before the next challenge, we hope that you're ready for Marriage Test Number Three."

Everyone groans. Us included, because hell. We haven't done so well on these tests. We've yet to get a question right about each other. Penny's eyes are wide because these are probably the first tests in her life she's ever failed. I lean over and whisper to her, "We've got this," as encouragement, even though I ain't sure.

She goes up with the rest of the women, and a crew member hands her an electronic board. Will smiles his big, fake grin. "First question, ladies! What or who is your husband's biggest inspiration?"

Holy shit. We really have got this. Behind her, I see the muscles of her back tense. She starts to scribble feverishly.

Amazingly, Penny and I are the only ones who get the question right.

"His granddad." She grins at me as she shows her scribbles and I show mine.

I grin back at her, because she's A fuckin' right.

"Annndd that is correct!"

"YES!" Penny jumps up and high-fives me.

Then she gets the question right about where I'm from. Easy question. Most everyone gets that one right.

But still. We're making up ground. We are turning this fucking thing around.

"This last question was taken from your last confessionals. What would your husband say is your best feature?"

She doesn't hesitate. She writes it down immediately, then looks back at me and winks.

Does she really know what I said?

Will Wang goes down the line. Natalie goes next, suggesting her courage, which is wrong. Brad had said her sassy attitude. Marta gets the answer right—she wrote her tits. I'm sure he said his cock. The two of them once again proving they have absolutely zero regard for the "keep things clean" rule.

Still looking a little flustered, Will comes up to Penny. "Okay, Dr. Carpenter! What is your answer?"

She flips her board around. "My intelligence."

The buzzer sounds almost before she gets the last word out. "I'm sorry, that is incorrect. What did Mr. Cross say about his lovely wife? Her . . . freckles! Ladies and gentlemen, her cute little freckles."

She looks back at me, blushing and feeling her face. She seems astonished that I didn't choose her brain. But hell no. Those freckles are what got me from the minute I set eyes on her.

Doesn't matter.

I can't wait to find out what she said was my best feature. I figure it must be my dick, but knowing her, she'd be too embarrassed to write that or any other part of my anatomy. So I play it safe and write my eyes. And what did she say? "Your smarts, Mr. Cross!"

Me. Smart.

When she's the one with all the degrees. I turn around and stare at her, shocked as hell, thinking she must have heard the question wrong.

We end up getting four out of six right, tying with Ace and Marta. Now the little trash talk from Ace bounces right off me. I said I'd clean the floor with someone's ass . . . and it's going to be his.

"Well, this next challenge is going to eliminate one team, and it's a bit of a mucky one." He smiles broadly. "You and your partner will both be working together on this one. Let's go on inside and see what you'll need to do."

We go inside and strip off our outerwear so we're in our regular clothes. As we do, I murmur to Penny, "What were you, drunk in confessional?"

"What do you mean?"

I laugh. "You said smart. What, you think they were talking about you? Ain't no way I'm smart."

"Yeah. You are." Then she lowers her voice an octave and says, "Ain't no way freckles are my best feature."

Is she pretending to be me? Is that how she thinks I sound? It's kind of fucking adorable.

"Oh hell yes they are. That and a few other parts of you, but it wasn't a shopping list. And I didn't want to make you blush too much when you found out."

Her eyes widen.

Will says, "This here is an indoor fish hatchery, providing sustainable Alaskan salmon to the world. Salmon that are raised indoors provide more food to keep up with demand. The tanks that keep these salmon hold up to ten thousand fish!"

He's going on, but the rest of us aren't listening. We want the challenge.

We walk into a large room on a metal gangplank overlooking tanks. They're some big tanks, about five feet high, with fish practically sandwiched together. There are five of them.

When we signed the agreements for the show, we were told that we could be exposed to potentially dangerous situations. I'd say this is definitely one of them.

I'm fucking game.

"When you are given the okay to start—we'll go at three-minute intervals, starting with the first-place team, based on when you arrived at the camp yesterday afternoon—both team members will choose a tank, climb into the tank, and attempt to find the clue. I'm not saying what this clue is, but you'll know it when you see it. Once you retrieve the clue, read it and proceed on to the next leg of the journey.

"However, please note that since only four of you will be proceeding on from this point, only four of the tanks will actually have a clue. Good luck. Teams ready?"

We all applaud.

As expected, Ace and Marta were first, so when the whistle blows, they rush down the stairs, jumping into the first tank. I look over at Penny. She looks ready, rubbing her palms together, her brows narrowed in concentration. "You know, girl, you have a competitive side. An inner beast."

She nods. "I want to win. And I'm so happy you're feeling better. I was really worried."

She's so damn cute. Worried about me?

"You *could* take a break this challenge," I suggest. "Since you did almost all of it yesterday."

"No. You dragged me all the way up the hill. Plus, if the two of us go in the tank, we'll find it faster." She points to Ace and Marta's tank, where the guy is cussing up a storm. "It must be hard. They've been looking for five minutes and haven't found a thing. We should work together."

"All right. You said it." I hold out my fist.

She stares at it.

"Bump?"

"What?"

"Or . . . should we have a team handshake? Put out your hand like this."

She does. I bump it, grab her hand, give her skin, then let go and run my hand through my hair. She's still staring. "I don't get it."

"I forgot. You ain't into sports. It pumps you up. Gets you riled. Ready to go." She's still confused. I shake my head. "Forget it. Let's do this."

By then, it's our time to go. Will Wang counts down and says, "Team Prince Charming and His Doctor, are you ready? Annnnnd go!"

We race down the stairs. I get to the ladder of the last remaining tank first and climb in, diving headfirst into a murky tank full of fish. I reach in, trying to find who the fuck knows what, but all I keep feeling are handfuls of fish and the flat sides of the tank.

Penny climbs the ladder and slowly slides into the water. "It's freezing!"

She looks around carefully, like she did that first day in the swimming pool, her face twisted in disgust. Meanwhile, I'm splashing around her, reaching blindly down into the bottom of the tank, trying to take ahold of something that doesn't feel scaly. I dive under, but the water is green and putrid and I can't see a goddamn thing. I look over and notice that the other teams are having the same luck.

Suddenly, she says, "Luke. Luke!"

I push the water out of my eyes. She's holding a tiny white canister, only about the size of her thumb.

"Look at that! The lovely doctor may have just been the first person to find a clue!" Will Wang shouts as the cameras zero in on us. The rest of the teams stop what they're doing and watch as she unscrews the lid and pulls out a long piece of paper.

And just like that . . . we're in first place.

HEAD OF THE PACK

Nell

> *It's funny. Luck brought us to the bottom of the pack that first day. And then luck went and brought us to the top of it. So I guess things are evening out. We're not ready to go home yet.*

> —Nell's Confessional, Day 10

We ended up putting on our snow gear again and taking a speedboat to our next destination, around the glaciers and icy outcroppings in the lake as we sped toward Anchorage for our flight to the next place. Because we were still wet from our dive in the tanks—It. Was. Freezing. I was afraid of Luke getting sick again. At the Anchorage airport, we checked in for our flight to the next place, where we were told that we could lose the coats and boots.

Warmth! Huzzah!

As I came back from washing up in the bathroom and changing into the only clean clothes I had left—the capris, workout bra, and a T-shirt—I saw Ace and Marta running in wearing their winter gear. Ace looked at me and said, "You were lucky, Poindexter. You ain't gonna be lucky for long."

Poindexter? Really? I'd thought about giving him the middle finger like Luke showed me, but I couldn't bring myself to. Besides, just being in first place should've been enough. He's worried. About us. We're his big competition.

Me. Competition. Hilarious.

Now we're in another airplane, hopefully headed toward a warmer climate. Our lead isn't really a lead, because most of the teams, who are on the flight with us, must've found their clue right after we did, judging from how quickly they arrived at the airport. I'm trying to read my *Les Mis* right now in the original French, but I'm keenly aware of Luke's eyes on me. He's wearing a T-shirt now, and so his powerful arms are on display, his defined chest muscles peering through the thin black fabric. As big as he is, though, he still lets me have the armrest. I'd let him have it, but then I think neither of us would use it, and I like the feeling of his skin against mine, even if it is just our arms touching. His skin is dark caramel, and I'm light peach. I can't stop looking at that, the contrast of our skin, pressed together that way. It's strange, but also natural. The goose bumps on my skin are most pronounced right where our bodies meet. I wonder briefly if he'd have that effect everywhere he touches.

Then . . . right. Victor Hugo. Must concentrate on the reading.

He breathes out, and I venture a look at his face. He's staring at me, his eyes assessing, framed by lashes so thick and dark I could get lost in them. The setting sun casts an orange hue on his skin and amber flecks into his eyes. His lips are curved in amusement. "Having trouble reading?"

I blush. So he noticed. "Why do you say that?"

He puts a finger on the book. "Because you haven't turned a page in a while."

"No." I turn the page, even though I hadn't really finished the preceding page.

A small chuckle erupts from his throat, like he's so onto me.

I close my book and look at him, my eyes shifting over him uncomfortably. If I spend too long on any one part, I worry I might be blatantly staring. But every part of him is so strong and masculine and begs to be adored; he's raw, dirty sex on a cracker. I bet the camera loves him, and when we watch this season months from now, he'll make all the females weak in the knees. And they won't know the half of it, because they can't smell his delicious, soapy, woodsy smell. They won't know the way he can make their world quake just by one look in their eyes. They won't know the way he kisses, or says their name . . .

I need to stop this. Otherwise I'll go insane. I tamp down the emotions inside me. "Are you feeling okay?"

The amusement turns into a full-on smile, his eyes sparkling, and I notice a dimple poking out from two days' worth of dark scruff that's bordering on a full beard. "So you really were worried about me, baby?"

I bite my lower lip in response.

"I'm good. It's all good." His voice is low and rumbles inside me, and I almost hate how everything he says and everything he does makes my body react.

"I was worried for a little while," I confess to him after a minute. "I thought that because . . . that night . . . that you and I . . . you know . . ."

His eyes are back to mine, holding me. "That you and I what?"

I take a breath. "We almost . . ."

He laughs, his eyes drifting to those damn freckles—the bane of my existence—that he loves so much. "We didn't *almost* anything, baby. We weren't even close."

"Oh." I shrink back, doing my best to separate myself from him. "I know. I mean, I just thought you were upset at me or I'd done something wrong. But you weren't feeling well, right? You're not angry at me?"

"Nah." I start to relax, until he reaches over and takes my hand, entwining his fingers with mine. I feel the calluses against my palm as his fingers stroke the back of my hand. "You ain't done nothing wrong with me. I doubt you could."

I blink at him. "I'm *sure* I could. I'm always—"

"No you ain't. What was wrong was with those other people, Penny. I can't be angry at a sweet girl like you." He squeezes my hand gently, then pulls it up and kisses my knuckles, his gaze holding mine. "And if we were that close, sweetheart, close like I wanted to be? I wouldn't have been able to turn back."

Oh my goodness. I'm undone. Completely undone. My nipples are hard and my sex is clenching, and all he's done is grab my hand. And part of me wishes I could remember that night in Boston just a little better because the hazy drunk memory of his mouth on my skin barely feels real. It feels as far away as one of my fantasies, almost like it never really happened.

I want to be able to talk about that night. I've been dying to. But I haven't been able to find the words, and he's always looked like he couldn't be bothered. Now he's looking at me, his eyes studying me with intense concentration. Now is the time.

"So that night . . . ," I start, hoping that his eyes will spark with memory and he'll finish for me. That doesn't happen. And I realize I don't have the words, even now. "Was it . . . what was it?"

One eyebrow cocks up. "I think it was called getting shitfaced."

Right. That's all it was. My stomach knots.

"I know. But was it like, just fun, because I was there and we were drunk, or was it . . . more?"

My insides clench as I realize what I said. Oh god. Did I just say that?

His eyes dance playfully. "What did you want it to be?"

I frown. What am I doing? Of course that night meant nothing to him. Of course he makes out with drunk girls on a regular basis. He owns a bar, after all. Lives to be shitfaced. "Forget I said anything. I'm just tired because I didn't sleep much last night," I mutter, turning so he won't see the lie on my face. I slept great last night. Because of him. "I should turn in because I'm sure tomorrow will be busy."

Soon it'll be dark, so I pull down the shade to block out the sunset, which would probably make me think the romantic thoughts I shouldn't be thinking, especially where someone like Luke Cross is concerned. Luke Cross, who lives to be shitfaced, is a thug, loves to fuck, and probably doesn't have a romantic bone in his body.

A moment later, I hear, "Penny."

Oh, I want this conversation to be over. I can't be near him when every single part of my body reacts to him. My sex is still clenched from his closeness, and even though I separated from him I can still feel goose bumps on my arm.

A bit after that, more insistent now. "Nell?"

I can't just ignore him, so I turn, letting out a "Hmm?" but his mouth is there, and he captures mine for a slow, sweet, nibbling kiss that turns my entire world upside down. No tongue, just his lips and mine, his scruffy beard tickling my chin. There are cameras—I know there are usually two or three on each plane we've been on. But he doesn't seem to care as he gently licks at my lips.

His mouth lingering by mine, he says very softly, "Good night, sweetheart. Want to sleep on my shoulder?"

I look up at those green eyes so close to mine and nod gratefully.

I lean against his broad shoulder, inhaling him, and he dips his head. I think he's smelling me, too, his lips and nose in my hair as his chest expands, and that causes a weird little flutter in my tummy that I've never felt before.

Romantic or not, he does have a way about him.

And I'm falling for it. Hook, line, and sinker.

Luke

What were we talking about on the plane to San Diego? Hell. I don't know. I don't remember. Did we get along? Yeah. By now, we have a lot of the kinks ironed out in our strategy. We've been getting along pretty damn well.

—Luke's Confessional, Day 11

When we step out of San Diego International Airport into warm ocean breezes, whatever sickness had been hanging over my head for the past few days leaves me completely. And I feel strong. Good. Ready to take on the world.

In the taxi line, I wrap my fingers around Penny's small hand as she reads the clue. "We have to get to the MCRD," she says, wrinkling her nose. "Where is that?"

"Marine Corps Recruit Depot," I whisper to her. The other teams are also in the line, and I don't want to give them any help.

"Oh, really? How do you know?"

"I have cousins who went there."

We get in the next cab, which has a busted air conditioner. I've been pining for warmth for so long, and now that we have it, it's too much. I'm wearing a T-shirt and cargo pants, and I'm sweating my balls off. I look over at Penny, who's still wearing her jacket, fanning her face.

"Hey. Doc," I say as I tug on her jacket. "Take this off."

She does, swiping her hair back off her face as she shrugs the jacket down and wraps it around her waist. She sticks out her tongue, panting. "It's still hot. Gosh, it's brutal. I thought San Diego was supposed to be perfect weather."

I pull on her T-shirt. "Take this off."

Her eyes widen. "No. I can't."

I wonder if she remembers anything about that night in Boston. I wonder if she remembers that she let me pull down her shirt in that alleyway and suck on her perfect pink nipples. I wonder if she knows I'd kill to do that again. "You got a bra on underneath it, though. Right?"

She nods. "But—"

"I want to know who put it in your head that you've got a less-than-perfect body. Was it that prick boyfriend of yours?"

"No. It's just that . . . I'm self-conscious. I don't like people looking at me."

"Dammit, really? Because I love looking at your sexy body. In fact, when you were pressed up against me in that igloo, that's all I was thinking about. Your body."

She blushes, stiffening, turning her head to look out the window as she continues to fan her face. Then, suddenly, she reaches down, lifts her shirt, and pulls it off. "Happy?"

Hell yes, I'm happy. Because she. Is. Gorgeous.

She has the curves you wouldn't expect on a buttoned-up, book-ish girl. I've felt them before, but seeing them only makes me want to bare her more. She bites on her lips and balls her T-shirt in front of her tight, bare abdomen. She's so damn lickable that my mouth is watering, my body tightening with need. The sexiest thing about her is that she doesn't know how beautiful she is.

When she realizes I'm staring, she crosses her arms over her chest.

"You said you don't like people looking at you," I murmur. "But believe me, when they do, ain't no way they can be thinking anything bad."

She flushes straight down her chest, straight to the top of her bra. I stare at her perfect cleavage. What I wouldn't give to see where that flush ends again, to draw her top down and take those hardened nipples into my mouth again.

We pull up to the depot and are greeted by men in military fatigues. Not greeted. More like assaulted. The second we get out, they get right in our faces and start yelling at us as they usher us into a room. They tell us that we are the lowest scum of the earth and the worst pieces of shits who've ever breathed. Penny gives me a nervous look, like she wants to cry. She starts to open the envelope as I catch a glimpse of the marines who just verbally tore us new assholes.

They're now looking her over like she's something they want.

Red-hot anger shoots down my spine, and I feel possessive, like I want her to put that shirt back on. I scowl at them, gritting my teeth. Marines or not, I'd fuck them up. *Put your fucking tongues back in your mouth, or I'm gonna do it for you.*

Then the door opens, and Charity and Tony walk in. Good. That'll give 'em something else to look at. Because this girl? This smart, beautiful, hot-as-hell girl in the ponytail and freckles?

She is mine.

I don't know when I started feeling that way, but I'll be damned if I let any other man get close to her now. We're a team, in this race together, allied. The only alliance that matters. All my other alliances can go to hell.

She gasps suddenly, and I turn to see her staring with horror at the card she's slipped from the envelope.

"What?"

"One of us has to go through the confidence course," she says, not lifting her eyes from the paper.

The confidence course is balls hard. I saw things about it in high school when I was thinking about going into the service, before I got wrapped up in drugs. "Okay. No problem. Just one of us? I can handle that. What . . ."

She lets out an uneasy breath, and the envelope falls to the ground. "The other one has to get his or her head shaved."

Oh.

Fuck.

Now I see what she means.

"Okay." The door opens, and Brad and Natalie come in. We don't have much chance to make up our minds.

The marine sergeant hands us military fatigues to change into. "Changing rooms for males and females. Once you come back, we expect your answer."

They shove us in separate directions, and all the while I'm zeroed in on Penny's horrified face. "Look. It's up to you. I'll do whatever you want."

She doesn't respond. She looks dazed. I want to follow her, tell her it'll be all right, that I'd fucking think she was the hottest thing ever even with a bald head. But I'm not so sure it's my opinion that matters to her. The world will see her, the thirteen million fans who watch this show on television.

I throw on the tight T-shirt, the boots, the military cargo pants and hat, and then I go outside, where I finally see Ace and Marta arrive. Somehow, they're dead last. I don't even have the urge to rub that in his face, because I'm getting enough satisfaction watching him get his ass yelled off by a marine sergeant.

Penny comes outside into the sunlight. She's wearing the military fatigues, her cap pulled down low over her eyes, so I almost don't recognize her. The getup makes her look like something from one of my fantasies. I wouldn't mind her getting in my face a little and yelling that cute button nose off at me.

"I've decided. I'm going to do the confidence course."

"Penny," I start, because I'm not sure she knows what she's getting into. "Do you—"

"Don't. I know it's not the best strategy, but I made up my mind," she says, setting her jaw, staring straight ahead. A marine is already guiding her away, toward the course.

Another marine approaches me. "Ready?"

I just watch her go as I rip the cap off my head and run my hands through my hair. I couldn't give a shit about losing my hair; it's just hair. But damn, I don't want Penny hurt. "Can I watch her?"

"We'll take you out there when you're done. Come on."

When I can't see her anymore, I nod. "All right. Let's get this over with."

CONFIDENCE

Nell

> *Do I like Luke's new hair? Yes. I mean, what is hair? I'm not concerned with physical traits. That's not sufficiently interesting to me. The simple reason I decided on the confidence course is because I wanted to prove to myself I could do it. But yes. Luke makes a good-looking marine, I suppose . . . Actually, I guess he makes a good-looking anything.*

> *—Nell's Confessional, Day 11*

I walk with a camera crew out to the course, wishing only my palms were sweating. But all of me is sweating now. A river of sweat is trickling between my breasts, down my ribs, everywhere. I wonder if I made the worst decision ever.

My thinking was this: I was going to embarrass myself either way. I could do the confidence course and be embarrassed for an hour, or get my hair shaved and be embarrassed for six months while it grows out.

So . . . here I am.

Confidence course.

All the obstacles look a lot higher and more insurmountable as I draw closer. There are ten different obstacles I'll need to conquer in order to finish and be given our next clue. But as I approach, I start to shiver despite the sweat leaking out of my pores.

"All right," the marine says to me. Thank goodness they're not yelling like they were when we first got here, or I might give up. "On the count of three, you start. I'll follow you through, giving you directions. Got it?"

I nod, tugging on my ponytail, then get into ready position at the starting line. *I hope I made the right decision.*

Now part of me is wondering if the only reason I decided to keep my hair is because I loved flipping it and twirling it and watching Luke's eyes dance as I did.

No, no. Physical traits do not interest or stimulate me.

What a lie. Luke's physical traits stimulate me better than any intellectual conversation ever has. His eyes, his muscles, those powerful legs, that ass . . . everything about him pushes my buttons unlike any man ever has. It drives me wild, just thinking about—

"Ready? And . . . go!"

The camera catches the first thing I do, which is stumble forward, nearly falling on my face. I can sense the marine behind me wondering what kind of clumsy oaf he has running his esteemed course. But I jump to my feet as I hit the first obstacle, which is a long line of monkey bars suspended over a mud pit.

I haven't done these since I was about ten on the playground, but I *have* done them. And though I have no muscles whatsoever, I manage to get across the bars without falling into the mud. I scramble down the ramp to the next thing as the marine yells at me that I need to go over it. It's a chest-high wall with a rope attached to it. I take a running leap, grabbing the rope, and somehow manage to propel myself over it without coming out dead on the other side.

And then something happens.

I actually start to think I might be able to do this.

The next few obstacles are almost easy. I run through tires, then have to grab onto a rope dangling over the center of a mud pit and leap over the pit. I get it done. And soon I start feeling invincible. The theme from *Rocky* starts to play in my head as I get to the next obstacle, a series of wooden balance beams I traverse, only falling off once.

Then I see it. A rope, suspended horizontally over a pool of mud.

I have no idea how to get over this thing.

"Wrap your arms and legs, keep it tight, and go over, hand over hand, foot over foot," the marine shouts at me.

I climb the ramp and tackle it. I am not going to be the weak link in this challenge. I am more than halfway through. I am going to get this done.

Somehow I end up falling over, so that I'm hanging under the rope instead of on top of it, but I slowly make it across, aware of another person on the course, gaining ground. I see a flash of black hair and tanned skin.

Marta.

Then someone whistles and shouts, "Get it, Penny!"

I tilt my head to the side and see a handsome, formidable marine, clapping his hands for me. He has his hat down low over his eyes, but few men have a broad chest that looks as good in a T-shirt. Luke.

I bite down hard on my lower lip, nearly drawing blood as I move over the pit, until I reach the end.

I did it! And I didn't get a face full of mud either.

I rush down the ramp to the next obstacle, a series of low walls, which I climb over, not as gracefully as I'd like, considering I can feel Luke's eyes on me. He's cheering and wolf-whistling and clapping for me, and I take on the next obstacle, a series of metal bars. I have to hoist myself up with my feet before I can get up, but I do so only because I want it bad. I'm determined to get this shit done.

I cross the finish line before Marta, and Luke is there, grinning at me. He gives me a high five and pulls me into a celebratory hug. "How the fuck did you do that, beast?"

I reach up and tug on his hat, yanking it off his head. All that messy dark hair is gone, as is the beard. He's . . . clean. And just as hot as ever. "Nice buzz," I say as he swipes his hand through it.

I start to walk toward where our next clue is, but he stops me, and when he does I follow his finger and realize that I have a tear in my cargo pants and I'm bleeding. I roll up the fabric to reveal a huge gash on my shin, and the blood is running down into my sock and boot. I don't think I've had an injury like that, ever.

"Let's have medical look at that."

I peer over at Ace, who's trash-talking Marta through the rest of the obstacle course. "No. We've got to go now. Let's go."

He takes my hand, and we grab the next clue. We don't bother to change into new clothes. We grab our bags and get the first cab. I rip open the envelope and read, then gasp breathlessly to the driver, "We've got to get to someplace called Julian. Please. As quick as you can."

"Julian? What do we got to do there?" Luke asks me as I check to see if any of the other teams are coming.

I shrug. "It doesn't say." I lean over and ask the driver how long of a ride it is, and he tells me it's about an hour into the San Diego mountains. I sit back, feeling wired and restless but most of all . . . pumped. "Did you see me?"

Luke motions to my leg. I lift it up onto his knee as he says, "Yeah, I saw you, killer. What, you gonna give up your French poetry and become a marine now, Dr. Cross?"

I shrug happily. "Maybe."

He laughs and carefully and methodically rolls up the fabric of the pants, his gentleness so uncharacteristic of his big hands. He reaches into his pack and pulls out the medical kit they gave us at the beginning of the race. He opens up an antiseptic wipe packet with his teeth, shakes it out, and applies it to the cut. I squirm a little. "Hurt?" he asks.

I shake my head. One of his hands is tending to the cut on my shin, but the other is on my bare knee, so warm and solid, and I can feel his calluses on my skin. I can feel his touch drawing up the goose bumps, making every nerve ending come alive. When he's done cleaning the wound, he dips his head and very softly blows on my skin.

Those goose bumps start to sizzle, and when he raises his head, he's smiling just a little hint of a devilish smile, like he knows he's gotten to me by the way the electricity is practically zinging off my body. Like he knows that every sexual organ in my body is aching for him.

It's the adrenaline, I tell myself.

But that's a lie. Because I've felt this before, and it didn't take an obstacle course to do it.

The gash isn't so bad once it's cleaned. The bleeding has nearly stopped. He applies cream and an extra-large bandage. "You'll be all right, killer. You tired?"

I look down at myself. Somehow, for someone who didn't fall in the mud once, I'm covered in sweat and dirty and muddy and probably look gross. Not to mention that neither of us has showered since Boston, which was four days ago. There's only so much that quick cleanups in airport bathrooms can do for a person. "Exhausted. What are the chances that we'll be able to sleep in a real bed tonight, with an actual bathroom we can shower in?"

He fixes me with a lazy smile. "Is that an invitation?"

I blush and start to move my leg off his knee, but he doesn't let me at first. He strokes his thumb lightly over my knee, up my thigh. I like it.

And when his gaze meets mine and he says, "Anywhere else need my attention, Dr. Cross?" I nearly die. Because I want to say all of me.

I want him in the shower, in my bed, everywhere. Wherever I can get him.

Every last inch of me needs every last inch of him.

Luke

I knew she could do it. She thinks all she's got to flaunt is that great big brain of hers, but I never met a girl who's so damn hard on herself. Truth is, she's tough as nails.

—Luke's Confessional, Day 11

We pull in front of a bed-and-breakfast in the little mountain town of Julian. When we get there, we see Will Wang waiting on the platform. We jump out of the cab and throw our shit on the platform at his feet.

"Congratulations, team," Will says. "You are in first place."

Fuck yes. We've held our lead.

I turn to Penny and engulf her in a hug. We're covered in sweat and dirt, and yet she smells damn good. I pull her scent into my lungs, and suddenly I want to keep her against me for the rest of the night, just like this.

No, I want more than this.

I want her. Me. In a room. All night long. I want to drag her body to me and undress her and explore her every inch with my mouth.

And I don't think even that will be enough to knock her out of my system.

Fuck yes, we're in first place. We get to continue this adventure. But right now, I just want to take her up to bed.

Will grins widely and says some stupid shit about how Julian is known for their apple pies and how tonight we'll be treated to a relaxing dinner with a dessert of pie à la mode as well as a night at one of the town's best bed-and-breakfasts.

But the thing I zero in on? Bed.

As in, Nell and me. In bed. Together.

And I sure as fuck plan on not sleeping over the covers this time. From the way she's holding my hand as we go inside, I don't think she'll mind.

"I'm so glad," she says as we take a creaky elevator to the top floor of this little Victorian house. "I feel so gross. It'll be so nice to take a shower and have dinner and relax right now. I'm . . . starting to feel a little sore."

"Oh yeah? Where?"

"My shoulders, from the monkey bars, and . . ."

I run my hand up her spine to her fragile shoulders and knead the muscles of her neck. Her head drops back.

"That's nice."

Our room is small, but it has its own bathroom. The second I close the door, we drop our bags, and I draw her to me. I crush my mouth to hers and press her up against the door. She lets out a moan as I run my hands under her shirt, cupping her tits. She feels warm and sweet, and my mind is whirling. I spit out half-formed thoughts as I kiss her. "I want this. Want you."

"Take me."

Sweet invitation. I intend to. As soon as I can.

And then it hits me.

I half assed it when I packed for this trip and forgot a bunch of things that could have come in handy. But the thing I'm regretting most?

Protection.

I kiss her hairline and force myself to tear away from her. "Fuck. I've got to get something. For us. Okay?"

She gives me a confused look, which morphs to disappointment. She drops her eyes over her dirty fatigues and cringes. "That's okay. I guess I'll go take a shower, then. I really need one."

I cup her chin in my hand and settle a soft kiss on her lips. "I won't be long."

The cameras are swarming over every last inch of this tiny bed-and-breakfast, making it more like a zoo. There's no gift shop, so I go outside the back entrance, trying not to call attention to myself so that I get a camera following me. Once I'm sure I haven't been followed, I search up and down the hilly streets for a drugstore, all the while thinking of Penny, naked and showering in our room. It may be that the world is plotting against us, because all the stores I go past are either closed or they don't carry condoms. Twenty minutes later, I end up finding a gas station that sells only one kind, extra-large Crowns, suspicious because the package has a layer of dust on the top and I can't find an expiration date, but fuck it. It's better than nothing.

Penny's just coming out of the shower as I get in. She's wrapped in a towel, her wet hair back, her glasses gone, giving me a really good look at just how beautiful her face really is. She looks at the box of condoms as I pull them out of the paper bag and blushes. That sweet blush makes me crazy with the need to touch her, taste her, take her.

I pull her to me and tug at the towel. The smell of sweet shampoo and her damp skin is driving me wild. My cock strains for her. The air crackles with static and tension and heat.

"Success," I tell her, opening the box and pulling one out. It's a value pack, not that I think I'm getting that lucky tonight, or that I need the extra-large size. "Ain't no fair, though, you being so clean. Guess I should take a shower first."

I strip off my clothes and jump into the bathroom. I take the quickest shower known to man, all the while thinking of Penny, waiting for me in that little towel. By the time I get out, my cock is rock hard, tenting the towel I wrap around my waist.

I step out of the shower to find her sitting on the edge of the bed in her towel, in the same place I left her, gnawing on her lip.

"Um . . . Luke?" Something's bothering her. She looks so shy and like a little girl, but that body is all woman, the way her breasts heave under the towel, those generous curves I just want to feel every inch of.

She's so *clean*. So rosy-cheeked and sweet-smelling and fresh, and it's driving me insane.

I sit down on the corner of the bed and draw her onto my lap. The water droplets are still dancing on her lovely, feminine collarbone. She drops her head onto my shoulder. Holding my hand, she lets out an uneasy breath and kisses my fingertips. "You make me crazy. Like, really crazy. Crazy in a way no one has ever made me. I can't even think when you look at me like that."

I chuckle. Then I scoop her into my arms and lay her down on the center of the bed. I have her now, right where I want her, right where I've thought about having her since the minute I saw her in the line in Atlanta. She looks up at me, biting unsurely on those pretty pink lips as I reach for the towel. I want to touch her. Touch her first, then taste her, eat her, swallow her whole.

I start to pull on the towel, but she flinches suddenly. "Luke . . . I'm afraid."

My fingers stop tugging, but my cock pulses with the need to fuck her. "Of . . ."

"Not of you. Of the way you make me feel. Of losing control." She lets her head fall back and stares at the ceiling. "I've never . . . you know. With a man. Before."

She's blushing deeper now. It's the cutest damn thing. And she isn't telling me anything I didn't already suspect. "You can say it, sweetheart. You've never come."

She inhales sharply at the word. "I mean, I don't think I have."

"You don't think? Baby, you'd know if you did. Let me guess. That prick ex of yours made you think it was your fault?"

She shrugs. "Well. What if my body just isn't able to?"

I crawl up onto the bed next to her and prop myself up on my elbow as I study her lovely, near-naked form. "No such thing. You and that asshole were just wrong for each other."

She gives me a doubtful look. "But that's the thing. I thought he was so right for me. I thought I was in love with him. And I was so wrong. Because you . . . I never thought that *you* . . . What I'm saying is that all my life I've been the one who knows everything, but when it comes to this . . . I know *nothing*. I really feel stupid."

She's babbling right now, and it's the cutest thing. I dip my face to hers, licking a drop of water from her earlobe. "You want to wait. Is that what you're saying?"

She shakes her head. "I can't. I need you. I want you right now. But I just want you to go easy on me. Please. And don't be upset if I'm a horrible lover. I waited before, and it was because I wanted to make sure I was in love. And look where it got me."

I push the wet hair out of her face. "Ain't gonna happen, sweetheart. If you want to wait, you should."

She let out a nervous laugh. "But I already—"

"Fuck that. You're allowed to make a mistake. But you don't need to settle. There are about ten million guys in this country that would happily and easily take you to bed, and I bet every single one of them could make you come. You don't need the prick. What you don't seem to get through your head is you're worth waiting for. Just stop hiding behind those glasses and shine that little light, and you'll see that men all over will be panting for you."

"But . . . I don't care about them. I want . . ."

I lower my head to kiss each cheek. "How about this. Just relax. You don't gotta do nothin', killer. You did that whole course, so you deserve a little rest. Let me take care of everything. Okay?"

She nods slowly. She looks like she's about to protest, so I put a finger up to her lips.

I replace it with my mouth, nibbling at the pretty pink rosebud of her lips. She sighs against me, relaxing, her hands wrapping around my neck. "That's right. Hold on to me, baby."

She meets my tongue, tentatively pushing hers inside as I drag my hand down the terry cloth–covered curve of her hip to her bare thigh. I reach for the sensitive skin between her legs, and she gasps.

"Ain't nothing you got to do but spread your legs for me," I tell her as I kiss her, my mouth traveling over her chin, down her jaw, to her earlobe. I take it into my mouth and suck as I part her legs, slowly moving upward. Her skin is so damn soft and untouched, and I'm going fucking mad at the thought of being there. But this is for her. I stroke my way through downy-soft hair between her legs, finding her slit.

She shudders, her eyes widening.

"Shh. Anything you don't want, you tell me to stop." I delve a finger between the warm, wet folds. Yes, she's so wet for me already. I won't believe she can't come. When I find her clit, she lifts off the bed, bucking her hips a little.

"Oh." Her breathing is coming harder now, and she looks like a goddess before me. All I want to do is watch her. As much as I've wanted her, fucking her isn't my goal anymore. Now I think I'll be sated by getting her the release she needs, seeing her lose control at my hands.

I start to move my finger in light circles over her clit, and now she's closing her eyes and biting her lip and getting into the feeling. I lean over and lick at her throat, making my way down to the tops of her breasts as they heave along with the motion of my hand. "That good, sweetheart?"

"Yes. Very." I feel her every muscle tensing, something coiling inside her that's readying to explode.

I slowly tug the towel off her perky breasts and suck one hardened nipple into my mouth as she groans. Then I gently push a finger inside her, applying pressure to her clit with the pad of my thumb. Seconds later, she throws herself forward, fisting the towel, breathing out all the air in her lungs. Her pussy contracts again and again on my finger, hard as hell. And holy god, she's fucking gorgeous as she comes, her face all rosy and her eyes all smoky and sexy.

I lean toward her ear and murmur, "See? You're perfect."

She falls back onto the bed, looser and more relaxed than I've ever seen her. "Oh my *god*. You did that so fast. And I can't feel my toes." It's fucking delicious, how sexy she is, lying naked and flat across the bed, wiggling her feet. She suddenly sits up on her elbows and looks at me. "Done that a lot, have you?"

I shrug. "I told you. There ain't nothing wrong with you."

"I can't believe it. All this time I thought I couldn't, and . . ." She's babbling again. Somewhere in there, her sense of shame comes back, because she tightens the towel around her body and gives me a sheepish look. "What do we do next?"

I laugh, because if I don't, I'll go batshit. There are so many things I want to do next to her, and every single one of them will only make me feel like I'm taking from her more than I can give in return. I may have made her come, but I'm not a doctor. I'm not husband material. Hell, I can't even carry on a halfway intelligent conversation with her. I'm sure as hell not the type of person a woman like her should go falling in love with.

I sit up. "First, we'd better get dressed," I tell her. "Then we'd better go down and get dinner. We don't want anyone wondering what we might be up to."

She gives me the cutest pout. "But then . . . can we come back up here?"

Yeah. And the glint in her eyes almost makes me take her, right there. But god help me. She should save herself for the man she's in love with. The man she deserves to be with. The man she's going to spend the rest of her life with.

And that fucking can't be me.

SWEET AS PIE

Nell

I was so tired after that confidence course that I could barely move a muscle. After dinner, we just crashed.

—*Nell's Confessional, Day 11*

We go downstairs to the dining room, where we find out the other remaining teams are Ivy and Cody, Brad and Natalie, and Ace and Marta. Charity and Tony were eliminated back in Alaska, and the outpost in Julian was a non-elimination round. The other remaining couples, sans Ace and Marta, are there, eating, and they greet Luke like he's their best friend.

"Hey!" he says to Brad and Natalie as we're led to our table. I hear him tell Natalie that she's a total badass, because she shaved her blonde hair off in the last challenge. They wave at me. I let the hostess guide me to the seat as he crouches down in front of them, telling one of his more animated stories.

I watch him from my seat. The new haircut bares the back of his neck, and it's incredible to realize that every little part of him—even those parts he keeps hidden—is perfection. My fingers itch to touch him again. And god, I want him to touch me. I want it with a fever.

A couple of minutes later, he turns around, strides over, and sits across from me. "Ace and Marta are in second again. Fuckers," he says with a smile. "That's okay. We'll take them."

Luke is pumped that we're down to the final four. He seems to think that the prize schedule in the folder said that we should each be getting $100,000. He's back in game mode, trying to talk strategy with me as we feast on baked chicken and mashed potatoes.

But all I'm thinking?

I came.

Holy god, did I come. I came, and all those clichés they say about orgasms happened to me. The world shook, mountains moved, planets collided.

And I can't wait until I do it again.

I was nervous, once the adrenaline from the confidence course wore off. I mean, he's Luke Cross. I can't even look at him and his beautiful body without blushing all over. But he was so good. So sweet. So patient. He gave without expecting anything in return.

Our table could be considered romantic, since it's in a corner away from the others. We're sipping on wine and toasting the fact that we've kept Ace and Marta out of first place for the second leg in a row. I'm not drunk, just pleasantly buzzed. I can't stop grinning goofily at Luke. Our legs are tangled under the table, and we're sharing the apple pie for dessert. I haven't even thought about the cameras, though I know they must be catching all of this.

I don't care.

Let Gerald and my father see. If they do, they'll only see good—me, blissfully happy for the first time ever.

So what if it's a cheesy reality show?

So what if the ring and the marriage aren't even real?

So what if Luke looks like a thug and we're complete opposites on paper?

He's the first person who gets me. The first person who took the time to take care of me. And the first person in this world I think I might actually trust.

So as I sit there listening to him tell a story about his days growing up on a farm outside Atlanta, I decide that I'm going to stop being so uptight. I'll let the chips fall where they may. Let this crazy journey take me wherever it wants. And leave the driving to someone else for once in my life.

I lean in closer to him, just wanting to absorb him into my skin. His skin is a warm caramel in the firelight; his eyes sparkle. Even with the buzz haircut, he looks ridiculously sexy. I want to rub myself all over him tonight. As I take another sip of my wine, I decide that yes, I will.

Like Luke said. Fuck them all.

"Why did your parents throw you out?" I ask him, swirling my wine and feeling oh so relaxed and content. "You never told me."

He shrugs. "I was a junkie. They had every right to. I started with pot when I was twelve, then I was taking my father's painkillers, then it just spiraled out of control and I was shooting heroin every chance I got, just to get myself through the day. I was stealing from them all the time to pay for my habit and making their lives a living hell. I tried to come to them and get clean, but they were done with me. So I lived on the streets for a couple of years."

"A couple of *years*?"

"Yeah. Every day I woke up, I thought it'd probably be my last. I thought I was gonna die, and I was okay with it. Then my grandpop took me in. My grandfather never got along with my parents."

I gasp. "You were so young."

"Yeah, but . . ." He reaches over and shows me the track marks on the insides of his arms. "I was hardcore. The scars don't go away. It's been ten years, and I still got them."

He has such magnificent parts, even scarred. I run my finger up his strong bicep, down to the crook of his arm, taking in the corded muscles. He's so beautiful, and the scars only make him more so. "Are you ever scared you might go back? I mean, you work at a bar. Don't you ever worry about relapse?"

"Every damn day. I did drugs because I was bored, but also because I didn't know who I was. I didn't know how to cope with shit either. When I was working at the bar, handling things for my granddad, I learned who I was and also the person I wanted to be."

"You want to be like him. He's your inspiration."

"Yeah. Try to, at least. But we all have limits of how much bad shit we can take being piled upon us before we break. I know it better than anyone, because I've been there. I try not to think about it, but I know I'm always only a couple of hits away from falling back down again. It scares the shit out of me."

His arm trembles. I blink when I realize I'm still holding his arm in both of my hands, mesmerized by him, by his sincere words. I let go. "And your granddad?"

"Died a few years ago, not before teaching me everything he knows about tending bar," he says, tucking his arm against his side. "Though, like I said, the place is a shithole now. My fault."

"I truly doubt that," I say to him. I can't believe that anything this man touches could possibly turn bad. "So your parents still don't talk to you. Do you have *any* family at all?"

"Gran. She's a tough old lady. I told her I was going on this television show and I wouldn't be around for a little bit, and she thinks I've gone to Hollywood to become a famous movie star. She was telling everyone that before I left." He grins, his eyes dancing. I can tell how much he loves her, just from the expression on his face, and it makes my heart do a little flip for him. "Anyway, paying for her in the home was really cutting into my ability to pay the mortgages on the bar, and the banks are closing in, which is why I'm here to begin with. I'm kind of at the end of my rope. Part of me thinks I should just call it a day and turn the place over to the bank, but then . . ."

His eyes darken, and I know what he's thinking. The bar is all he has. If he doesn't have that, then he's not much better than that aimless kid he was at sixteen. "You shouldn't do that. It's your grandfather's place. It's probably not as much of a shithole as you think. I bet you just have really high standards for the place, because it was your hero's."

One corner of his mouth twists up. "Could be. All I know is, never saw myself running a whole business on my own. What the fuck do I know about that? Nothing."

I drain my glass of wine. "You know more than you give yourself credit for."

"Nah. You give me too much credit. I'm not smart. I don't know a hell of a lot about anything. I didn't even know what this competition was. I don't watch reality television—didn't even know what the hell this show was."

"I don't either. I'm so in debt with my college loans, mostly because I'm too afraid to enter the real world. I just kept burying my head in the sand, not wanting to face it. So when I found out about the show from my friend, I decided it might be my chance to get out of the hole I'm in. It was like fate, you know?"

"Yeah. I never would've even known about it if it weren't for Jimmy."

"Jimmy?"

"James Rowan? YouTube sensation? He's my closest bud. Kind of like my brother. You saw him at the auditions. Remember?"

"Yes. But I am not that familiar with YouTube," I confess. "I didn't even know there was such a thing as a YouTube star."

A slow smile spreads over his face. "Goddamn, girl, you're like a blank slate. There is so much I could teach you."

I'm thinking a thousand and one thoughts, many of them surprisingly dirty. Whatever a YouTube star is doesn't even make the list. "I'm willing."

"There's way more you could teach me. All those sexy words in French you can say."

My mind's never in the gutter. I'm usually the last one to get a dirty joke, and even then, it has to be explained to me. But it's the way Luke's looking at me, with that devilish glint in his eye, that has the strangest effect on me. I'm a total gutter rat where he's concerned. "Oh. Like, *Voulez-vous coucher avec moi, ce soir?*"

He doesn't get it. "Yeah. Like, whatever that means. What does that mean?"

I raise my eyebrows.

He narrows his eyes. "Are you shittin' me? So you won't talk dirty in your native language, but you have no trouble talking dirty in French?"

I shrug innocently. "It's easier when you have no idea what I'm saying."

"So. You gonna tell me what you just said, or am I gonna have to guess?"

I wink at him. "We should probably go up to our room. Maybe I'll tell you there."

I don't have to suggest it twice. He doesn't hold my hand, doesn't put a hand at the small of my back to guide me, because cameras are capturing our every move on the way to the elevator. He's protecting me. Us.

As the elevator rises, I tamp down any nervousness inside me. I've made the decision. I'm doing this. I've spent twenty-five years of my life afraid. So tonight, I'm telling everyone and everything in my life to go to hell, and I'm giving myself to the only man who has ever made me feel anything.

We go inside our room, and I expect him to pin me against the door like he did before. But he slowly walks to the end of the bed, ripping the T-shirt over his head. "What side do you want?"

I gaze at his beautifully muscled frame, so warm in the low light, at his new haircut that I've already begun to get used to. I'm so ready for him I think I might burst. I need him to bridge the distance and take me. But when I don't answer and he doesn't look at me, I know something's wrong.

"Did I do something wrong?" I ask, my voice fragile because I swear, if I did, I might kill myself.

He sits on the edge of the bed and starts to unbuckle his pants. "No, sweetheart. But we'd better get to bed. Tomorrow's going to be tough if we want to keep our lead."

"No," I tell him, gathering my courage. "I'm not tired."

So I take a step forward. Then another. And when I am right in front of him, his knees touching my quaking thighs, I lift off my shirt, freeing my hair from it and tossing it to the side.

He gazes at me in my bra top, his eyes hot with desire. I see it. I feel it. But something is holding him back. I want him to touch me with his hands, but he curls them into fists at his sides. His voice is tortured, desperate. "Don't do that."

My every nerve ending is tingling as I unsnap my jeans and wiggle my hips out of them. It's hard to speak without my voice trembling, but I want him to see that I have control and I know exactly what I'm doing. "Do what? I'm getting ready for bed."

Suddenly, his hands fly out from his sides and he grabs my wrists, holding them immobile. "Don't fuck with me, Penny. I can't fucking do this now. You said you want to save yourself for the man you marry."

I'm breathless, my body quaking for him. "Right. I'm married to you."

He shakes his head, his eyes full of a pained desperation that makes me want him all the more.

"But not for real," he says with a ragged breath, and my heart drops. "You're saving yourself for the man you love. Mr. Perfect. And you should."

I knew it. Knew I'd say something to ruin things. I said too much. If I hadn't told him about my past, he'd be all over me now, making love to me. A thousand emotions roil in my chest, and I can't seem to get one out. "What if I never find him?"

He exhales, his nostrils flaring. "You will. Even if you don't, that's no reason to settle."

"You think I'd be settling with you?"

He squares his shoulders and grits out, "I am one hundred and ten percent sure you will be settling if you let me fuck you."

"Why? How can you think that?"

He sits back, his chest heaving. "It doesn't matter."

"Yes, it does. It matters to me, Luke. Haven't you ever wanted something so bad it made you change your mind about everything you once thought was true?"

He shakes his head slowly, his eyes on the ground. "If I fuck you, it won't give you what you're looking for."

He means that fairy-tale love that I believed in back when I was dating Gerald and naively thought he was it, that it would be me and him for the rest of my life. "Maybe I'm not looking for that anymore."

"You should be. You deserve that. You deserve someone who appreciates every last little fucking amazing thing about you, Penny," he says. "If we do this, it'll just be a fuck. That's all. That's all I'm capable of. All that's possible here. That's not what you want."

"Don't tell me what I want!" I shout at him. "Give me what I *need*."

It raises something in his eyes I've never seen before. Something hot and almost feral. His hands are still clasped on my wrists. He pushes off the bed, coming to his full height and towering over me. My breasts rise and fall with every breath as he holds my gaze. I'm nervous I might have done something to really hurt him, to make him reject me once and for all, and it eats me raw as I wait for him to make the next move.

In a sudden motion, he drags me aside and throws me down on the bed.

He leans over me and, placing both big hands at my hips, drags my jeans and panties down together in one swift movement, baring me completely. I try to sit up, but before I can, he scoops his hands under my ass and drags me to the edge of the bed, resting each ankle upon his bare shoulders.

And he dives in. Without warning. He plants his mouth so full on my core that I cry out.

"This what you want?" he says, his angry words muffled by my body, his breath hot and hard. No one has ever done this to me before. I'm half-surprised, half-embarrassed . . . but all turned on when his tongue circles my clit, in just the way his fingers did hours before.

But this is that times a thousand. He licks me from bottom to top, not a place unexplored. Embarrassment gives way to a clutching need. The wet heat of his tongue has me twitching with pleasure. I venture a look at him, and he's gazing at me with a dark, hooded, angry look that only serves to make me hotter. He's delivering just what I asked for, and damned if he'll stop until I'm done.

"Oh god!" I cry out, my moan nearly shaking the walls as he flicks his tongue over my most sensitive spot, then dips it down to probe deep inside me. He lifts his head and then adds the pressure of one finger inside my canal, pumping me, sending all coherent thought out the window.

All I can think is *More. More. More.*

And he gives it to me. His tongue licks in faster circles, and his finger pulses inside me, and the friction is growing to a head. The coiling inside me is suddenly unfurling, and his licking is only become wilder and faster. I wish he had hair for me to pull on. I buck against his mouth, and suddenly I'm screaming and coming, and he plunges his tongue deep inside me as I come. Holy god, do I come. I turn liquid around him, and every little part of me that had been starting to ache feels suddenly cured.

"Is that what you wanted, sweetheart?" he says to me, his voice gruff, his eyes glinting. I look at him, his mouth covered in my juices, this sexy, masculine pride on his face.

It actually wasn't. At least, not when I started.

But I doubt that anything could feel much better.

So I nod, dazed and wild eyed and ready to let him take the lead. Ready to let him do whatever else he wants to me.

Luke

> *Yeah. We overslept and missed the start of the leg out of Julian.*
> *What can I say? We were bushed.*

—Luke's Confessional, Day 12

In the morning, I wake, sunlight streaming through the stained-glass windows over our bed.

We made out like teenagers all fucking night. I made her come, then we kissed silly, kissed our lips raw, kissed and touched and massaged each other until we somehow fell asleep. I don't know what the fuck is wrong with me and why I'm so protective of this girl, but she's not like any other woman I've ever had, in a million ways other than the most obvious. I want her by my side, in my veins, everywhere.

Penny looks fucking fantastic, her head resting on my biceps, her hair tickling my chin, her lips like a ripe strawberry where I marked her with my own. I've been staring at her for the past hour as she sleeps, not wanting to wake her, completely into every little expression that crosses her face as she floats from dream to dream. She looks completely at rest. Completely satisfied. Completely happy.

And she feels like she's completely mine.

Even if she isn't. Can't ever be.

But holy god, I want to be inside her, with a passion that shreds me from the inside. I feel like I know her body intimately, every little beauty mark and curve, and all that's left is that last hurdle. I can't do anything with it. If I claim her, if I take her where she wants me to take her, it's like putting punctuation on this sentence, and I'm not sure if that's a period or a question mark.

I thumb the plastic ring on my finger. Only in a screwy game like this would a girl this classy, sweet, and gorgeous be wed to a bum like me.

That's probably why I can't bring myself to wake her.

I don't want this dream to end.

In a few days, it will. We'll have to make our decision and go back to our lives, in the same city but on opposite ends of the world from each other. And this dream will float out of my life forever.

Her eyes flutter a little and slowly open, drifting up to me. "Oh. Hi. What time is it?"

"No idea." My first words of the day are a rumble. "Sleep well?"

"Amazing." She's smiling. She stretches her arms up above her head, and the smile fades. "Oh god. Ouch. I'm so sore."

"That ain't nothing a good massage can't fix, sweetness. Roll your cute little ass over and let me have at it."

I'm salivating to touch her by now, to feel those soft lines and muscles in her shoulders and back. She starts to roll her naked body against me, then reaches her hand out for the portable clock on the night table. She lifts it up, and I feel her muscles tense under my fingers. "Isn't our check-in time at eight?"

"Yeah." I skirt my hand down the curve of her back, massaging the orbs of her ass, my dick getting harder yet. I've been sporting a permanent erection around her for days, and just when I think I'm used to it, my balls get tighter and my cock swells more against my boxers. The pressure is bad now, and when I get my hands on her again, it's just going to get worse.

But I'm game. She lets me touch her everywhere now. She'd let me do anything I damn well want, in the name of pleasing her. It's me that's in the way, treading a fine line between sanity and madness.

I don't get the chance. She jumps into the air, pretty damn limber for a girl who wrecked that confidence course yesterday. "Oh hell! Oh fuck! It's eight thirty! We missed check-in!"

I don't know how we do it, but we manage to get dressed, throw our stuff together, and race downstairs to the check-in platform in five minutes. Will Wang is nowhere to be found. He couldn't be bothered to wait around for our sorry asses. The only people standing there are a backup staff member and a single cameraman. He scolds us as he hands us the next envelope, then says into the camera, "Our first-place team is now in last place, thanks to oversleeping! Whoops! And so late in the game! Let's hope this doesn't mean doom for Dr. and Mr. Cross!"

Fuck you, she's Dr. Carpenter, I think as we grab a cab and slide into the back seat. Fucking great. I'd wanted more time with Penny, and now I'll probably never get a chance to finish that massage. Put a fork in us. We're probably done.

Or are we? All we've ever done is talk about getting back to Atlanta and annulling the marriage. But wouldn't it be so crazy, wouldn't it totally blow everyone's mind if we . . .

I can't think about that right now. "Slab City," she barks at the driver in a voice I never knew she had. "We've got to get there. As fast as you can. Please. Step on it."

Our driver doesn't mess around. He guns it ninety down Interstate 8, getting us up to the place in what has to be record time. As he does, Penny sighs. "I can't believe we did that! I can't believe we were so stupid. We gave up our lead! For what?"

For what? It's still hanging in the air as I wait for her to realize what she said. She doesn't.

Does she really not think it was worth it?

Maybe it wasn't. It's a hell of a lot of money in the balance. The chance to pay off her student loans and get out of that hole. Maybe that's more important.

She looks at the clue in her lap and reads, "This place used to be a naval base. But now it is an art community where many people live. We need to find the toilet bowl sculpture. Our next clue is in there."

"That shouldn't be hard."

The driver laughs a little but doesn't say anything, and when we pull up, I see what's so funny. The place is overrun with junk, as far as the eye can see. The hunks of gleaming metal in the California desert may pass for sculptures to some people, but all I see is a bunch of shit it's going to take forever to get through.

And it's balls hot. Like a hundred, at least, the sun beating down on us full force, no trees or any source of shade anywhere. There are no other cabs in sight, though, which tells me the other teams have already found their clues and driven off.

Shit. I don't want to tell Penny, because I don't want to make her think last night was a mistake any more than she already does.

But it's true. We fucked up. And it might be a million dollar mistake.

"Let's go!" she says, rushing off into the scrub brush. We end up climbing over mountains of discarded landfill shit that people have set out on the desert floor. It's fucking insane. The sweat's pouring off me, and all I can think is that an hour ago I was in heaven, and this sure as hell feels like the other place.

Then I hear her calling to me. "I found it! Luke, I found it!"

I run down the hill toward her. She's standing at the edge of a large, crumbling concrete slab, reading the clue.

"Yuma," she says. "We've got to get to the airport in Yuma."

Another flight. To think I'd never set foot in an airport before a couple of weeks ago, and now I feel like a goddamn world traveler. I've lost count of how many hours we've spent on airplanes. I'm just glad that it's not ending yet. That we get to go on, somewhere else.

We get to the airport just as the flight is boarding. When we sit down at our seats and finally have a chance to rest, she looks for any other members of the race and, finding none, says, "We must be so behind. Do you think they'll send us off when we get to wherever we're going?"

"I don't know," I say. Because I don't.

I don't know anything anymore. Even the things I thought I knew. I feel like it's all up in the air.

ALOHA, HAWAII

Nell

Yes. We are back in last place. Made it through by sheer luck again. I'm looking forward to spending our downtime on the beach. I've never been to Hawaii before.

—Nell's Confessional, Day 13

After a brutally long connecting flight, we end up on the platform in Maui at eleven the next morning, covered in leis from the girls welcoming us at the gate. We throw our bags down, waiting for Will Wang to tell us we've been eliminated, because he's giving us the puppy-dog sad eyes again. "You are, sadly, in last place, but once again, you're in luck," he says to us, his face magically brightening. "This is a non-elimination round!"

I turn to Luke, tired and still sore, and we hug again. I feel all jet-lagged and weird, like I could sleep for a day.

Then Will gives us the best news ever: We'll have the entire day to hang at the hotel and relax before the game picks up tomorrow. There will be something called a farewell luau at night with the other three remaining couples, which makes me look at Luke, my eyes widening.

Farewell. We're almost done.

It's so funny. It's been nearly two weeks since I said goodbye to Courtney at the Georgia Tech rec center. And yet I feel like I've changed and grown and become this completely different person. Like when I get back to my apartment and try to fit into the life I left behind, I'll be a square peg in a round hole.

As much as I miss Courtney, when I think of home, a deep, depressing sense of dread settles in. I'm trying not to think of it so much, to just live in the moment.

"Remember to set your alarm clocks so you don't oversleep!" Will says to us with a wink.

Luke mutters something under his breath at him and then says to me, "What do you want to do? Beach?"

I nod happily. I can't wait. To just sit out on the beach under a palm tree with one of those fruity little umbrella drinks and my beautiful hunk by my side? Sounds perfect. I even brought a bathing suit just for this purpose.

The *Million Dollar Marriage* staff really outdid themselves this time. For this site, we're staying in a little cabana on the beach. It's a beautiful place with open windows to let the breezes blow in and a lanai that steps right out to the ocean. I quickly get changed and come out as Luke is going through his stuff. He looks up at me and shakes his head. "Sweetheart. That ain't you."

I look down at my racerback tank bathing suit. It's modest, and I thought it'd be good for challenges. "What do you mean?"

"I mean," he says, reaching into his bag and pulling out a tiny red bikini, the strings of which dangle down, "you should wear this." It looks practically microscopic.

I blink. "Hell no. Where did you get that?"

"Just now. In the store. I saw it and thought it had Penny Carpenter written all over it."

I gape at him. "That money is to get us from place to place, not to be buying—"

"Put it on."

I take it, biting my lip as I look at it. It rivals the underwear he bought me. Cameras are going to be on me. And I've never worn stuff like this in my life. I mean, I've actually tried them on, wondering if I could pull it off, but I never got out of the dressing room.

But . . . fine. Time to live in the moment.

I go back into the bathroom and return wearing the bikini. "Happy?"

He nods, reaching out and wrapping both big hands around my waist and pulling me to his hard chest. He cradles my face in his hand, the pad of his thumb running over my lips. "I don't think I can let you leave looking this way."

"Fine by me," I say, blushing. "There are cameras out there."

He lets me go and reaches for his own suit. "You and me, alone, in here? With you wearing that? Don't tempt me."

Tempt him? Really? He's the one who gave me the bathing suit. It appears that for the past day all I've been doing is tempting him. He groans when I come too near or when I look at him a certain way, and he is always muttering under his breath that I'm going to be the death of him. And yet he knows I would let him do whatever he likes. But he still insists on torturing himself, and nothing I say seems to change his mind.

He thinks he's the only one being tortured by this. Sure, I've come. He explored me so well the other night that he knows my body like it's his own, and his touch has a way of setting off fireworks instantly. But I want more. He knows exactly what I want.

And the bastard won't give it to me.

No, instead, he's intent on driving me insane.

We go out to our private lanai, and I sit under the shade of the palm trees, gazing at the aqua water, while he goes for a swim. I watch him in the water, the beautiful curves of his broad back, the way he moves, like a panther stalking its prey, the way the sun clearly adores every last inch of him. It's hot and sticky, and yet he gives me cold, chilly goose bumps.

He comes back while I'm curled up on the lounge chair, finishing up *Les Mis*. "Come in with me. It's warm."

I shake my head, thinking of the way Courtney called me a flailing insect in the water. "I don't really swim."

He sits down beside me. Droplets of water create a mosaic on his skin, and I desperately want to lick them off, to taste the salty sweetness of him. "What'll you do if we have a swimming challenge tomorrow?"

I give him a grin. "Let you handle it?"

I go back to my book, but he's there, silent. When I look up, he's staring at me, silently discerning, his gaze so intent it nearly takes my breath away.

"What?" I motion to the ocean. "Even if I went out there now, there's no way you'd be able to teach me to swim in an hour."

"Right. Like there's no way you can come, either, baby."

Well, isn't he cocky? I scowl at him. "We have to get ready for the luau."

"We don't got to get ready. The producers said we can wear our bathing suits."

I cringe.

"So, sweetheart, you're out of excuses." He studies my face, and I can see where recognition dawns. "Oh. So that's it. You don't want anyone to see you?"

I point down the beach at the two cameramen who are lurking there. "That's right."

He goes inside and comes back with one of his balled-up T-shirts, which he tosses to me. "Then put this on. Don't let stupid shit get in the way of you living life to the fullest."

I can't argue with that. I pull his massive shirt onto my body, inhaling the heavenly scent of him as I make my way down the white sand. He's right. The water is warm and relaxing and perfect. It'd be more perfect if the cameras weren't here. He even gives me a few stroking tips that make me feel less like a drowning insect. But he's careful not to touch me or do anything that might get on camera, which I guess is a good thing.

It's also driving me insane.

"You're right. The water was great," I tell him when we get to the luau.

It's right on the beach, not far from the cottages. Again we're given leis. The sun is setting and the sky is orange, and the salt feels tight but not unpleasant on my skin.

They're serving mai tais, so we each take one and sit down as lilting ukulele music plays. Women with flowing hair are wearing grass skirts and hula dancing.

"I could get used to this," he says, sipping his drink as we wave to the other competitors, who are all watching the show. He has a new tan and looks even more delicious in this light. The island lifestyle definitely agrees with him. To think, not so very long ago I thought he was a thug. Now he's so sexy it physically hurts me to look at him, knowing he'll probably deny me what I want.

We listen to the music a little, and meanwhile, the sun sets, leaving a sky full of pink streaks. We're served native foods like mahi-mahi and poi, and everything just seems right with the world. He may be the wrong guy, but . . . I don't know if that's even true anymore.

He might just be the right guy. No matter how much he denies me. Maybe I just need to convince him.

"I had fun today. I should stop worrying about what other people think," I tell him, "and just live in the moment more."

"You should," he says, dragging me out into the line of hula dancers, with Ivy and Natalie. The dancers give us grass skirts and tell us how every movement tells a story. And they show us how to move our hips in time with the music, in a sultry and sensual way. I'm terrible at it, but I'm in good company.

I think I've finally found something that Luke can't do.

But it doesn't matter. We're up here, not giving a crap what anyone thinks.

And it feels amazing.

It feels even more amazing when he turns to me and hooks a finger toward me, drawing me to him like a puppet on a string. The cameras are on us, capturing the act of him taking the lei off his chest and putting it over my head. But they can't possibly capture the way his eyes glint at me, like I'm the only girl in the world. They can't see the need in his expression as he tugs on the edge of the T-shirt.

I know what he's asking, even though those eyes make it impossible to think sane thoughts. It's getting dark, and the mai tais are dulling my nerves, and the T-shirt is still kind of wet, which is making me chilly.

So I reach down, peel it off, and hand it to him. "Good?"

"Yeah. Good." His voice is a low rumble as his eyes drift over my body appreciatively. His arms wrap around me, his skin melts against mine, and his fingers dig into the bare skin at the small of my back. "Very, very good."

Luke

Well, yeah. It felt like we were almost at the end. The game was stressful. It was good to just let go for a night. We all needed it.

—Luke's Confessional, Day 14

It's after midnight by the time the torches of the luau fade and it's time to go back to our cabana.

The rest of the competitors have been getting along well. But none of them, not even Ace and Marta, have what Penny and I have. I didn't want to leave her side for a second. I stayed next to her, holding her near me, cameras be damned, wanting to brand her with my touch, mark her with my scent, make every last damn person on the beach know she was mine.

We're still in the game, and that means she's still mine.

And there were plenty of other fuckers sneaking looks. Doubt that Penny—sweet, naive Penny—had any idea how she made their tongues wag in that little bikini. She had them all on a string, like a little fucking temptress, and the craziest part about it was she probably didn't see a thing because her eyes were on *me*.

I drank like a fish, trying to get a little buzz going so I wouldn't be so hyperaware of every last thing she did. Even the smallest, most insignificant moves fixed me with the need to taste her, even right there in the open. I kept leaning toward her, scenting her, drinking her in.

By the time we walk back on the beach, alone in the full moonlight, frustration and anger are surging hot through my veins. Anger directed at her. At myself for unleashing this monster in her, for being half the man she wants.

She's happy, which is only feeding my shitty mood. Holding my hand, moving her hips in the way the hula dancers showed us. Wearing that little grass skirt and that bikini and flowers in her hair and around her neck, and I just want to throw her on the sand and sink into her.

We get to the lanai, and I drop her hand and fall down onto the lounge chair, facing the moon.

She spins in front of me, still hula dancing. Moving her hips in mesmerizing circles and her hands in the way we'd just been taught means *come to me*. She holds my gaze, and I'm not going to give in to her. Give in to this temptress who has no fucking idea what she's getting herself into.

I'm about to lose it. I rub the new scruff on my jaw as I watch her, my fingers shaking from want. "You come here."

She does, still dancing her hips in those tantalizing circles, right before my eyes. When she's close enough, I wrap an arm around her, drawing her to the side of the lounge. She lets out a little gasp and stills.

It only takes one pull on the string of the skirt and it falls in a puddle at her feet. I lay one hand flat on her belly, feeling her tremble underneath. I lift my head to kiss her navel, then take ahold of the string at her hip with my teeth. "Take this off—now."

"What if there are . . . cameras?" she asks, her eyes darting about.

"There ain't."

"But how do you—"

"Because I paid off the cameraman to leave us alone for one night."

"Oh. Transportation money again?"

"Yep."

She's still frozen there, so I pull on the other string, letting that swath of fabric fall to the ground, and now her bottom is bare to me. I run my fingers lightly into her slit. So wet. So ready and primed for me, and . . . fuck. So not what I need right now. But the scent of her arousal hits me, and she lets out a little moan, wobbling on her feet.

Feeling her come, seeing her totally lose control . . . that's my new addiction.

"Sit on my face."

"What . . . ?"

"You heard me. I need to taste you, Penny. Sit your pretty little ass on my face and let me taste you." *Let me punish you for being so fucking tempting.*

Her eyes flash with worry, but I can tell she wants it as much as I do. Breathing hard, she climbs onto the lounge, straddling my face with her thighs. She sinks down onto me and gasps when my tongue hits home.

As I lick her, she's moaning, grabbing onto the sides of the lounge in desperation. She's tense and sounds almost like she's crying when she says, "You can't keep doing this to me, Luke. Give me your cock. I need your cock. *Please.*"

I dig my tongue into her as far as I can, biting and nibbling on her clit, feeling her juices flowing out of her. I pull her down hard onto my face, and she wriggles, sliding her bottom where she wants me to be.

She comes in a rush, falling forward on me, then slinks off to the side of the lounge and is quiet for such a long time that I have to sit up and look at her.

There are tears in her eyes.

"What's your problem? You fucking came. Isn't that what you wanted?"

Her eyes turn hard. She sits up and grabs her bikini bottoms. "No. I told you what I want! What are you trying to accomplish? Are you trying to be some kind of a martyr?"

"No. I'm trying to save us both from making a massive mistake."

"It's not!" She jumps off the lounge and stares at me, her chest heaving, her hands fisted on her hips. She's nearly naked, and in the moonlight she's a fucking goddess. The urge to take her in my arms and hold her against me is so strong that I'm physically shaking. "Yes, the rings are fake. But why don't you believe that this is real?"

Because I know more of how the world works than she does. And it doesn't work like this. Brilliant doctors with bright futures don't marry ex-junkies with nothing to offer them.

I don't answer. Can't, because I know she'll argue with me and try to convince me that this can work. I have to get up and leave her now before I do something we'll both regret.

I slip off the lounge and try to storm inside, but she stops me. It's embarrassing how easily she does. A touch on my arm, and I stop. Time stops. Nothing else exists. I'm hers.

I turn to her, and she's already zeroed in on my board shorts. She drags a finger down my abdomen and reaches under the seam, pulling at the tie. She lifts them open, guiding them carefully over my cock, letting it spring free, as hard as it's ever been for her.

She sinks to her knees.

Her fingers close around my cock, like she's been doing this all her life. I can only watch in complete fucking disbelief as she takes it in, her eyes hungry, hungry for me. My body jolts from her touch. I let out a growl of protest that dies in my throat, becoming a moan of ragged desire. I will my hands to push her off me, but they don't go anywhere.

She has me.

She's had me since the day I met her.

And now she's under me, gazing at me, wanting me like I'm her oasis in the desert.

I fucking can't deny her any more than I could deny myself her. This was inevitable.

And maybe I'm not the man she'll want forever. But god help me, if this is all I get, it's good enough. I'll settle for being the man she wants to be with right now.

I scan down to see her stroking and teasing my flesh with her palm, curiously, like the tempting little kitten she is. I think of the way she begged for my cock, and my knees nearly give out. I brace myself against the wall as she slips her hands down my hips to my thighs.

"You're so big. So . . . alive here," she murmurs to me, awestruck, my little dirty vixen who's got me on a string. "Luke . . . do you, um, want my . . . Oh god, you're so beautiful. I really want to . . ."

And then she trails off and starts to lick the shaft, her tongue flicking, experimental. Unsure. My head falls back, but not because I want it to. I want to see this, want to see every little thing this girl's tongue can do. But the feeling of her lapping at me, tasting me, teasing my cock is beyond even my hottest wet dreams. Mindlessly, I clutch at the back of her head, tangling my fingers in her hair, completely at the mercy of this woman.

"Am I . . . ," she suddenly says, her voice as sweet as music. "Is this okay?"

Jesus. Is it okay? If there has ever been a better feeling on earth, I don't know what it is. I think of that asshole ex of hers and how she's got the last laugh because this is fucking glorious and he doesn't know what he's missing. "Yeah, baby. You have a sweet mouth. Give me more."

Emboldened, she pulls my body closer and then takes the head into her mouth, tonguing my skin in soft, slow circles. She sucks me in deeper and my mind spirals out, and I'm not even sure what fucking planet I'm on. She starts to bob her head on my cock, finding a rhythm, making me fuck her pretty mouth, and now her hands are on my ass, gripping me into her mouth. And I'm twitching, getting close. Getting so close that she seems to know it.

She releases me, only to deliver soft, teasing kisses to my length. Fucking temptress. Fucking beautiful temptress, kneeling before me, worshipping my cock. When she gets to the base, she dips her head and slowly sucks one of my balls into her mouth.

My body seizes. I tense, letting out a groan that people on the other side of the island can probably hear. "Holy fuck," I groan. "You said you've never done this before?"

She stops lapping at my balls and nods as our gazes lock and hold, and then she takes my whole length into her mouth again. I'm beyond sane thought right now. I thought I'd be teaching her, but she's been schooling me from the very beginning. Her tongue flicks over the ridges of my length, and she holds there, her lips firm around the base of my cock as my breath catches.

"Penny," I warn her in desperation, because I'm close, and I know that after the sheer torture she's put me through, when I start coming, I ain't gonna stop. I nudge her away, but she doesn't let up. She takes me deeper, sucking me in as I let out a moan and start to spurt my hot come into the back of her throat. I can't help it. Can't stop it. Coming harder when she moans softly. She's so into this that she doesn't even flinch when I go. She fixes her mouth on me, swallowing eagerly, lapping up every last drop, and she doesn't let go until I'm done, sagging against her, gasping for breath.

I lift her up into my arms, my beautiful goddess, and I hold her on the lounge in my shaking arms, cradling her as much as she's cradling me. I can't find the words. Can't find a single thought.

All I know is she's fucking done it.

She's gone and made me fall in love.

BEYOND THE SEVEN SACRED POOLS

Nell

Yes, I'm nervous. Nervous about things ending. Nervous about the upcoming challenges. We're so close. But I'm just trying to live in the moment and appreciate every moment we have in the game. This really is a once-in-a-lifetime opportunity, and I doubt I'll ever experience anything like this again.

—Nell's Confessional, Day 14

We need to report to check-in at six in the morning. This time, we don't oversleep.

Before we leave the cabana, Luke kisses me breathless, cupping my face possessively and awakening desire straight down to my toes. "You ready?"

I nod. Even if I'm not, we're doing this. It's hot and sticky, even this early in the morning, so I'm wearing the bikini—just because Luke gave it to me—and the one pair of shorts I brought. He's just wearing his board shorts. For a moment, I wonder if it's possible to just stay here and seal out the outside world and hibernate together.

But we've got a race to win. We're determined now.

The sun is just rising as we report to the platform and see Will Wang and the other couples. "Welcome back, remaining couples! We're now going to bring you Marriage Test Number Four! In this challenge, we'll be finding out how well the two of you have become aligned over the past two weeks. We're going to have couples standing back-to-back, women on one side, men on the other, wearing earphones to drown out any sound. At the count of three, we'll begin showing you sets of two words. Your job, simply, is to shout out one or the other. These words are going to come lightning fast, so you'll need to be quick. The couple who has the most matches at the end of the round will receive a fifteen-minute boost on their starting time. Contestants, take your places."

I look over at Luke, and he winks at me, as if that fifteen minutes doesn't matter in the least. It does matter, though. We're dead last. If we want to win, we need all the help we can get.

I take my place on the wooden platform and affix the earphones to my ears. I venture a look over at Luke, who's doing the same thing behind me. Taking a breath, I stand with my back to him, almost but not quite touching.

Until I feel his hand graze my hip, touch my elbow, and slip down my wrist, finding my own hand. He entwines his fingers with mine and squeezes.

I melt.

"Ready?" Will Wang says, raising a hand. "Set! And go!"

They weren't kidding when they said the words were going to come fast. I barely have time to think before the screen flashes with a new one. ROMANCE/SEX, LIGHT/DARK, SWEET/SEXY, FAST/SLOW, ROUGH/SMOOTH. I shout out my answers in a jumble until my mouth goes numb. Then, suddenly, the screen goes blank, and Will Wang's voice is piped through our ears. "Contestants, please remove your headphones and see how you and your spouse did!"

I drop his hand only to pull off the headset. When I turn around, I see the giant scoreboard. Ace and Marta matched only twelve times. Natalie and Brad, sixteen. Ivy and Cody, twenty-seven.

Luke and I? We matched fifty-six times. Out of sixty.

My eyes widen as I take it in, but he's already hugging me. Hugging me and lifting me up off the ground, pressing me up to his bare chest in a way that makes me wish we could go back to that cabana. He buries his face in my neck and says, "That's my girl."

"How did we do that?" I ask, shell-shocked, as the other teams start lining up for the next leg of the race. "Are we psychic?"

He shrugs. Ace and Marta get to start out first, and then the other teams, but now we're not so desperately far behind as we were when we left Julian. We have a good chance. As Will says, right now it's anyone's game.

A few minutes after Brad and Natalie leave, it's our turn. We step onto the platform, holding hands, and get our clue from Will, who winks at us. "Are you two glued together?" he says, pointing at our joined hands.

At this point, we've both gotten good at ignoring his cute comments. I tear open the clue and read it.

"We have to get to the highest point on the island," I say.

He scans the lush green foliage around us. There are a lot of hills. "Fuck. Where's that?"

"Haleakala," I say, happy I took a minute to read the brochure in the cabana. "The dormant volcano."

He gives me an appreciative thumbs-up, and we pile our stuff into the rented Jeep Wrangler, then take off, following the signs for the volcano. We climb high into the clouds, passing pastures with grazing cows. When we finally get to the parking lot, we see a Jeep with Ivy and Cody just leaving. I hope that means we're catching up.

When we climb out, we rush into the welcome center. Someone at the welcome center tells us that we need to proceed down a route into the crater. We rush into the barren, moonlike landscape, and up ahead we see the outpost, which makes us run faster.

I'm feeling good. Almost athletic. Like we can do this. I keep up with Luke now, or maybe he's just falling in with my pace. But we make a good team.

We get to the outpost and see Brad and Natalie there. I get a thrill of excitement, thinking yes, we really are catching up, when I hear Brad let out a torrent of curses. He starts to kick and pummel at the wooden post in front of him.

As we near it, I see it. Four posts, one for each team. There is a little glass-faced cabinet with the clue visible inside, but it's locked with a padlock. I come up close to it and lift it. It's a combination padlock, looking for five numbers.

"What do you think this is?" I ask Luke.

"Hell if I know," he says. "Did we get a combination?"

"No!" Brad growls, punching his palm. "We've been here an hour, trying every fucking combination we can think of."

I look around, then at the clue. It hits me right away.

I put in one, zero, zero, two, three, then yank the lock.

It opens.

"Holy fuck," Luke breathes. "What did you just do?"

I grab the clue and rip it open as Brad and Natalie stare at us. "The height of the mountain," I tell them. "The highest point on Maui."

"Oh!" Natalie says and starts to press in the number. I grab Luke's hand, and we rush back to the parking lot.

I pull the clue out of the envelope and read. "We have to take the Road to Hana. When we get to the end of the road, beyond the Seven Sacred Pools, we'll get our next clue."

"The Seven Sacred Pools? Shit."

We jump into the open-topped Jeep and take off. *Road* sounds a lot tamer than what this actually is. It turns out that the road is a narrow, twisty one-lane dirt path, with traffic going in both directions . . . on the side of a high cliff over the ocean. If you take any one of the hairpin curves too fast, you might find yourself careening straight into a tour bus coming the opposite way. Swerving to miss it means hitting a cliff wall or plummeting a hundred feet into the rocks below. So the speed limit is only five miles per hour.

Luke drives forty, his hands gripping the wheel, his body tense, like he's got something to prove.

"Do you see that?" I say, pointing across the inlet. "I think that might be Ivy and Cody."

Luke presses on the accelerator, swerving narrowly to miss a stray cow on the road. "Hell yeah. We're coming in right behind them."

I grip the handle on the door, hoping we do and don't somehow end up falling to our deaths, because that would be a really great way to finish this season.

We end up driving past the very crowded and touristy Seven Sacred Pools, but the road continues on, and we manage to catch up to Ivy and Cody, ending up right on their tails. We climb out and see the marker telling us which trail to take. It's simply a bunch of arrows on the path that we need to follow.

Once again, our two teams are neck and neck on the trail, which is mostly uphill and rocky. Luke gives me a hand during the really steep parts, and we don't lag behind.

We all stop and look up in wonder at an ice-blue pool with three narrow, beautiful waterfalls cascading into it. Cody points to the arrow.

Which is pointing straight up the waterfall.

Fear tightens my chest.

"How do we do that?" I ask Luke. "There's got to be an easier way. I'm not Spider-Man."

He rakes his hands through his scrubby buzz cut and frowns. "Nah. I bet it's easier than it looks. Come on."

We wade into the pool of warm water. It grows deeper and deeper, almost hitting my chin before we get to the waterfall. There we notice a cord hanging down the waterfall. Cody grabs it first, hoisting himself up and almost straddling the narrow falls as he looks to find a foothold. Ivy goes next.

Luke places a protective hand on the small of my back under the water. "Go first. I won't let you fall."

I cast him a worried glance but nod, rubbing my hands together as I take hold of the cord. I try to remember where Ivy's setting her feet as I pull myself up.

The first few feet aren't a problem. It's only when we get up higher and the pool starts to shrink beneath me that my fear of heights kicks in. The footholds are wet, and my sneakers keep slipping. More than once I have to rely on the cord—and Luke—to keep me from falling. And he does just as he promised, always keeping one hand hovering nearby to catch me.

At one point, we climb to one side of the falls, then have to cross over sideways to the other side of the surging water. I stop and watch Ivy make the difficult jump, gaining her foothold. She reaches up for Cody's hand but suddenly slips. She reaches for the rope, but it falls through her fingers, and down she goes. Luke reaches out for her, but her hand slips from his grip.

We all stare open-mouthed as she falls at least thirty feet, shrieking, splashing into the water below.

"Holy shit!" Cody calls out. "Ivy?"

She surfaces a minute later, waving. "Shit, that hurt! I'm coming."

"She's okay," Luke says, letting out a sigh of relief as we continue the rest of the way up.

When we get there, the path abruptly ends at a cliff. We see a sign that says **WELCOME, TRAVELERS. TAKE THE LEAP OF FAITH!** with a giant arrow pointing off the cliff.

Oh hell no.

Luke goes to the edge of the cliff. "It's about sixty feet. You can't really see what's down there because of the tree cover. But it's got to be okay."

I stare at him, then try to go and peek over myself, but even craning my neck to look over makes me dizzy and sick to my stomach. "It's got to be?" That really isn't the guarantee I was looking for. "Are you sure?"

He nods. He gives me his hand. "Do you trust me?"

I nod. I do. I really, really do.

"Then let's go."

So we do. No hesitation. Holding hands, we charge off the cliffside, falling down, down, down, into the warm, fresh water of the pool. We surface in each other's arms, and I don't need breath because he kisses me, and it turns out, that's all the sustenance I need.

He takes my hand, and we wade as fast as we can out of the pool and to the next grouping of clues. "Come on, killer. We have a race to win."

Luke

We didn't know when it was going to end. We figured soon, but we had no idea it would be like that.

—*Luke's Confessional, Day 14*

I rip the envelope of the next clue with my teeth and pull out the slip of paper. It tells us we need to head back around the island again. My voice loses its timbre as I say, "And listen to this. Make your way to the Maui Ocean Center, where your adventure will come to an end."

"An end?" Her eyes widen.

I don't know what I was thinking. Not that this would go on forever. We'd fucking die. But I thought we'd have a little more time. Now it feels like everything's about to come crashing to a halt, and I want it to keep going.

I want us to keep going.

We climb into the Jeep. The other teams are still on our tail, and Ace and Marta are still ahead of us, so we can't lag like I want to. Talking to her. Making plans.

I want to know what the fuck she's thinking.

She doesn't say anything as we set off around the island again.

The silence is fucking slaughtering me.

We have to talk about this. We can't just end with the cameras on us. Here in our Jeep, we're alone. There's so much I want to say, and this could be my last chance to say it.

"Look," I say, at the same time that she says, "You know . . ."

We both laugh. I say, "I'm sorry. You go first."

"No. It was nothing," she says softly. Was it? The game is about to end, and she's saying *nothing*? "I was just saying it's crazy that we're almost at the end."

"Yeah." I tighten my hand on the steering wheel and upshift. I can't take it anymore. "What are we going to do? At the end?"

She blinks. "What do you mean?"

"I mean, if we win. What do you want to tell them?"

She shakes her head. "I think we need to concentrate on beating Ace and Marta first. We can cross that bridge when we come to it. Don't you think?"

"No. Even if we don't win. What do you want to do?"

She's wrinkling her nose. "You mean . . . what? Do you mean do I want to stay married to you?"

When she says it like that, it sounds as fucking batshit as it sounded the first day it was brought up back in Atlanta. It's just why I've been keeping her at arm's length this whole time and didn't take her when I desperately wanted to.

She's too fucking good for me. She deserves so much more.

"I'm just making sure we're on the same page." My voice is stiff. "That's all."

"Um . . . ," she says softly, staring straight ahead. "I don't know. What do you want to do?"

Holy fuck. Is she . . . seriously considering it?

I laugh. "What would people say? If we actually said we wanted to stay married?"

She shrugs. "What difference does it make? Fuck 'em. Right?"

"Right," I say. "We should just do it."

"Yes. We should."

Holy shit.

Did we just agree on what I think we agreed on?

A car's coming at me head-on, so I have to swerve. Penny grabs the door handle, and I get us back onto the road, then pull over at the first chance I get. "Come here," I murmur, sliding my hands around her back and pulling her over the console toward me. I slam my mouth onto hers and kiss her. I trace the outline of her lips, which are still red and swollen from the thousands of kisses I've given her in the past few days. "This is insane, you know that?"

She nods and sighs with total contentment, entwining my hand with hers and lifting them to gaze at the two fake rings, small and large, touching in our joined hands. "Luke . . ."

"Yeah?" I nuzzle her neck, lost in the smell of her and the feel of her and the overpowering need for her. I'm ready to go and be her husband and make her the happiest wife on the planet.

"I'd love to go on a honeymoon with you. So let's go win this race."

I laugh. "Yeah. Let's go."

I let go of her and pull out onto the road again, never releasing her hand, and we make it down to the aquarium. As we descend the hill, we see it. A small crowd of onlookers, as well as the cameramen and the flags for the *Million Dollar Marriage* show. They're waiting for us and start to cheer as we pull into the lot.

It's the end of the line.

As we near the platform, I see Ace and Marta standing in a large square. At first I think they've got us beaten.

But then I realize Marta's frantically directing Ace, who's moving colored cinder blocks into a line. They stop and throw up their hands. Will Wang runs over to them and says, "Sorry, but that is incorrect . . . again!"

They haven't won this thing yet. We coast to a stop at the edge of the lot. "Come on," I shout to Penny as we climb out and run through the crowd.

Will comes over to us and leads us to our own square. I see the colored cinder blocks, ready for us to line up.

"Your next chore is simple—and the final task of the race," he says. "Arrange these cinder blocks in order of the color of the flag at each of your previous check-ins."

Oh fuck.

There were flags at the check-ins?

I rake my hands through my hair and crouch down, thinking we're fucked. Who the fuck could remember all that?

But Penny, very quietly and methodically, is studying the colored blocks. She taps on the green one. "Luke. Can you help me?"

I stare at her. "Wait. You know?"

Then I remember who I'm talking to. This is Penelope Carpenter, who, among all the millions of other things she is, has a fucking huge brain in that head of hers, with an insanely good memory.

She. Knows. Everything.

I grab the green one and put it in the first slot. She's already picking up the purple one. I take it from her hands and stick it into the second slot. She goes right down the line, directing me which one to pick up, one after another, not even pausing to think or break a sweat.

When I have them all down, she nods.

"That's it."

There's no question at the end of that sentence. She's all confidence. She just knows.

That's *my* fucking badass *wife*.

FINISH LINE

Nell

> *I had so much fun. It was easily the best experience of my
> life. I'm sorry. I'm not allowed to say more until the final live
> episode.*

> —*Nell's Final Interview, Day 14*

Ivy and Cody are just arriving as I step away from the puzzle and Luke
and I raise our hands.

Will Wang approaches us with the microphone. "Let's see if the
brilliant doctor and her stud are up to the challenge."

He pauses for effect, but I don't need the pause to know I'm right.
Everything else I just survived at. *This* is what I'm good at.

I catch a glimpse of Ace, who's hefting a cinder block into his arms
and watching us carefully as Will checks our work. The crowd seems to
be holding its collective breath.

"Ladies and gentlemen, I give you the winners of the first season
of *Million Dollar Marriage* . . . Penelope Carpenter and Luke Cross!"

I can't help it. I start to cry.

There's cheering, but I don't pay attention to that. People wildly
flying banners with our names on it. Cameras zeroed in on us. Ace
throws a cinder block with impressive force at a parked car, and its
alarm goes off.

But in all this?

Luke comes gently up to me. He engulfs my face in both of his big warm hands, and he dips his head, leaning his forehead against mine. I focus on nothing but the feel of him, the desire that I have for him that permeates me to the very core. We don't talk. I'm not sure we do anything else but breathe each other in as chaos erupts around us.

"Penny," he finally whispers, and all that bravado is gone. It's like he can't believe it himself. "We did it."

I love that he calls me Penny. I love that his competitive side never took over and made him a total ass, like Ace. I love that he thinks of me before he thinks of the game. But more than anything, I love that we are going to be man and wife. More than anything, I love Luke Cross and the idea of spending the rest of my life with him.

I guess that doesn't make very good television, because a second later, Will pulls us apart and puts one arm around each of us.

"You look very cozy like that. And of course, the whole world is waiting to know your answer!" he says, and I'm already missing Luke's touch.

Besides, the answer is yes.

Yes. Yes. YES.

Let's get it over with. We want our happily ever after to start now.

I peer past Will, in his bright Hawaiian shirt, and find my husband. He winks at me. He looks just as impatient as I am to get this show on the road.

We both open our mouths, in complete agreement.

And then Will says, "But we're going to ask you to hold that thought as we wait for our live finale! Yes, our live finale, airing direct from Hollywood on December seventeenth! Don't miss it!"

I balk at the date. December 17? I've lost count of the days, but we're not even anywhere near Thanksgiving yet. Is he saying we need to . . . wait?

What?

Luke's looking just as confused as I am as the rest of the audience cheers and the cameras stop rolling. They all abruptly start packing up to leave.

"Hey, wait. What the fuck was that?" Luke fixes him with a hard stare. "What are we supposed to do in the meantime?"

Will completely ignores Luke. "Congratulations, you two," he says, giving me a perfunctory pat on the back. "Someone will be here shortly to explain things."

Random people come up to congratulate us. The crowd starts to disperse. Luke grabs my hand. "Don't worry. We'll get this settled."

Eloise Barker appears. "Hey, guys! Congrats."

"So, what?" he asks. "What's this about not giving our decision until December?"

She nods. "Right. Well, the season doesn't start airing in the States until this Sunday. Ten episodes in all . . . December seventeenth. It's in your contract, hottie. But I have to say, you performed well. You both did. *Million Dollar Marriage* is shaping up to be the biggest hit of the season!"

Luke grits his teeth. "Okay. But . . ."

Eloise gives him an annoyed look. "Sweetie. Did you even read the contract? If not, I'll lay it out for you."

She talks to him like he's an idiot. Like he's just a hunk of good-looking meat and doesn't have a brain, which makes me hate her all the more. I clench my fists, but I'm all but invisible to her.

"The gag rule is pretty solid. You two are contractually obligated to remain mum and not disclose anything about this season until after the finale. That means that you two may not be seen together or communicate in any way from now until December seventeenth. Understood?"

My heart catches in my throat. Luke speaks before I can find the words. "No fucking way."

"I'm sorry," Eloise teases, clinging to his formidable biceps, and that does it. I instantly hate her, like I've never hated anyone. "I didn't realize you were doing this because you didn't want the money?"

I swallow. I possessively grab his arm and take him away from her. "It's okay," I murmur, trying to smile for him. "It's only a little while. And nothing's going to change this, right?"

He nods distractedly, still scowling at Eloise. He manages a smile and reaches out to touch me, but suddenly Eloise grabs his arm again, giving me a condescending look. "It starts at the conclusion of on-location filming. Thus, *now*." She starts to drag him away. "Come on, stud. Don't make me put you in violation of the contract."

No. No, this is all wrong.

"Fuck, you mean I can't even say goodbye to her?" he says as she guides him toward a waiting limousine. "You're fucking kidding me, right?"

Apparently not.

They lead him into the back of the limo, and he turns to wave at me. I wave a little, and then the door closes, and he's gone. I can't see him through the tinted window.

December 17. A lot can happen between now and then.

I pick up my bag and wander back toward the parking lot, fielding congratulations from people, trying to ignore the massive hole that's opening in my heart, growing bigger and bigger by the second. One of the staff members greets me and gets me my own limousine to the airport. I hope I'll catch a glimpse of Luke on the way, but apparently they're dead serious about keeping us apart. I don't see him anywhere.

I have a sleeping woman who hogs the armrest on my way back to Atlanta. No one to talk to, to share music with, or with a broad shoulder I can sink into while I sleep. The flight back goes on for a miserable eternity.

By the time I get home and the cab drops me off at my apartment, it's after midnight. Courtney isn't expecting me, since we had no idea when we'd be allowed to come home. I left my keys at home, so I have to ring the doorbell. A sleepy-looking Joe, in rumpled boxers, opens the door and lets out a surprised, "Hey!"

He opens the door a little more, and Courtney is there. "Oh my god! Look at you! You have color! You no longer look like a zombie from the living dead!"

She runs to me and hugs me so hard, and suddenly I'm crying, and it's not because of the living dead comment. I don't know why. I had an amazing experience. Luke and I won the whole fucking game. We've agreed to stay married. I should be floating on air.

But I can't stop blubbering like an idiot. I cry so much I'm in danger of getting snot all over her T-shirt.

"Aw, honey, what? Did you come in last place? Embarrass yourself on national television? What?"

It occurs to me that they don't know because the season hasn't started airing yet. I can't believe that after all we've been through, I have to sit and wait and keep my mouth shut about it. Even to my best friend. "I can't tell you," I wail. "It's in my contract."

She puts an arm around me and brings me into the kitchen. She motions to Joe to put on a pot of tea. "Sure you can. You just have to make sure that the people you tell aren't going to blab it to the world. You know Joe and I will keep it under wraps."

"Oh. Okay." I wipe at my nose.

We sit down at the kitchen table, and I look around. Everything looks smaller, somehow. Colder. Like it doesn't belong to me anymore. "I think I'm just really overtired," I tell her, wiping my eyes as Joe sets a cup of tea in front of me. I dunk the tea bag and sigh. "I know it's only been a couple of weeks, but I've been planning for the appearance for months. Now everything feels so different. I've just spent the entire flight trying to decide what's going to happen now. *After.*"

"Well, you do what you have to do now. I'm sure it will be a little weird, since you're going to be on television. But then it'll calm down," she says as Joe sits beside her. "So can you tell us what episode you got kicked off?"

"Yeah," Joe adds. "How far did you get?"

I think about that last moment, when Luke was pulled away from me, and my heart twists. "I won."

Courtney leans forward, then cocks an eyebrow at Joe. "Excuse me? It sounded like she just said she won."

Joe nods, confirming. "She did." He looks at me and shakes his head. "She's pulling our leg."

"I'm serious!"

Courtney crosses her arms. "Fine! Don't tell us!" She says with a pout. "Can you at least tell us what the big twist was? Did the winning couple have to get married?"

I shake my head, more confident now since I doubt they'll believe anything I say. "We all had to get married. I married Luke Cross. The guy behind us in line?"

Her jaw drops. "The smoking-hot dirty guy? OH MY GOD!" Joe flashes her a hurt look, which she ignores. "So did you have to do challenges with him and stuff?"

I finger the place where the plastic ring was up until they ripped it off me. "I had to do just about *everything* with him."

She's fanning her face again. "I seriously can't wait to watch this season with you. So was he hot? Sweet? Sexy? Did you . . . get cozy? Was he every bit a swoony as he looked? Please tell me he made you forget Gerald."

Yes yes yes yes yes. A thousand yesses. The more he runs through my head, the more I just want to be with him again. The more horrible I feel. I can't believe we have to wait until December 17 to even see each other. This is cruel and unusual and . . .

I'm crying again.

I swipe at my tears with the back of my hand, and suddenly I don't want tea. I want my bed. Even though I'm sure that from now on my bed will be missing something if he isn't in it with me. But I just don't want to face this anymore. I want to go to sleep, hanging a sign on my head that says **DO NOT WAKE UNTIL DECEMBER 17.**

"I think I should just turn in," I say, standing up. "I'm sorry."

I can tell Courtney wants more gossip. Of course she does. This is the most exciting thing that's happened in my boring life, and I'd ordinarily be able to speak volumes on it. But I can't. Not now. Not when every single story I could tell her would be tinged with the memory of him.

So I go up to my small room, with my small bed, and crawl under the sheets. Without him. Without my husband.

Luke

It was great. I have no complaints.

—*Luke's Final Interview, Day 14*

Eloise sits beside me in the limo, crossing her legs to give me a glimpse of her toned thighs.

But all I can do is look out the window as the girl of my dreams disappears in the distance. She's watching the car leave, and she looks so damn sad, I already want to go back and hold her and take her with me.

Eloise snaps her fingers at me, and I realize she's asked me a question.

"So, how does it feel to be the winner?"

I nod. "Good."

She gives me a look like she expected a little more enthusiasm.

I add, "I'm just confused as to what happens next."

She grins and reaches into a refrigerator, pulling out a couple of beers, one of which she hands to me. "The sky's the limit for you, baby. I guarantee you, the footage we have of you is pure gold. What do you want? Endorsements? Modeling contracts? Want to try your hand at acting? Once the world gets a load of you, they'll be all over you! And I can say I discovered you."

I stare at the beer, then set it down in the cup holder. "I don't want any of that."

She takes a sip of her beer. "Are you kidding me, baby? You've just been given this amazing opportunity. In the next couple months, the whole country is going to be in love with Luke Cross."

I look out the window at the line of blue ocean in the distance and think of yesterday, swimming in the waves with her. Maybe two weeks ago stardom would've been something I'd be up for. But now? There's only one person I want to be in love with me.

"Now, don't worry about the marriage. We'll be able to get it annulled immediately, as we have a little loophole involving the coercion clause," she says with a sly smile. "I know it must've been hard for all the contestants, having to work through a marriage with someone they have nothing in common with. But we knew it would be good for ratings, and the early buzz is incredible. You going to watch on Sunday night?"

I frown and shake my head.

"Aw, you nervous? Don't worry—I had the final word in editing down the footage, and I made you look very, very good, if I do say so myself," she says, leaning over and patting my chest. Her hand is still lingering there, clawlike fingernails trailing down my abdomen, and I can feel her eyes on me, expectant. "You could say thank you, you know."

"Thank you," I reply woodenly.

Her hand is still on me, trailing lower.

"Or maybe you can just show me," she says.

I shift my eyes to her. There's no mistaking that wolfish look. I grasp her hand in mine and throw it off me. "No. I can't."

She sits back, astonished. "You . . . can't?"

"You heard me," I grind out. "I'm in love with Penny. I want to stay married to her, and she wants to stay married to me."

She shakes her head. "That's not the way this is supposed to work. We paired you—"

"I know. You paired us up so that there was no way we could get along and want to be married. You thought you'd be able to save yourself the money, right? But we don't want the annulment. That's what we were going to say at the end of the race, and it's what we would've said if you hadn't played this fucked-up ratings-grab game. We want to be together. You're fucking with our lives, making us wait until the finale, you know that?"

"I don't think so. You're just not thinking clearly. Of course you're going to want the annulment."

"No. We're not. And we're not going to change our minds at the finale either."

I'm aware of her staring at me, her mouth slightly open, as the limo pulls up at the Maui airport. I grab my bag and climb out, and she hands me my ticket and says, "That's too bad."

No, it's not.

I might feel like shit now, but it sure as hell is not because I made the decision to be with Penny. No, that's the only fucking thing I've done right.

I board a flight right away and end up getting into Atlanta at around ten in the evening. I know Gran's probably sleeping, so I have the cab drop me at Tim's Bar, where I know I'll find Jimmy, right where I left him.

The bar's just getting crowded as I push open the door. They all cheer in surprise, which draws a smile from me, despite being fucking exhausted. Couldn't sleep on the plane at all. I spot the guy I hired to temporarily replace me behind the bar—some poor slob like me who needed money, at least whatever he could get. And I spot Jimmy at the end of the bar, in the corner booth he uses as his office. He's with Lizzy now, so I think he comes to this office out of habit more than necessity.

James comes over as Flynn—my mini-me—pours me a shot of tequila and says, "How the fuck are you? We all missed you around here."

I toss back the drink, trying to keep at bay any memories of Penny in Boston, dancing up close to me, giving me those sweet, innocent looks through her thick lashes as she lapped at my fingers with that magic tongue of hers. I slam the glass down on the bar and motion to Flynn. "Yeah. Another."

"So, it was that good?" Jimmy grins, pulling out the stool beside mine with his feet. "We're all fixin' to have a viewing party here this Sunday. It's gonna be the biggest thing this neighborhood's ever seen."

"You should probably count me out for that," I say, tossing back the next drink.

"What the fuck did they do with you there? Shock treatments? You look like shit. Nice fucking haircut."

I scrub my hands over my face, then through my hair. My beard is as thick as the hair on my head these days, and my eyes sting from the jet lag. "Need to get my ass to bed. I'll talk to you tomorrow."

I feel the weight of every eye in the place on me as I trudge to the narrow staircase to my apartment and start to climb the stairs. When I get up to my place, I throw my shit down on the floor and collapse on the sofa, staring up at the water-stained ceiling.

I think of Eloise tugging on my pants, and nausea thickens the back of my throat. Two weeks ago when I met her, I'd have been game to give her anything she wanted. But Penny's so under my skin and in my veins that I can't even look at another woman. This isn't about sex or release or any of that. I need her like the air I breathe.

And I'll be damned if I'm waiting until December 17 to tell her that.

THE REAL WORLD

Nell

> *It was hard, trying to keep everything under wraps for that*
> *long. Everyone kept asking me. I'm glad it's over.*
>
> —*Nell's Finale Interview, December 17*

"What are you doing?" Courtney asks me while I'm sitting in front of my Mac, trying to put together my résumé. "Get your ass over here. It's about to start."

"No," I moan, my stomach roiling with dread. "I have to get this out. There's a position opening up in the English department at GSU that I think I might be perfect for."

Joe walks in, and Courtney says, "Let's get her."

They double-team me, grabbing me and throwing me on the couch. Joe sits on my legs and Courtney on my stomach. I might die. "Stop!" I moan.

She grabs a handful of popcorn from the big container she just made and tosses it at my face. "You promised you'd watch."

I groan. "Fine. Just get off me before you crush me to death."

It's been a week since filming ended, and today is the premiere of the first episode of *Million Dollar Marriage*. Courtney is a superfan already. She has been scouring the online news sites and knows all the competitors, and she has even mapped out their chances of winning. I keep trying to tell her that Luke and I won, but she's living in denial, possibly because she still has the mental image of my drowning-insect flailing in her head.

They peel off me just as the opening credits roll. I watch with my hands over my face, half shielding my eyes. There's Will Wang, running down the hallway of the Georgia Tech rec center as the camera follows him, announcing the beginning of the show. As the camera scans, I think I see my elbow, and then I get a second-long glimpse of Luke.

Courtney squeals, "Oooooh! He's so hot!"

My thoughts exactly.

That's all it takes.

I can't watch this.

I jump off the couch just as my phone starts to buzz. It's a text, but I pretend it's a phone call and say, "I've got to take this!" then run as fast as I can into another room, leaving the cheers of the fake *Million Dollar Marriage* audience behind me.

And oh my god. It's Gerald. Hi, superstar.

I drop the phone on my lap and sigh. I don't feel a thing for him right now. Not love. Not anger. He's nothing but an annoying insect to me now. I think about deleting the message, but then I'll have to go into the living room and watch my romance with Luke play out in detail.

No thanks. So I type in: What do you want?

Just thought it's been a long time since we caught up.

I sigh. A month ago I would have killed to know he was thinking of me. For so long, he knew he had me on a string. He'd say jump, and I'd do it. But I have nothing for him now. No animosity. I just want him to leave me alone. I type in: I really don't have anything to say to you.

I hear Courtney gasp and say "NO!" in the other room, then "Kill that asshole, Luke!" and I realize she must be talking about Ace, and they must be at the point where Luke's balloon gets busted. A moment later, Gerald texts back: I'm watching the show. You look good, Nell.

I clench my fists. He's playing his regular Gerald game, trying to dig his way under my skin. I'm done. Enjoy it. I have to go.

I throw my phone down on the chair beside me and shake my head. Somehow I knew he'd text me back now. Maybe that was even the reason why I signed up for the show in the first place.

No, that *was* the reason I signed up. To get in his face again.

But somewhere along the line, I stopped caring. And now I really couldn't give a fuck.

Courtney squeals again, and I hear her yell, "I always thought I'd be your maid of honor!" So we're on *that* part. My phone buzzes with a text a moment later: Holy cow. Did you really marry that guy?

I quickly grab the phone and race to block the number.

But not before another text comes through. I brace myself to read it and realize it's not from Gerald. It's from a number I don't recognize.

It says: Vooly voo coochie a le moi croissant?

I jump nearly to the ceiling.

This can't be . . . can it?

Of course, it has to be.

My fingers tremble as I type in: Are you asking me to sleep with your breakfast pastry?

A moment later: So THAT's what that means? Fuck, girl. You're turning me on.

I grin from ear to ear. Courtney's shouting something at the television, but all my attention is on my phone now.

Me: You know you're not supposed to be talking to me.

Him: That's why I'm texting from my buddy's phone. Took me a while to find your number.

Me: How did you do that?

Him: It's easy for us felons. You watching the show?

205

Me: Can't bring myself to. You?

Him: Hell no. Never seen the bar so packed, though. I'm in the back closet. Doing "inventory."

I smile. I like the fact that we're in the same boat, even if there is distance separating us. Not much distance, though. He never said where his bar was, but I looked it up on my GPS and mapped it out, and it's less than three miles from me. I keep thinking that if we were meant to be, maybe we'd run into each other somewhere.

Sometimes I think about trying to "accidentally" run into him, say, by going down to the bar and pretending to be in the neighborhood.

Then I remind myself that he needs the money, and I don't want to jeopardize things for him.

Him: Has a good girl like you ever broken the rules before?

I grin at the thought.

Me: What do you have in mind?

Him: I'll text you when I can get away. Good night, sweetheart. Sweet dreams.

I throw my head back against my chair and let out an excited little squeal, just thinking about breaking the rules with my yummy husband. My whole body's tingling, quivering for him, for the possibility of seeing him before the finale.

I'm practically brimming with delight when I walk out to see Courtney and Joe, with their eyes glued to the screen. She doesn't look at me, but her voice is full of suspicion. "How was your quote-unquote phone call?"

I grin. Nothing can stop me from smiling now, nothing. Not even . . .

I catch a glimpse of Luke being tethered to me for the corn maze mission. The camera isn't focused on me, though. It's focused on Luke's bulging biceps, the look of concentration on his face as we line up at the starting line.

And now I'm not just grinning; I'm wet. Wanting. Delirious. I actually have to put my hands on my thighs to keep my knees from knocking together.

"Oh my god," Courtney says, jumping up and down on the couch. She's clutching a pillow on her lap in both hands, twisting it anxiously, and I think she may end its life pretty soon. "You not only married Mr. Hot, Dark, and Dirty, you went through an entire corn maze tied to Mr. Hot, Dark, and Dirty like *that*?"

I nod, sporting that smug smile she hates. The one I use to gloat when I know something nobody else knows.

Because really.

She hasn't seen anything yet.

Luke

Yeah, it's tough. It's like being in a holding pattern. I just want to get it over with and get everything out in the open.

—*Luke's Finale Interview, December 17*

It was a shitty week. I was surrounded by the parts of my life that didn't in any way fit with Penny's. I tried to get back into minding the bar, but I felt like I was being forced to sit still when I should be moving. The days dragged on like years, driving me half-mad.

Texting with Penny was my touchstone, bringing me back to where I wanted to be. Reminding me of what I needed, what I was working for.

After that, I had purpose. I knew what I had to do.

I knew I could probably get through the next couple of months if I could just see her. Once. To do that without raising suspicion and violating the contract, I had to accomplish two things. One, I needed to talk to Lizzy, Jimmy's girlfriend. And two, I needed to find the time and the place.

Lizzy made it easy. She was a peach, and I knew I could trust her to keep it a secret. She helped me with the shit I knew nothing about, showing me pictures on her phone and helping me find the best source. She even made the deal for me and delivered the goods. All I had to do was make a choice based on what I knew of Penny and provide the credit card number.

Finding the time would be another challenge. My grandmother ended up having a stroke the night after I got back, so it was touch and go for a while. But eventually, she got back with it. When I go into her room one morning, she's sitting up, waiting for me. She looks like she's back to her tough old self. "How're you feeling?"

"Luke, you're late," she says.

I laugh. "Late for what?"

The nurse smiles at me. "She's been wanting to discuss last night's episode of *Million Dollar Marriage* with you. I think she wants to give you a piece of her mind."

"We all do!" Gran says. "We can't believe what you did to her."

I lift an eyebrow. So all the old people have been discussing my love life, is that it? "To who?"

"To your wife! What are you doing cavorting around with those sluts when you have a beautiful wife back home?"

I scratch the side of my face. That's overdoing it, isn't it? I talked to some of the women on other teams to form alliances, but that's as far as it went. But my Gran has always been black and white. "I don't know what you're talking about, Gran."

I fluff her pillows, but she nudges me away. "I *like* that Penny girl. When do I get to meet her? I'd like to meet my own granddaughter-in-law." She smacks me on the hand. "Why have you been keeping her from me?"

"Gran, it's . . ." I sit on the chair across from her, my Braves cap in my hands. "You see . . ."

I look at the nurse, who whispers, "We've tried to explain it. She doesn't understand that it was just for television."

I lean forward. Gran is a traditional woman; she was married to my grandfather for sixty years. "Yeah. Well, see . . . the thing about the show is that after you leave the race, you can choose to get the marriage annulled."

She's not following me. "Annulled?"

"Yeah. Like broken. Declared invalid."

Her eyes widen. "But you didn't, did you?"

"Well . . . not exactly, not—"

"Good! You're married to her. You make it work. You don't give up when the going gets tough. She's good for you, Luke. I see the way you look at her. The way she looks at you. You belong together." She pats my hand.

My Gran. The only person besides Penny and me who believes we even have a shot in this world.

She motions me closer, and I lean in. "And don't fuck things up," she growls into my ear.

The nurse bursts out laughing.

"I won't," I tell her. "I promise, I won't."

The nurse taps Gran on the foot. "I'll let you guys visit," she says and leaves.

When she's gone, I look around to make sure we're alone, then reach into my pocket and pull out the case and open it. This is the only piece of jewelry I've ever bought, so I don't know much, but it's pretty. It'll be prettier on her hand. I don't think Penny's much for jewelry, but I think she'll like it. "You think this is good, Gran?"

She studies it. "Well, it's a step in the right direction. The first ring you gave her was a Cracker Jack prize!"

"Actually, I . . ." I trail off. No sense telling her I didn't exactly give her that first ring. Gran wouldn't understand. I pocket it and exhale.

"Why're you so nervous? She already said yes, boy."

But not for real, I think. "Because she's too good for me."

"Oh, honey," she says, leaning over and touching my cheek. "Your grandfather said that to me until the day he died. With that attitude, you're going to make a wonderful husband."

SECRET MEETING

Nell

> *Of course. Yes. I had no communication with anyone from the show in the interim period between filming and the finale. Those were the rules.*

> —*Nell's Finale Interview, December 17*

Three weeks.

Three agonizing weeks.

That's how long it took before I received another text from Luke.

I was going mad. I interviewed for the position as adjunct faculty in the Department of English at Georgia State but didn't get it, so I was still looking for jobs. But the stress of my rising debt barely bothered me, since I knew that come December 17, we'd get our big million dollar payoff. My mind was completely muddled by all the chaos surrounding the television show—and of course, thoughts of Luke. I kept my phone with me every moment, waiting for that elusive text.

By the time I got it, it was November.

It wasn't sweet. Wasn't even nice. All it said was: 8 p.m. this Sunday. Follow Carver Mill Road from Atlanta to the S curve, then take a right into the first wooded drive and drive about 100 yards.

I stared at it. How did I know it was even from him? It could've been from a serial killer, luring me out into the middle of nowhere.

But I took one look at the time—eight p.m. on Sunday, the regular airtime of *Million Dollar Marriage*—and decided I'd rather chance it than be forced to watch. I've actually done a great job of avoiding every episode, even though Courtney keeps trying to get me to sit next to her and endure it. She is even more of a fan now than before, and she can't believe I'm still in the game. One Sunday, she scrunched her nose and said, "You don't really win, do you?" and I just shrugged.

So I borrow Nee's car on Sunday and drive out of Atlanta into the country. I have no idea where I'm going, and the road is creepy and dark. It's autumn and the leaves are falling as I drive into the S curve. Sure enough, there's a small road to the right, gravel and full of ruts. I drive along, squinting in the light from my headlights, until I see the back of an old Ford pickup truck.

I apply the brakes and cut the engine, hoping to god that's him. I don't get out, just in case.

And then the door opens, and a big form steps out, comes around the back of the truck, and leans there, arms crossed.

Can't mistake those biceps. It's him.

I forget to take off my seat belt in my excitement, and it nearly strangles me. I finally snap it loose, bound out of the car, and run to him, throwing myself into his arms. I straddle him, and he lifts my ass, so I wrap my legs around him. He kisses my hairline, kisses my face, my mouth, and I bask in him, his smell, his body, everything.

"I missed you so much," I say, burying my face in his neck.

"Missed you too."

He holds me for the longest time, against his warm body, and we don't talk, even though I've been saving up a million things to tell him since I left. Funny, when we parted, I kept seeing things I thought he'd like or thinking of things I wanted to tell him, and now . . . I don't want to talk. I just want to be near him.

When after an eternity he finally lets me down, I look around. "Where are we?"

He points behind him. "My parents' farm. Their house is just over that ridge. No one ever comes out here, though. I used to come here to get high."

"Oh." Okay. Enough talking. More kissing.

I reach for him, but he says, "You have to go back soon?"

I shake my head adamantly. "I don't *ever* want to go back."

"Good. I might just keep you." He opens the tailgate on his truck, climbs in, and spreads out a sleeping bag. Then he gives me his hand, hoisting me up. We kick off our shoes and slip into the bag together, on our sides, facing each other. "Bring back memories?"

"As I recall, the last time we did this, it was ten degrees. But we were wearing a lot more clothes and were a lot closer."

"Hmm. Let's address that," he says, unbuttoning the buttons on my blouse. I shrug it off. We slowly help undress each other, and when he wraps an arm around me and pulls me into the warmth of his body, I feel like I've died and gone to heaven. "You feel good, Dr. Carpenter."

"Call me Dr. Cross," I say, nuzzling against his chest. "It's more of an honor to me to be your wife. It feels more real, more right to be yours than anything else."

He drags his hands down my back, cupping my ass. "Sweetheart . . . my wife . . . you're so many things," he breathes. "I've fallen so in love with you, I don't know what to do with myself. *Sans toi, je ne suis rien.*"

I gaze up at him, my every pore thrumming with love for him. "Where did you learn that?"

His eyes scan my face, and he reaches up to swipe a lock of hair behind my ear. "Tell me I said it right. I've been practicing for weeks."

I smile. "You did. Without you, I am nothing too."

"Good. Did you tell anyone about us?"

I nod. "My best friend. She didn't believe a thing I said."

He chuckles. "I had a hard time believing this myself. That's why I had to see you. I need to know you're not just a dream in my head." He kisses my forehead. "God, you're so beautiful."

He drags his hand between us. "Touch me there," I murmur. "Just touch me everywhere."

He nudges my thighs open with his knees, spreading me wide. I'm dripping. His hand slides between my legs, fingering my clit, and then he slowly delves a finger into my wet core. I gasp as a fever shoots through every one of my nerves. Luke laps up my gasp, groaning as our mouths fuse and his finger slides slowly and rhythmically in and out of me, making me moan and wriggle under his touch. His touch on my clit is gentle and soft and lingering, circling surely so that now the wetness is coursing out of me. I feel an ache in my belly, a craving inside me that can't seem to be appeased, yearning to get as close to him as I possibly can.

I touch his cock. His beautiful, perfect cock. "I want you. I need you. Please, Luke."

I expect resistance, but there is nothing but a male growl rumbling against my chest. He kisses me harder and then pecks my lips as he eases back and positions himself between my legs. He reaches for his pants, and I know what he's looking for, so I grab his hand. "I'm protected. And I want to feel you completely. Just fuck me."

"Goddamn, Penny. You know how many times I've dreamed about this?"

"I know." I kiss his forehead. "I have too. I've thought about you every single second since I left Maui."

I rest my weight on my elbows, watching him take his shaft in his hand and guide it between my legs. He pauses at my entrance and looks into my eyes. "Sure you want this?"

I nod. More than anything.

He covers me with his body, and suddenly I feel him sliding slowly into me, inch by inch, filling me. It's so good, so delicious, him inside me, in the right place, fitting into me like the final missing puzzle piece. It makes my whole body quake.

"Fuck, Penny," he murmurs, voice ragged. His hands are gripping my hips, fingers digging in. "You fit me so well."

And then he is flush against me, hips against hips. He's huge, stretching me, and I feel him inside me, throbbing with his heartbeat. I let out a shuddery breath and savor the feeling of his hot skin totally against mine, blanketing me. I kiss the side of his face, salty with his sweat, and wonder what he's going to do to me next to drive me absolutely wild.

"This okay?" he asks unsurely, timidly, like he doesn't know how amazing he is and how every last thing he does makes me fall more and more in love with him.

"I love it. I love your cock. You feel so good."

Pressure is building, an explosion just waiting to happen. Before it can, he releases his grip on my hips and pulls himself out. I feel the tip of his shaft at my entrance for a mere breath, and then he plunges inside, slowly and steadily.

I can't help it. It rips a shriek from my mouth.

"Okay?" he asks me, searching out my eyes.

How can it be wrong? It's my husband and me. Together. Making love. Nothing could be more right. "Yes. More. Faster."

Another slow slide out, and this time no pause. He thrusts into me, hard this time. The pressure is building, blooming deep in my core like a volcano, ready to erupt. His muscles are tense as he pulls out and thrusts again, harder, faster, deeper, fueling the desire to get more of him as far into me as possible.

I have never been fucked like this before. Thoroughly, completely, fully fucked so that every pore in my body is a firework ready to explode.

"Yes. Yes," I cry out. "God, Luke. Oh *god*. Don't stop, don't ever, ever stop, please don't ever stop, Luke." I'm blabbering.

"You like it hard?" he says, voice strained as I'm now lifting my hips off the truck bed, meeting his every thrust in a steadily hastening rhythm. We're both covered in sweet sweat, and the friction is threatening to make us burst into flames.

"Yes. However you want it—just please give me *you*," I gasp, a frisson of pleasure radiating out from low in my belly, threatening to take over every inch of me. Now I feel shameless. I want his mouth on me, everywhere. I want him to fuck me forever. The pressure in my belly is now thundering through me, and I know something monumental is about to happen.

He slows his thrusts, sliding in and out, testing the rhythm, getting even deeper. His chest slides against my hard nipples, and suddenly I let out a cry. He's found the right place, because the pleasure is almost too much to take. I'm getting even hotter and closer to that edge than I dreamed possible. I hook my legs around his hips, and he buries himself impossibly deep inside me. I'm frantic as I go off like a rocket, clutching his big body as my only lifeline tethering me to this earth.

My entire body ripples with such intensity I let out a primal scream, my nails scraping down his back. I come. So hard. So hard that I keep screaming and sobbing his name, over and over again, even as I start to come down. He rips me apart.

He must've been holding out on me, because the second I find myself coming down, he plunges deep into me, holding me there, and I feel him pulsating inside me. He lets out a long, muffled groan into my hair, then whispers my name over and over again.

"Penny," he murmurs as the shuddering subsides, gazing dreamily into my eyes. He falls then, completely limp, into my arms, and I hold him close as the stars and the moon and the whole world seem to be shining on us, smiling at this perfect moment.

There's no doubt in my mind. This so-wrong-for-me man?

Is so, so, so *right*.

Luke

Right. It was tough waiting until December 17. But here we are. So let's get this done.

—Luke's Finale Interview, December 17

Later, she's lying against my chest, completely spent.

My fucking beautiful wife.

The sun is breaking over the horizon. What felt like an hour has been ten.

Her breath on me is a feeling I wish I could bottle and save. The smell of her shampoo and her arousal is heavy in the damp morning air, and I inhale it into my lungs, wanting to drown in it. I stare at her light eyelashes fluttering, the bridge of freckles over her nose, her red raw lips, and I want it all so bad, in my pocket, all the time.

I run my hands down her bare back and tangle my legs with hers. Her eyes open, and she lifts her chin to look at me. "Good morning."

There are so many things I still want to do to her. Again and again. I want to suck and lick and touch and taste her, all of her, every last piece, over and over. I will never get enough.

But our time is up.

"Morning, sweetheart. I think we have to go."

She pouts, but she slips soundlessly out of the sleeping bag. We find our clothes in piles all over the back of the truck and dress slowly, as if that will help us extend our time together.

I watch her slipping on her shoes on the tailgate, and for a minute I imagine her all in white, walking down the aisle toward me.

I take a breath and let it out, and it clouds in front of me in the chilly morning air.

"The day the show started you said that you wanted a real wedding, with the dress and the cake and the rings?"

She smiles. "Yes. But it's okay. I wouldn't have changed a thing."

I reach into the pocket of my jeans. I sink to my knee in front of her. I open the velvet case. "But I would have."

She gasps. "Luke . . . how did you . . . ?"

"You need a real engagement ring. A wedding. A dress. A honeymoon. You need all of it. And I'm going to give it to you, baby, the second this is all over and we get that money. I promise. From now on, all I'm going to do is live to make you happy. That's all."

"I am already so happy," she breathes out. "The answer is already yes. Of course. Forever."

She slips off the tailgate and pulls me up, easing into my arms, kissing me.

"Don't you want to try on the ring?" I ask.

She looks at it again. "It never was about the ring. It's pretty. You picked it out?"

"I had a little help," I confess, taking it out of the box and sliding it onto her finger.

She wiggles it about a little, admiring it, then slips her hands around my neck and kisses me. "Thank you. It's perfect. This makes it feel real. I can't wait until I can wear it all the time."

I kiss her goodbye. She gets into her car and waves at me through the windshield, the diamond glistening on her finger as she backs out of the driveway and disappears.

She'll have to take that diamond off. For now, at least.

Six more weeks. Six more weeks. Six more weeks.

I feel better equipped to handle it now. To survive.

But I'll still be on edge. I can't wait until she can wear that diamond and never have to think about taking it off.

I can't wait until the whole world knows she's mine.

FINALE

Nell

Yes. I finally get to say it out loud. Luke and I won the first season of Million Dollar Marriage. *I never would've believed it when we started. But we wound up making a good team.*

—Nell's Finale Interview, December 17

December 17

It's finally time.

I've been sitting in a greenroom in the back of the studio with the other contestants for two hours, waiting for our chance to go on stage. Right now, the studio audience is being treated to the first hour of the two-hour finale, which is the final episode in Maui.

Luke is here, making his rounds and talking to just about everyone. Only . . . not me.

Because though most of the contestants know it was Luke and I who won, no one—not the producers or even the contestants—knows what our answer will be. I was told when I arrived not to make our answer obvious.

He keeps looking at me, though. Giving me those intense eyes that shoot my temperature to the ceiling, his gaze possessive and heavy on me. And I've been my usual wallflower self, making friends with the crudités, full of nervous energy, but mostly, unable to take my eyes off him. He's wearing a suit.

He. Is. Wearing. A. Suit.

And he looks like a million dollars.

My husband is damn hot. I'm drooling a little.

As I sit on the couch in the corner, someone tugs on my sleeve. I look up and see Shveta. "Congratulations," she says, giving me a hug. "The buzz is that you won. Who would've thought?"

I smile. "Yes, thank you. Oh, gosh. I'm so nervous."

"Me too. Though you have more of a reason to be. All the cameras are going to be on you and Luke."

Yes, I suppose so. My stomach twists at the thought. But then I catch a look at Luke and—instant calm. His lips lift in a smile, and I swear I wish I could bottle the way he makes me feel. Sparks of excitement flicker down to my toes. In less than an hour, I can put on that ring that's currently in my purse and never take it off again. I can kiss and hug and hold my husband and never have to hide it again.

I can be Mrs. Luke Cross. His wife. Forever.

At five to nine, they start to line us up to go out onto the stage. The butterflies in my stomach become bats as everyone gets paired up with their "spouse" in the order they were eliminated, and they finally pair Luke and me together at the very end. I look up and he takes my clammy, trembling hand in his own.

"Fancy meeting you here, Penny." His voice is smooth as melted chocolate, completely relaxed.

I laugh. There are so many things I want to say to him.

But then the audience starts to cheer, and the producers signal for us to go out onto the stage.

So we do.

The arena is packed to the gills with reporters, cameras pointed at us. Flashbulbs go off, and my future seems to flash through my eyes with them.

Everything depends on what will happen in the next hour. We could give our answer in a split second, but not now. I know the announcer will drag things out to the point of sheer madness. Recaps of poignant moments from the season, interviews with contestants, performances by "special celebrity guests" who are also fans of the show.

It's all meant to build up to the moment of truth.

Every one of the people in this arena, every one of the thirteen million people watching at home—they're all waiting on the edge of their seats with the same question.

Will they . . . or won't they?

I wish to god we could just give our answer and be done.

He's so close, but he might as well be a million miles away. Our fingers entwined, he waves at the crowd cheering our names. His hand isn't the least bit clammy. I manage a peek at him, his chiseled features, his relaxed smile, and my throat catches.

No wonder the world is in love with him. No wonder he's been the fan favorite since week one.

This is it. The end. Or . . .

I look over at him and say, "Luke . . . I'm not . . ."

He shakes his head almost imperceptibly. "It's okay," he murmurs, his fingers stroking my palm. "Breathe, Penny. Just breathe."

So I do. But air is not the only thing I need to make me okay right now.

We've been through so much, more than most couples will go through in entire lifetimes.

And now we're about to make the decision that will shape our future.

We move closer to the stage, and as we do, I hear the announcer announcing the full names of the contestants eliminated before us. And then the spotlight is on us. The announcer says, "And here are your *Million Dollar Marriage* winners, Penelope Carpenter and Luke Cross!"

Mr. and Mrs. Luke Cross.

The crowd erupts into thunderous applause. Luke squeezes my hand and leads me out to the center of the stage, waving at his adoring fans. I see signs everywhere that mention Luke's name, held by beautiful women who probably ogled him all season long. And rightly so. I wobble on my feet as the applause starts to die. Luke doesn't drop my hand. He helps me, all the way toward the director's chair at the front of the rest of the contestants. He sets me down in the chair, helps clip my microphone to my collar, and whispers, "Relax, sweetheart—they love us," before sitting down beside me.

I catch a look at him in the video monitor. Damn, he looks good. And who's that pale, weird-looking ghost in the glasses and freckles next to him?

Oh, right. That's me.

I scan the audience. There are so many signs waving for him. **LUKE LUKE LUKE**, everywhere I look. They love *him*, that's for sure.

The applause ends, and I can hear my heartbeat thrumming in the prevailing silence. Will Wang strides up to the front of the stage and says, "Well, well, well, I'm sure there are a lot of questions for our contestants, but let me just ask the winning couple . . . how does it feel?"

Luke looks at me, and I nod at him, because my vocal cords are not working. He squeezes my hand. "Phenomenal."

Everyone cheers as if he's just discovered a cure for cancer. Women wolf-whistle. It's overwhelming how much they love him. Well, except for Ace, who's sitting a row behind us. The cameras pan to him for a split second, revealing his scowl.

I smile at that. Luke must see it, too, because he squeezes my hand, and I squeeze back.

"The people out here want to know . . . how did you two really get along? Looked like it was touch and go there for a while."

"It was," Luke says. "We were trailing a lot of the time. But we worked it out. There were some great competitors on this stage. Any one of them could've won. I think we came out on top by sheer luck."

People applaud politely. That's Luke, so diplomatic.

"And let me say," says a voice from behind us. I think it's Cody. "Luke's really a class act. Always trying to help people. Sure, he was competitive, but if anyone was in a bind, he'd help them first. The money really couldn't have gone to a nicer guy."

Louder applause. People on the stage and in the audience nod in agreement. They seem actually happy to have lost to him. It doesn't sting as much to lose the money because they're glad it's going to him and not someone like Ace. And I agree too.

Totally.

But did they forget that I was a part of his team?

It's okay, I tell myself. I'm used to fading into the background and being the wallflower. And Luke always gets attention. That's just who he is.

"Obviously there were a lot of fights on the journey!" Will Wang says. "Take a look at this."

The screens around the arena light up with a montage of couples screaming at each other during various challenges. There's one of us in front of the locked gate in Colorado, trying to find the key. The part where I went off on Luke with "Maybe I'm not because my name is *Nell!*" my eyes wild and fierce. People laugh at that. But what about what happened a minute before that, when he was screaming at me?

Then it cuts to the part where I say, "I don't worry about anything where he is concerned. He is not my problem. The only thing I'm focused on is winning." Luke's standing in the background, looking genuinely hurt by my response. It almost hurts me to see his stricken expression. I hadn't seen it then, but . . . I can't even remember when that was.

Someone in the audience says, "What a bitch."

I swallow.

These people who are cheering? They're on Luke's side.

But is anyone on mine?

The montage comes to an end, and everyone claps. My hands are sweating so badly that I have to let go of Luke's hand. I see an image of me on the video monitor, and my forehead is glistening with sweat. I look terrified. Luke leans forward and mouths, "You okay?"

I nod.

But am I?

"But it wasn't all hate at *Million Dollar Marriage*. There was actually a lot of love to go around," Will says, pointing to the video screen. There's another montage, this one of couples hugging during various victories. Ace and Marta making out, to which half the audience says, "Wooooo!" and the other hisses, "Booooo!" It's clear they're the couple people love to hate.

Then, big as life, on every one of the twelve screens around the place, I get a full-on view of my first kiss with Luke, at the zip line in Colorado, from every angle possible.

My heart jumps.

The audience reaction? A few people cheer, maybe, but what I hear is a long, loud boo from the women in the audience. One woman in the back shouts, "She isn't good enough for you, Luke!" and someone else calls, "Take me instead!"

I stiffen.

Then I catch a look at Luke on one of the monitors. He's smiling, like he's flattered by the attention. He doesn't seem to notice what it's doing to me.

Now I really feel like I'm going to throw up.

Thankfully, the montage ends, and I'm wondering just how much worse this can get. "But let's take an in-depth look at the leading couple of the hour. First, she's a PhD from Atlanta—here's Penelope Carpenter!"

Oh god.

They cut to a montage that is all about me. It's all the interviews I've done in the past, scattered with some information about my background. There are a few extremely unflattering shots of me falling on my ass during the marines confidence course, covered in snot trying to make the igloo, and freaking out about zip-lining. Then a few contestant remarks, mostly people thinking that I'm stuck up, stiff, or don't stand a chance in hell.

When it's over, people clap politely, while I cringe.

Could they make me look any more like the Wicked Witch of the World?

"Now, let's take a closer look at America's heartthrob, the man women all over the country are going crazy for . . . Luke Cross!"

His montage almost makes me fall in love all over again. It's shots of him riding his horse like a knight in shining armor. Diving shirtless into the water. Handing Shveta her balloon. Between those clips, there are interviews with various contestants, all putting him as a favorite to win. Then Ivy is there, smiling, fanning her face. "Oh, he's hot, isn't he?" she says with a grin.

I watch as, after Ivy, about ten more female contestants say the very same thing. Hot. Smoking. Wouldn't mind sharing a room with or getting a ring from him.

Then there's video of him hugging some of the other girls, women tackling him in the parking lot.

And then there's some grainy nighttime video. I recognize Luke's form as he walks between two buildings, along with a blonde . . . Charity? I hear her saying something like "You know, there's a place over there we could be alone" as she's touching him, stroking him.

He's not moving away from the beautiful model.

There's a voiceover that I recognize as Charity's squeaky high voice. "Oh yes," she says, whispering conspiratorially. "Luke and I had quite the secret romance when the cameras weren't rolling. He's every bit the stud people think he is."

I stare, the nausea inside beginning to burn as I see Luke shifting uncomfortably next to me. The montage comes to an end, and then Will Wang goes to a commercial break.

Luke reaches for my hand. "Hey. You okay?"

I can't even bring myself to look at him.

He gets up and stands right in front of my chair, shielding me from the audience. "Hey. Penny. Look at me. You don't believe any of that, do you?"

I look up at him. I don't want to believe it. I know what he told me that night. That he loves me. That he's nothing without me. I want to believe that.

But the more I look at myself through the eyes of the camera, the more I can't possibly believe that I'm worth it.

There's absolutely no reason for him to lie, though. No reason.

Unless he wants to collect the half a million. If we decide to get the marriage annulled, we'll only get half of that. But if we decide to stay married . . .

No. He wouldn't do that.

Would he?

I mean, it sounds ridiculous—just about as ridiculous as the two of us getting together in the first place.

I shake my head, but it's not because I don't believe what they're saying. It's because I need to get away. From him. From all of them. I can't make this decision now. I need more time. I have a ring in my pocket that says I'm his. But am I?

"Back from our commercial break!" Will Wang says, striding across the stage. "Before we ask Luke and Penny the all-important question, I'd like to give you some statistics. You've heard the saying that opposites attract. But in the real world, people tend to seek mates who are similar to them. This social experiment we performed proves that. After each couple was eliminated, we gave them the opportunity to remain together for a cash bonus, and all eight couples decided to have their marriage annulled. Even Ace and Marta, who appeared to find love at first sight, decided to call it quits after the taping. Which just goes to prove . . . opposites might attract, but they definitely don't stick!"

Opposites don't stick. Opposites don't stick . . .

"Okay! And now, for the moment you've all been waiting for!"

I feel the cameras on me. The temperature skyrockets. My head feels fuzzy. I can't breathe. Can't think.

"Penelope Carpenter and Luke Cross . . . what is your answer? We do, or no way?"

There is a silence so pervasive that I swear everyone must be able to hear the beating of my heart. Will Wang tilts his microphone toward us. People shift to the edges of their seats. Time seems to still, and the world freezes. I look over at Luke, the man I've stupidly fallen head over heels for, and he looks at me with that same steady gaze that makes my heart skip. I open my mouth, and he does too.

I know what he's going to say.

So I beat him to the punch.

I hear myself say it: "No way."

Then I stand up, rip the microphone off my collar, and rush off the stage.

Luke

It was bullshit, pure and simple. The things they showed on television isn't the way it went down at all. They cherry-picked footage to fit the story they wanted to tell. It's fucking bullshit, how they fucked with our lives for ratings.

—*Interview with Luke Cross for TV Buzz Daily,*
after the finale

I jump from the chair, trying to run after Penny, but I forget the mic tethering me to the chair. By the time I loosen it, she's gone. The camera catches my furious expression.

"Oooooh," Will Wang says. "Looks like Luke did not expect that answer at all!"

I see red. "Fuck you," I tell him, storming off the stage.

The first person I see when I get behind the curtains is Eloise Barker, who's reaching out her hands to me to calm me down.

"You!" I growl, pointing a finger at her. "You fucking did this! What the fuck was that? What did you fucking do to her?"

She gives me a condescending smile. "Luke, my dear. I have no idea what you're talking about. That was reality. Whatever you think you may have had with Penny? That was the fantasy."

What. The. Fuck? "Why would you . . . ?"

"Because," she says, breezily, "the world loves you. But they want you single."

I rake my hands through my hair. "This is fucking ridiculous. You wanted to save the studio half a million dollars, is that it? I don't care about the goddamn money. Keep it. I *love* her. I want to be married to her."

She shakes her head. "Apparently, she doesn't want to be married to you. I'm sorry, Luke. She gave you her answer, and that's final. And she already signed the paper." She holds it up to me, with Penny's scrawled signature on it. "Your marriage will be annulled."

No. This is a nightmare. I had it planned. After the live finale, when all the confetti poured down on us, I was going to take her in my arms and kiss her for the world to see. And then I was never going to let her go. I had a hotel room booked with our name on it. I'd been practically salivating for the moment I'd take my wife up there and sink into her, where I belonged.

Instead, on stage, the audience applauds, and no confetti is thrown. Canned music plays. The rest of the contestants file off the stage, looking at me with more fear than pity, like I'm a time bomb that's about to go off.

They're damn right about that.

Charity steps off the stage, blinking like a deer in the headlights when I corner her. "What the fuck was that?"

She gives me a disgusted look. "I didn't say anything you weren't thinking. You wanted me from the start. That was obvious."

I raise my hands up in fists, and they're shaking, I'm so angry. "*What?* I never fucking touched you!"

I push away from her. I can't fucking breathe from this suffocating tie. I want to lash out, hit something, hit someone, but everyone's keeping their distance. Ripping the tie off my neck, I race to the back of the stage, calling for my wife.

But I can't find Penny anywhere.

She's fucking gone.

And she's not my wife anymore.

MOVING ON

Nell

> TV Buzz Daily *has attempted to contact Penelope Carpenter on numerous occasions for her take on the shocking* Million Dollar Marriage *finale, but she could not be reached for comment.*

It's Christmas Eve.

It's been a week since the finale, and the outside world is a bigger minefield than it's ever been.

I sit in my darkened bedroom with my laptop. This is my fortress. I've been in bed most of the last week. The sheets are dirty because I haven't showered. I don't eat, can't even bring myself to do the normal things that used to make me happy, like listening to classical music and reading my books. Everything I do that once brought me joy just reminds me of him.

When I came home from the finale, Courtney tried to talk to me, but I told her I wasn't feeling well, and I locked myself in my bedroom. I've seen her maybe twice since, though she's always knocking at my door whenever reporters show up to ask questions. I ignore her or tell her I'm fine but need some time.

I've gotten—and deleted unanswered—at least two hundred emails from various news sources, wanting my take.

My take?

I wish I'd never signed on for that damn show in the first place. I have the money, which has helped take care of a lot of my bills. But if I could do it all over again? I'd take the bills, every time.

Because now I have this worthless broken heart that hurts so much, I think I might be dying. I keep trying to pull myself up, but I always sink back down. And because absolutely no one in the country was rooting for us as a couple or could see us together, I can't believe that anyone would understand.

I'm alone. Completely alone. And maybe that's how I belong.

My phone pings with another voice mail message from a 508 area code. I recognize the number. It's my father. Knowing I can't feel any worse than I already do, I press a button and listen to it:

"Merry Christmas, Nell. I . . . your mother and I want you to know . . . we saw the show. We've been trying to get in touch with you. We just want you to know . . . if you want to come home, we're here. We're here for you, Nell."

I swallow back a sob.

Home. Maybe that's what's wrong with my life. Maybe instead of coming all the way down here, I should've just stayed home and did what my father wanted me to do. Maybe he was right all along.

As I'm deleting emails asking me to come for interviews, I stop when I see one from the University of Massachusetts at Amherst. I'd interviewed for an English literature professorship there back in November. I open it and read with widening eyes.

Dear Dr. Carpenter:
We would very much like to welcome you to the faculty . . .

I stare at it, and suddenly I know my heart isn't all that damaged, because it starts to beat again. Maybe not the same or as fast as it did before.

Maybe I won't be happy. But I guess I can survive. I guess that's what I have to do.

Just then, someone knocks on the door. "Nell?" It's Courtney. "Please come out. It's Christmas. I made dinner."

I climb out of my covers, and she seems shocked when I open the door. She takes me in, and her eyes go sad. "Oh, Nell. You look terrible."

I smooth down my hair. "Thanks?"

"Oh, honey. It's been a week. Don't you want to talk about it?"

I go to my bed and collapse into it, face-first. "There's nothing to talk about."

She follows me and sits on my bed, her eyes skimming over the laptop. "What's this? You got a job? In Massachusetts?"

I nod, face still buried in my blankets.

She looks horrified. "You're not going to take it, are you?"

I swallow. "I think I am."

Her face pales. "No!" she shouts out. "But . . . what about . . ."

"I think I have to. I think it's the only way I can move past this."

"Past what? The fact that you're in love with Luke Cross?"

I jump up and shake my head adamantly. "I wasn't in love with him, I—"

"Right. You've been moping in bed for a week over someone you don't love. Sure."

I scowl at her. "I had a virus!"

"Yeah." She crosses her arms. "Right. Come on, Nell. I know you. Since you came back from filming you've been a totally different person."

"No, I haven't," I mumble. I've been a wreck since I got back from Maui, because all I've been able to think of is Luke, Luke, Luke. It's a wonder she didn't call someone to take me away to a padded room, considering how many times in the past two months I've caught myself staring off into space, flushed and feverish with thoughts of his body against mine. "What does that even mean?"

"I mean that the Nell I used to know was so afraid of anything if it wasn't found between the pages of a book. But look at you now!" She motions to the laptop. "You're the girl who was scared to death at the thought of lecturing a classroom. And now you're applying to be a professor at all these colleges. I've seen a girl who is happier. More adventurous. More outgoing. More relaxed. And at first I thought it was the game that made you that way. But as I watched the show, I knew it. It was the man."

All right. I figured it would be obvious to Courtney once she saw the show just how infatuated I'd become with Luke. He clearly had every woman in the country wrapped around his finger, and they didn't get to sleep in his arms every night. I'm not ashamed to have fallen under his spell; any other woman would have too. "Fine. I love him. So what?"

She looks at me like I'm utterly insane. "It's not just that. He made you love yourself, Nell. And you know how many men out there can do that? Like, none. If you love him, then for the life of me, I can't understand why you would say no way!"

"Because! Didn't you see all those clips from the finale? He clearly didn't feel the same way and was just wanting to marry me for the extra money. That's all."

"Nell. I watched the finale, yes. But I also watched the whole season. I saw him falling utterly in love with you. Utterly in love."

"That's not possible. No one in that finale saw that."

"Of course they did! They were jealous, maybe. We all saw you two staring into each other's eyes for an eternity when you finally won, and he was whispering to you, and it was like you were the only woman in the world. He's stupid silly in love with you. I have no doubt about that. Watch the clips again if you don't believe me."

I shake my head. "You're wrong."

"No, honey. You know I'm right. That's why you're destroyed. Because you found your soul mate, the man who made you your best self, and you were looking happiness in the eye, and instead you let other people tell you how to feel. You screwed up, sweetie. But it's okay. I have no doubt from the way he looked when you stormed off the stage that he's waiting for you, probably feeling as bad as you feel right now."

I cover my face with my hands, my whole body shaking with self-loathing and regret. "I did screw up, didn't I? And you know how pathetic I am? Part of me thinks that even if he wanted to stay married to me just for the money, I should have still stayed with him. It would've been better than this. Because this . . . without him? I hate it. I can't stand it."

"Trust me. It wasn't about the money for him. Go after him. Get your man."

I shake my head, feeling like a ton of bricks is sitting right on my chest. "I can't. I had my chance. I blew it."

She gives me a disappointed look. "Why? Because Nell Carpenter always has to be right and can't admit when she's wrong?"

"Yes. Pretty much."

"Even if it means the difference between happiness and utter misery?"

I nod. "I deserve utter misery for what I did to him. Did you know that I was the one who had to jump him? He kept refusing to have sex with me, because he didn't think he was good enough. And then when we finally did have sex, he proposed to me. For real. He gave me this." I reach into my bedside table and pull out the ring. "To tell me he wanted me. Forever."

I drop it in her palm, and she gasps at it. "Oh, gosh. Oh, Nell. That's probably the most heart-wrenching and romantic thing I've ever heard of. What the fuck did you do?"

I start to sob. "I don't deserve him. I'm a horrible person, and I don't. I spent all this time thinking I was too good for him, when he's too good for me. I think I deserve to be miserable for the rest of my life because of what I did to him."

"Sweetie, you don't. You deserve to be happy."

"And he does too. But he doesn't deserve to have someone walk all over him the way I did," I tell her, squaring my shoulders. "That's why I want to go to Amherst. I need to get away from all this. From him. Even if our paths never cross in this city, just knowing he's in the same town and what we could've had will kill me."

She hands me the ring. "You have to give that back to him, first."

My eyes drift to the ring. It's so pretty. I've known I need to give it back, but the thought of going to him and handing it to him fills me with dread. "I know. Maybe I can just mail it to him. I have the address of his bar."

Courtney shakes her head. "Cop-out. That's the old Nell talking. The one who hid from the real world and was afraid of her own shadow. You're not that woman anymore. You know it. You know hiding out here in your room isn't you. You have to talk to him."

She's right. And even if it's doubtlessly going to be the most painful thing I've ever done, I have to see him again. Just once. "All right. Fine. I'll go."

"Today."

"Today? It's Christmas Eve."

"So? You've put it off a week. You said it yourself—you treated him badly. You owe this to him."

I slide out of bed. "Fine. I will."

She smiles sadly. "Good. But god, Nell. Take a shower first. You smell like cheese. I'll have all the spiked eggnog you can drink waiting for you when you get home."

I reach for my robe, knowing for sure that I'm going to need a lot more than spiked eggnog to lift my spirits when all of this is done.

As I'm getting ready to go, I think about what she said. And I realize that while I might be lost in the throes of grief, I am a different person now. A better person. I'm stronger now. Because of him. Because he inspired me, helped me find myself, and never doubted me.

Yes, I got my heart smashed to pieces. But when I put it back together, it'll be stronger with the scars he left on it.

And the more I think about it, the more I know—I'd go back and do it again in a second. Because a scarred heart is better than one that never really beat at all.

Luke

It doesn't matter now because it's over. But yeah, I was angry at the finale. My answer would have been different. I can't blame her, though. I blame the producers.

—Luke's Interview with TV Buzz Daily

It's late. The bar is just about empty. I told customers I was closing up early so I could spend Christmas with Gran, but that ain't true. I spent the morning with her, and I'll be there tomorrow. Tonight I'm going to do what I've done the past seven nights in a row.

Get shitfaced.

I'm already halfway there.

In the past, I've made it a point not to drink until I've closed the bar. But not anymore. I've been sneaking shots of tequila from behind the bar since noon. The jukebox is spitting out "Rudolph," and there are twinkling colored Christmas lights everywhere, but I don't think there's a more depressing place on earth.

I have Gran. I have Jimmy, I have Lizzy. I have a thousand other people I call friends that I could surround myself with.

But they're not her.

Jimmy's been ironing out the details of his latest stunt for the past few hours over at his office table. He comes up to the bar to settle his tab and takes a hard look at me. "Jesus, Luke. Slow down."

I reach for the twenty he lays on the bar and don't meet his eyes. "Fuck you."

I've known Jimmy long enough that he won't take it personally. But even if I didn't, that'd be my response. A big old *fuck you* to the world. He shrugs it right off. "Yeah? Listen, Luke. We all know what this attitude is from. The girl. If you want her so bad, go out and get her."

I open the cash register. Put the bill in. "Don't know what the fuck you're talking about."

He does, though. He was with Lizzy when I asked her for help with the ring. He saw how fucking happy I was. How excited I was to have Penny as my wife. How I couldn't wait to have her with me all the time, like he has Lizzy. Then he and thirteen million other people saw when she tore my fucking heart out and stomped on it as she left the stage.

I pour myself another drink and down it. "Fine," I admit, staring at the bar. "Maybe I do. But I ain't going anywhere. It's over."

I pick up the bottle. Fuck the shot glass. I'm going to finish this sucker anyway.

Rowan's gaze follows the tequila as I wrap my lips around the bottle. "You should take it easy. I wish you'd come with Lizzy and me. We're going out to dinner."

I shake my head. What I want right now is to climb into bed and finish saying that *fuck you* to the world until I black out. "Nah. Go on. Merry Christmas."

He gives me a worried glance and then begs off. The last two customers leave, and I'm alone. I usually spend an hour after closing getting everything cleaned up, but I can't be bothered. I don't even lock the door. Soon this place won't even be my problem anymore. I grab the bottle of tequila by the neck and start to climb the stairs to my apartment.

"Luke."

The voice hits me in the gut.

I turn slowly. And she is there. Two of her. I blink until the two visions join into one. Penny. Beautiful Penny, wearing a little white coat with a furry hood. She looks like an angel.

For a moment I think she may have come for me, to tell me she made a mistake. I take a few steps down. But then I see the case in her hand. She sets it on the bar and says, "I came to give this back to you."

I look at it without interest and turn around to go back up the stairs.

"Luke." Her voice is louder now.

I turn around. "What?"

She lowers the hood and bites on her lip. "Well. Um. I'm going to Massachusetts in January. I got a job up there. I just wanted to tell you that, well . . . I'm sorry."

"You're sorry?" I repeat the words, because they sound so fucking wrong. Again and again. She's sorry. How?

I push forward and stalk over to her, slamming the tequila bottle down on the bar so hard that she flinches.

I get up close to her and wipe my mouth with my hand. "I'm sorry for a lot of things in my life, but I'll never be sorry for one minute I spent with you. Not one minute of it. Because that was the only fucking time in my life I was actually doing something right. When I was falling in love with and loving you."

She stares at me, her face pale.

"Regardless of what those clips show, I didn't fuck Charity. I didn't even touch her. I swear I didn't look at another woman. Because I was so into you. You were in my veins from the minute I saw you in line at the audition, reading that big textbook. You have to be out of your mind to think that any woman on that stage could even hold a candle to you. It's been you from the minute I laid eyes on you."

"But . . . ," she whispers, her brow wrinkling. "I know I was wrong. I know you can't forgive me."

I try to shake my head, but even that small movement makes me dizzy. I still myself against the end of the bar and try to focus on her so I don't end up falling over. "What'd I tell you? You're never wrong with me. Never. There's nothing to forgive."

She just stands there, like she can't decide whether to stay or go.

I pick up the case, grab her hand, and shove it into her palm, closing her fingers around it. "And I don't want this. I don't want the ring unless I have you. You, wearing it. That's the only thing that makes sense. Goddamn it." I wipe at my face because now my vision's bending and I'm fucking drunk off my ass, blubbering to her. "But that can't happen, so just get the fuck out."

"But . . . the money? You're not angry about me because of the money?"

I scrub my hands over my face. "I couldn't give two shits about the money. I'm gonna lose all my winnings. I wasn't supposed to disclose what fucking assholes they were and all the inner workings of the process, so now I'm in violation of the contract, and there's some lawsuit coming up and I got to get a lawyer. My bar's in foreclosure, and everything is shit. So really, you made a damn smart decision running away from me."

"Oh. I'm sorry," she says again, in that sweet little voice that tears me apart. There's pity in her eyes, and I don't fucking want it.

"Like I said. I'm not. I'm only sorry we couldn't last like I wanted. Have fun in Massachusetts."

I go back to the staircase, and she calls, even more panicked than before, "Luke! *Please . . .*"

I hang my head and brace my hands against the wall to stop the room from spinning. "Please *what*? What the fuck do you want me to do?"

I don't know how long it takes her to bridge the distance, but suddenly she's beside me, pulling me into her arms, and I'm powerless to resist. She takes my face in her hands, and then she's kissing my face, my cheeks, my forehead, gently. She's kissing me like I'm this sad little child and she wants to take care of me.

"Don't do this to me," I beg her, dragging in her scent, again and again. She smells like baby powder and toothpaste and that shampoo, and her lips are so fucking soft on my skin. "Don't do this to me and make me think you're mine and then leave again. I can't do that."

"I won't," she promises.

"You won't leave me?"

"No. I love you, Luke."

I cup her chin, holding her still for me as I look into her eyes. "I love you too, sweetheart. But I thought you were smart. I ain't got nothing to give you."

"That's a double negative. So you're right," she whispers. "*Sans toi, je ne suis rien.* Without you, I am nothing. With you, I have everything I need. We'll figure out the money, Luke. I promise."

I lift her in my arms, and she curls her limbs around me, clutching me like a monkey. We end up leaning our foreheads into each other. Her ass is in my hands, her breath coming in fast as I start nuzzling her.

I want to sink into her and prove to her that she's mine. I want to sink into her and prove to myself that she's mine. I'm shaking with desire and love and frustration as Penny strokes her fingers down my jaw. I groan and peck her lips once. Twice. Softly at first. Then harder. My beard bristling her skin as I start nibbling at her lips. All my emotions coming to the forefront.

"I'm sorry, Luke," she whispers as I nudge her coat off her shoulders.

I flip us around so her back is pressed up against the wall and my eyes are gorging on her. I visually rake her from head to toe as I drag my hands down her sides. Touching her gorgeous breasts. Squeezing and turning her on.

She wants it. That little hitch of her breath tells me so. She leans up and teases my lips with hers. We start kissing. For real. Holding nothing back. Almost an angry kiss. Almost. But not quite. Fuck, I love her too much. She squirms her sex against my hard cock as her little tongue duels with mine.

I'm nearly cross-eyed as we make out against the wall, kissing her harder and fiercer until I start softening it up. Making love to her mouth. She fucking heals me with her touch, sucking everything wrong out of my bloodstream and replacing it with her own little brand of magic.

I groan, shaking as I try to hold back from taking her right here and now. I could carry her to my bar and fuck her on the counter. Eat her up until morning. Get even drunker with her juices until I pass out.

But she's my wife. At least in my mind she is. She deserves better. She'll always deserve better than me.

Instead, I find myself carrying her upstairs to my room. I see the curiosity on her face as I shove open the door to my stink hole and walk us inside. I kick the door shut behind us and head straight to my rumpled bed with the rumpled sheets and drop her right in the center.

Penny pushes her hair back and bites down on this little temptress smile as she looks around. I'm surprised when she turns to inhale me on the sheets, sighing happily as she meets my gaze. She sits up and raises her arms in a slow, sultry move for me to undress her.

Fuck me. This girl will be the death of me.

I reach out and tug her top over her arms, pulling it over her head.

She's breathless as I grab a fistful of my shirt and pull it over my head.

We don't break eye contact as I peel off the rest of her clothes, then my own as I strip to my skin.

We don't stop looking at each other as I lean over her, careful not to crush her, and yank her legs up around my waist. I seize her wrists and guide her hands above her head, lace my fingers through hers, and plunge inside.

I groan at the feel of her warm, wet walls clutching me.

She starts crying.

"Why are you crying?" I stop.

"Because I love you. And I missed you."

"I love you too. I missed you too." She's crying, and I can't have it. "We won't be apart again. Ever, Penny. You're mine now. Where did you leave the ring?"

"Huh?" She seems dazed. Shakes her head, looks around. "In my . . . my bag."

I spot it discarded with her clothes and reach for it, flipping the lid open and taking out the ring again. I take her hand in mine.

A new tear leaks out of one eye. I peer into her eyes. "Third time's the charm. Yeah?"

She nods, sniffling, and dries up her tears as we both watch me slip the ring onto her finger. "Yeah, third time's the charm," she agrees on a croak. "And I do, Luke Cross. Forever. Tomorrow I want to get a real ring for you."

"I got it. You might not see it because it's invisible. But I got a ring right around my heart." I kiss the ring on her finger, then skim a kiss across each of her fingertips.

She puts her hand on my heartbeat. As if it grounds her. Then she leans up for a kiss. I kiss her forehead, the tip of her nose, and feast on her temptress mouth.

I want to take it slow. I want to make love to her. But I want to fuck her at the same time.

Instead, my Penny has other plans. She pushes me to my back. I let her and watch her straddle me. Cold sober now as she mounts me. Moves, finding the perfect spot.

I skim my hand up her sides. "First for you too?"

She smiles sheepishly. "I seem to like trying all kinds of new things with you."

She rocks her hips, and I bite back a groan. "That's okay. I like it. I love you. You're doing great."

Hell, more than great. If she keeps doing that teasing circular move with her hips, I'm not going to last.

She leans over, pressing her lips to mine, her sweet breath misting across my face. "Luke, you're so hot. You make me so hot."

I can barely talk, I'm so turned on. "You're gorgeous, Mrs. Cross. You can't possibly be hotter than I am right now watching you."

I cup her breasts and tease her nipples with my thumbs as I pepper her neck and jaw with kisses, hardly believing she's here as she lowers herself down on me and I sink into her, deeper and harder, like she likes it. Like I need it.

We start going at it harder, increasing our tempo.

Every cry she gives out, I suck into my body. Every sound I relish. Every lick of that sweet little tongue as she bends down and gives some love to my jaw, my neck, my shoulders.

"Fuck, Penny, tell me you missed it, you missed me."

"I missed you. I love you." She sits up and looks down at me, all sweaty and gorgeous.

I groan and cup her gorgeous tits, watching her ride me. Salivating as she rides me like a goddamn rodeo star. She's like a fucking beautiful dream, hovering over me. "I love you," I hear myself rasp. I can't say it enough. It's like I need to brand it into her. Any way I can. I skim my hands up and down her sides. Never wanting to come down from this.

"Me . . . *too* . . ."

She's breathless now, ready to go off for me. Tossing her head back, moving her hips faster. I help her with my hands on her waist, lifting and lowering her, my muscles straining as I try to wait for her to come first.

When she comes, I watch her. Awed. Awed by how gorgeous she is. Awed that I can feel this close to another human being. That I can feel this fucking whole even when I know myself to be a man who's been in pieces. I watch her for merely two seconds, and then I come with her.

When we sleep, we sleep pressed together.

In the middle of the night, I wake with a hard-on, courtesy of her sweet rear pressing up against my shaft. I smile when I smell her hair beneath my nose. Tilting my head to the side, I slide my hand down her arm and lift her hand to me, feeling with the pad of my thumb in the dark for her fingers. And yeah. Didn't dream her. Didn't conjure her up out of desperation. Hell, I wouldn't ever have come up with such a perfect Mrs. Cross even if I'd been asked to write down a wish list.

But it's true. Penny's wearing the ring that will tell the entire world that she is mine.

Nell

It's Christmas morning, and it really feels like it when I wake up to Luke Cross's kisses. I turn my head toward the warmth of his body and find his neck, burying my head in it as I wrap my hands around him and hold tight. I slept like a baby. Better than I have in a long time.

"Mornin', killer," he whispers softly.

"Morning." I'm smiling. I can't help it.

Even though the annulment was nearly instant—I suppose the show had that pre-prepared—we're getting married again. For real. My voice is groggy with sleep as I lift my hand and set it on the stubble of Luke's jaw. I'm just making sure that I am not imagining this or him, that I'm really here in his arms.

"Hi," I say when I touch his warm flesh.

"Hi." He chuckles.

"I didn't imagine last night. Or . . ." I lift my hand and gasp delightedly, staring at my engagement ring. "Or this!" I squee, throwing my arms around him again.

He chuckles and draws me to him, propping his back up against the pillow as he drags me to his lap. I'm peppering him with kisses the whole time he maneuvers. "Yes! A thousand times yes," I say.

"One's enough. One for a lifetime." He sounds sleepy too. Sleepy and sexy as he pops a slow, sweet kiss on my lips.

"It's a quote. You know. *Pride and Prejudice*."

His eyes start dancing mischievously. "Tell me one in French."

I laugh. *"Je t'aime."*

"Je t'aime aussi."

"Oh! You are learning French!"

I can't take my hands off him or stop dropping kisses on him. We didn't just win the game. We won the fucking soulmate jackpot. We found the kind of soulmate that everyone most wants.

"One day," I say when I finally ease out of bed and head over to investigate his small, messy kitchen, "I want you to show me how to pour a glass. Make a killer drink. Like a real bartender." I slide behind the kitchen counter and rummage through the fridge. Everything in there looks really old. I scrunch my nose as I try to find something edible. "Can I make you something?"

I lift my gaze across the room to the bed. He is slowly shaking his head. And then he wags his finger at me. Oh gosh. He is so hot. In bed, all rumpled from having sex with me. I can't believe I almost threw him away, threw *us* away out of fear and insecurity. I'm never going to be apart from him again. If the world doesn't get it, then okay. But I get it and I get him, and he gets me. I don't know what I'm going to do about Massachusetts anymore. I don't know what I'm going to do about anything anymore except that I'm marrying him and I hope we don't wait too long.

Leaving the food for now, I head back to bed. Obeying his sexy summons. My fiancé/ex-husband/future husband is more edible anyway. He draws the covers back and pats his naked lap. He's so hard for me already that my mouth waters a little bit as I climb up there and twine my arms around his neck once more.

We kiss for a bit. Actually, for a lot. With no rush, easily. Without any cameras on us. Without any checkpoint waiting. Just Luke and me.

His hot tongue and warm, caressing hands. And breathless little me. Eating all of it right up.

"So, when are you thinking," I prod softly, easing back to catch my breath. Wiggling the ring in front of his eyes.

"Now. Tomorrow. Soon." He doesn't hesitate when he answers, but then he frowns. "But not so soon that it feels fake like last time. I want you to have the wedding you always wanted."

"I will have what I want—*you*." I skim my gaze around his place, which, although messy, is quite charming. Even his bar downstairs is somehow so . . . him. And I can't help remembering his financial situation. Soon to be ours. "I also don't want us to throw away any money . . ." I keep visually skimming the place methodically, noticing there are absolutely no bookshelves or books at all except for a single book about learning French on his nightstand. My toes curl as I spot it. "This place isn't as bad as you said. It's cute. Will we live here?"

"For a while, yes. Until I can get shit sorted and we can get a bigger place for when the kids come. Hey." Seeing me distracted, he turns me by the chin to face him and look into his beautiful eyes. "Don't worry—I'll tidy up."

"I'm not worried." I exhale, press my head down to his chest, and hug myself to him again. "I can't wait."

Still. I think of all the money we lost—he lost—because of me, and I want to apologize again. "Luke, if it weren't for me, you'd be—"

He sets a finger on my lips, smiling as if he knows what I'm thinking. "I ain't sorry, Penny. Neither should you be. Okay?" He sounds stern until I nod. Then, more gently, he nods. "We'll figure something out. Together. Teamwork. Right? And there ain't a better team I know than us. Hell, we got first place."

I nod. "Yes. We did."

His smile is about a million watts in force. "Then we'll figure something out. Together. But for now"—he holds me against him and tips my chin up a little more—"tell me about this dream wedding of yours."

For the next hour, we talk about my dream wedding and his. He says that his dream wedding is anywhere and anytime, as long as it's with me. He's so adorable, I could eat him up by spoonfuls. Once we're finally decided on what we're going to do, he asks me something I didn't expect but am thrilled to do.

He wants me to meet his grandmother.

He's so excited when he sees my anticipation for meeting her that we head over to the nursing home before noon.

"Gran," Luke says as we arrive.

I spot a beautiful old woman in a wheelchair, with a book on her lap and her gaze out the window, her profile pensive as Luke's voice registers and the nurse wheels her around to see him.

Luke motions to me at his side, his face breaking into a smile. "This is her, Gran."

His grandmother cracks the widest smile I've ever seen. "Come here, Nell," she says, as if we've met before and have known each other forever. Which happens when you take part in a reality show, I guess.

She crooks her finger at me, and I walk over. "It's so nice to meet you, Gran," I say, kneeling before her and taking her hand as she ducks her head.

"This boy loves you very, very much. And I know you love him too. So when my time comes, I'll be at peace to leave my Luke, knowing he won't be alone. Far from it." She winks at me and my throat closes, but I nod and straighten.

"What are you two whispering about?" Luke shoots us a scowl as he shuffles through Gran's things. "So what do you want to do? How about a board game?"

We end up staying two more hours, until the nurse asks us to leave so Gran can rest. I exhale happily as we head out of the home, Luke's arm around my shoulder, my cheek on his chest while I hold him by that strong, lean waist of his.

"She's wonderful, Luke. I love her. Thank you for bringing me."

He remains silent, setting a kiss on the top of my head. He doesn't need to tell me how grateful he is that I came. I caught him watching Gran and me as we talked and played Life. I filled my car with babies, and Gran got to the end before we did, and we all laughed.

He had a great time tonight too.

And it only makes me wonder if I can somehow bridge the gap that I, myself, have with my own family.

"Would you be okay if you met my parents?" I ask hesitantly, tipping my face back. "I mean, if you want to. I know they're not winning any awards this year, but recently they reached out and . . ."

"I'd love to meet your parents, Penny." He cuts me off with this sexy little smirk, and I exhale, taking his hand and placing a kiss on the back of it. "I know they might find it difficult to attend the wedding, what with the crazy plans we have." I grin. "But I'd love for them to meet you beforehand."

EPILOGUE

REALITY STARS
Nell

> *Everyone in the country is clamoring for the release of the tell-all book from Million Dollar Marriage winners Penelope Carpenter and Luke Cross. We're all hoping to get some juicy insight into what was reality and what was envisioned by the producers, how they fell in love, and how he finally proposed—for real! Look for it on sale next week!*
>
> *—TV Buzz Daily*

Paris.

We are in the most romantic city in the world, posing for pictures with the Eiffel Tower glittering in the night sky behind us.

I'm wearing white. Luke is wearing a tux.

We are surrounded by those who truly care about us. Courtney—my maid of honor—and Joe. Jimmy—Luke's best man—and Lizzy. It's a small destination wedding on the terrace of the Shangri-La, overlooking the Eiffel Tower.

No, my parents definitely weren't up to flying all the way here. But when we visited them at my childhood home, I was surprised to feel their warmth toward me when greeting me, and even their warmth (and curiosity, yes) toward Luke.

We had pot roast for dinner. We told them about our plans. They congratulated us and wished us well, asked a lot about the show with genuine interest and almost in a fanlike way, and before we left, they made me promise I'd come back after the honeymoon for another visit.

It was . . . good.

I feel hopeful about that—and about finally having the courage to live my life, rather than plan it from a safe distance. I've found a more stable tutoring job, and I also plan to be helping Luke at the bar. It's all so . . . exciting.

We're doing it right this time. The wedding, everything. We're doing it our own way and not letting anyone tell us anything different.

Today is exactly what I envisioned in my dreams. Romantic locale, beautiful dress, giant cake, real diamond and gold rings, and the most dashing man in the world, who also happens to be in love with me.

When the photographer finishes taking the pictures, all six of us go onto the terrace so that Luke and I can exchange our vows. This time, there is no lime Jell-O. No harsh lighting or video cameras or cheering crowds or cheese. It's just us and our best friends, a full moon, and so much love. I'm wearing contacts for the first time ever, and I keep dabbing at my eyes with the handkerchief Luke's sweet grandmother gave me as my "something old."

The justice speaks French, so I told Luke not to worry, that he could simply say the vows in English. He insisted that I say them to him in French. (I wonder why?) When he takes my hand, I peer into his beautiful green eyes and say:

Moi, Penelope, je te prend, Luke,
pour être mon mari,
pour avoir et tenir de ce jour vers l'avant,
pour meilleur ou pour le pire,
pour la prospérité et la pauvreté,

dans la maladie et dans la santé,
pour aimer et chérir;
jusqu'à la mort nous sépare.

Luke takes my hand, his eyes shining. "I've prepared my own vows for you."

I blink. We've gone over the plans a thousand times to allow for no surprises, but this catches me completely unaware. "You did?"

I watch, expecting him to pull a piece of paper from his tuxedo pocket, but he doesn't. It turns out, he has them all memorized.

And then he tells me that he is so in love with me and he will live his entire life to do nothing but make me happy. He tells me that I am his greatest adventure. That he's never wanted anything as much as he wants me to be his wife. He tells me that I've gotten so under his skin that I'm a part of him. And that he can't wait to spend forever with me.

And he tells me all that . . . in perfect French.

If there's anything sexier than the French language, it's French coming from my sexy husband's wicked mouth while he gazes at me with intense, wet eyes.

The handkerchief is really coming in useful right about now, because I start to sob. I gather myself together, fanning my face, and manage to get through the rest of the ceremony.

When we're pronounced husband and wife, he doesn't wait to be told to kiss me. Pushing my veil behind my shoulders, he gazes at me like it's Christmas morning and I'm the best present he's ever gotten. He frames my face in his hands for a sweet, ceremonial peck, which is nice and all, but it's definitely not what I had in mind.

"You can do better than that," I challenge. After all, we're pros at the wedding thing right now, and we need to make up for our lack of a kiss during our first wedding. "We had thirteen million strangers watch our first kiss, so I don't think we need to be shy for this one."

"Yeah, I can. But I was trying to be respectful."

"Fuck respect," I tell him, wrapping my arms around him. "Give me the heat, husband."

And he does. Oh god, he does. He fucks my mouth long and hard, cupping and squeezing my ass until I'm completely breathless and weak in the knees. I squeak out, "All I can say is, *Mon dieu*. How did you do that?"

He smiles. *"Vous n'avez encore rien vu."*

You ain't seen nothing yet.

I know. And I can't wait. I clutch my heart, which can't take much more of this. If it's possible to die of happiness, I'm in trouble. "Stop. You're killing me."

We hug our friends when it's over. When we are finally married—forever, this time—Luke offers me his arm, and we go to the edge of the terrace, where a table is set for a lavish meal. We sit down, and Jimmy raises his champagne glass for a toast. "To Penny and Luke. You may not have gotten the million dollars out of that goddamn show, but I think you guys got somethin' a hell of a lot better."

We toast and sip champagne, and Courtney and Lizzy and I are giggling like schoolgirls from the excitement of the night. There's a buzz of romance in the air, and I can't stop looking across the table at my incredible husband.

And then there's dancing. A lot of dancing, though I'm not much better at that than I am at swimming. But we've danced before under the eye of the cameras, so this is nothing. Luke guides me onto the floor and engulfs me in his arms and says, "Hi, wife."

I'm grinning like a fool. "Hi, husband."

He whirls me around, his hands drifting down to my ass. "I seem to remember a dance floor in Boston where you got pretty crazy."

"That was someone else," I say, batting my eyelashes innocently. "I don't do such things."

"Damn. Are you telling me I married the wrong girl? Because I was really looking forward to getting her shitfaced. Makes her easy."

I laugh. "So I hear. But shitfaced or not, I think the girl you married will be pretty easy for you tonight."

He pumps a fist. "Yessss," he hisses. "Come on, let's go get you a drink. Just in case."

He goes behind the bar, surveys the ingredients, and starts to sugar the rims of cocktail glasses. Then he fills a shaker with cognac and lemon juice.

"What are you making?" I ask.

"One of the first drinks my granddad showed me how to make was a sidecar. Born in Paris."

I stare at him, mesmerized, as he adds ice and expertly shakes it, then picks up a lemon and a peeler and shaves the rind into the glasses. It's clear he's been making them for a long time.

"You look good doing that," I say. "Sexy."

He pours the liquor into the glasses, easily, and hands one to me. "Does it turn you on?"

"Oh, fuck yes," I say, taking a sip, then pulling back, surprised. My man can get me liquored up anytime. "Mmm. This is *good*."

He stares at me in mock horror as he lifts the glasses for the girls. "I don't approve of that kind of talk, Mrs. Cross. I find it low class." He gives me a wink.

"Hey," Joe calls from the table, where he and Jimmy are checking out Jimmy's latest YouTube video. "Word overseas is that a certain tell-all book is at the top of the bestseller list. *Again*."

Courtney claps her hands. "That makes two weeks in a row!"

I look at Luke, and we shrug. Haven't read the book. Haven't even thought of reading it. We sold our story at auction, did a few in-depth interviews with the writer, got the money to pay off my loans and his mortgage, and wiped our hands of it. Actually, we were kind of hoping it would bomb, because we've already gotten the money, and if it bombed, maybe people would stop caring and the media would finally leave us alone. When we left for the wedding, they were camped out at both Tim's Bar and Courtney's apartment, even though I've been living with Luke for several months.

But we say what we've always said, which has now become the Cross family mantra. I'm going to have it sewn in needlepoint and placed above the mantel in our apartment at Tim's when I get back to the States:

Fuck 'em.

I've been decorating, and the place isn't nearly the shithole Luke thought it was. The bar is actually quaint and homey, and people love it. With a little advertising and some clever marketing schemes Lizzy and I worked up, the bar that holds his grandfather's name is not just going to live on—it's really starting to pack them in. The night before we left for Paris, the line to get in was all the way around the block. Jimmy was joking that he was going to have to give up his booth.

"I don't want to go back home," I say to Luke over the bar as I finish my cocktail and he pours me another. "You know they're just going to hound us when we return from our honeymoon."

He grins and sips his cocktail, then leans forward and kisses the shell of my ear. "Who says the honeymoon has to end anytime soon, baby?"

I like the sound of that.

The celebration ends, and I'm a little sad about that, but I'm happy because I know what comes next. The wedding night. As much as I love these people, I'm giddy at the thought of being alone with my husband.

My husband, my husband, my husband. I'll never get tired of saying that. And I'm his wife.

I know, he's been my husband before.

But only now does it feel real. Right. Perfect. Forever.

We kiss our friends good night, tell them we'll see them tomorrow for the farewell breakfast, and he takes my hand and leads me to the elevator, his hand already roving under my skirt. We go inside and the doors slide closed, and he buries his face in my neck, lifting the fabric of my dress.

"Damn, this dress has a hell of a lot of layers," he murmurs as we head up to the penthouse. "Where is my wife? She under here?"

I am definitely *not* hiding from him. Sure, I wanted the dress, but that was then. I'm over it. I can't wait to get out of this infernal thing and feel his skin against mine.

His fingers get free of the tulle and slip between my legs.

He lets out a groan, and desire flickers through me as he strokes the bare skin of my thighs. "There she is. Mmmm, so warm and wet for me already?"

The bell above the door dings, and without warning, he scoops me up into his arms, carrying me all the way to our room. "Luke, what are you—"

"I'm taking my wife to bed, the fastest way I know how."

I can't argue with that. I tighten my hands around his neck.

He opens the door and kicks it closed, then settles me down on the bed. His eyes darken as he gazes at me, taking off his jacket, loosening his tie. "You sure are pretty in that dress, Mrs. Cross. But now I think it's time I took it off you."

I grin. "Good luck." I roll onto my stomach so he can take a look at the complicated hook-and-eye thing running down my back that has me basically sewn into the dress. "Also. I have about four hundred bobby pins in my hair. This mission, should you choose to accept it . . ."

He starts by slipping off my shoes, and then he begins to work on loosening the dress. "Since when did I ever back down from a challenge? And the reward's a hell of a lot better this time."

It's slow going. I start working on the bobby pins, uncoiling the ringlets of hair that I'd piled on my head, while he does the dress. Every time he bares a little bit of skin, he kisses it gently. Then, about five minutes into it, he lets out an impatient growl. "I hope this ain't grounds for divorce."

And he grips the fabric in his hands and rips the seam clear apart.

I laugh as he pulls the heavy white draping away from my body, leaving me in my frilly white thigh-highs, thong, and lace bustier with garters. "I wasn't planning on wearing it again, really."

Now he's standing at the edge of the bed, gazing at me hungrily. "That's more like it," he growls, reaching for my stockinged feet and sliding me across the bed to meet him. His fingers dig into my thighs, into the clips tethering my garter to my stockings. "I don't know what the hell these are, but they're fucking classy."

"I don't give a shit about class. Give me dirty any day," I say, reaching up and unbuttoning the buttons on his dress shirt, baring his smooth chest. When I am done, I splay my hand over his heart, feeling it pumping like mad in his chest. "No. Just give me you. I want you, Luke. Always, forever."

He stands between my open thighs, looking down at me, ready to claim me, but the truth is, I've already been claimed. I was claimed the moment I set eyes on him.

He cups my face in his hand, his thumb lightly tracing my lip, and breathes, "I'm going to live every fucking day of my life to make sure that you're happy, Mrs. Cross. My beautiful wife. You'll see. I'm going to be everything you've ever wanted in a husband and then some."

I kiss the tip of his thumb and lean into his touch. "Oh, Mr. Cross. You already are."

THE END

ACKNOWLEDGMENTS

Although writing is a personal thing and sometimes quite a lonely profession, publishing is a whole other beast, and I couldn't do it without the help and support of my amazing team. I'm grateful to you all.

To my family, I love you!

Special thanks to Lauren and Holly at Amazon Publishing and Montlake, for believing in me and taking me under their magic wings. Thank you to everyone at Montlake for being the very best team I could have ever hoped for!

Thank you to Amy and everyone at Jane Rotrosen Agency!

Thank you to all my writing friends. I appreciate each and every one of you so much.

Thank you to Nina, Jenn, Chanpreet, Hilary, Shannon, and everyone at Social Butterfly PR. You are amazing!

To Melissa, Gel, my fabulous audio publisher, my fabulous foreign publishers, and all my bloggers for sharing and supporting my work—I value you more than words can say!

And, readers—I'm truly blessed to have such an enthusiastic, cool crowd of people to share my books with. Thank you for the support. XO

Katy

PLAYLIST

"Trouble"—Pink
"Timebomb"—Tove Lo
"Say It Right"—Nelly Furtado
"Team"—Lorde
"Clarity"—Zedd (feat. Foxes)
"I Don't Know How to Love Him"—Sinead O'Connor
"Goodbye"—Miley Cyrus
"Far Away"—Nickelback
"Dancin' Away with My Heart"—Lady Antebellum
"Nothing Really Matters"—Mr. Probz
"I'm All Yours"—Jay Sean
"Never Gonna Leave This Bed"—Maroon 5

ABOUT THE AUTHOR

Katy Evans loves family, books, life, and love. She's married with two children and a dog, and she spends her time baking healthy snacks, taking long walks, and taking care of her family. To learn more about her books in progress, check out www.katyevans.net and sign up for her newsletter. You can also find her on Twitter @authorkatyevans and on Facebook at AuthorKatyEvans.